WRATH

WRATH

FAITH MCMANN NO. 3

T.R. RAGAN

THOMAS & MERCER

Text copyright © 2017 Theresa Ragan

Published by Thomas & Mercer, Seattle

www.apub.com

Amazon, the Amazon logo, and Thomas & Mercer are trademarks of Amazon.com, Inc., or its affiliates.

ISBN-13: 978-1503941410 (paperback)
ISBN-10: 1503941418 (paperback)

Cover art by Melteddashboard.com

Cover design by Rex Bonomelli

The Faith McMann trilogy is dedicated to all who work hard to raise awareness and increase understanding, and who struggle endlessly to supply services and help survivors of human trafficking. Organizations like the Polaris Project advocate for stronger federal and state laws and operate the National Human Trafficking Resource Center hotline. Truckers Against Trafficking (TAT) trains truck drivers to understand, identify, and report instances of human trafficking. We can all do our part. If you see something, say something.

For information about trafficking:
www.traffickingresourcecenter.org.

ONE

Twenty-four hours ago, Faith's son had come back from the dead.

Hudson was alive.

He'd saved another boy's life.

He was a hero.

And yet there had been no celebration. Hudson's father was dead, and his ten-year-old sister was still missing.

Faith's father and brother were also heroes. They had spent too many days in the Mendocino National Forest, but they had survived the elements and brought her son home to her.

Last night, Faith's father, brother, and son had been examined by doctors at the hospital. Her brother, Colton, was doing fine. Russell, her dad, was suffering from exhaustion and dehydration, while Hudson had numbness in his toes and fingers. Thankfully, he didn't have frostbite. After the hospital, they'd returned to Faith's parents' house and gone straight to bed.

Hudson's first full day back had been filled with lots of hugs and small talk, everyone happy to have him home. He'd eaten well, but overall he'd been quiet and appeared to be in a daze, still trying to find his bearings.

It was seven o'clock at night, and Faith was getting ready to tuck her son under the covers. All he had to do was lay back on the pillows and go to sleep, but he seemed to be fighting it. She could see the exhaustion creeping into his shadowed eyes. Eyes that had seen too much horror in the past two months. She wished she could hold him close and take away all the fear and confusion he must be feeling.

She leaned over and kissed his forehead.

"Mom?"

"Yes?"

"You haven't told me about Dad."

"What do you want to know?" Faith took a seat on the edge of the bed, pushed strands of flyaway hair from his small face, and waited.

"Did he bleed a lot?" Hudson asked.

Her heart dropped to her stomach. She didn't want to think about the human traffickers who had taken Craig's life. She couldn't think about her husband without seeing images of the sharp blade of the knife as it sliced through his throat. She didn't have to close her eyes to see all the blood as her husband's life seeped away.

Hudson didn't blink. "Did Dad suffer?"

"No," she said softly. "He didn't suffer. Beth tried to save us both, but Dad was already gone. He went quickly, and he's watching over us now."

"How do you know he's watching us?"

"I just do. I can feel him close by everywhere I go. He was next to me while I was looking for you, encouraging me to never give up searching for you and Lara. He loved you both so much."

"I miss him."

"I do, too."

Hudson pointed a finger at her scar, which ran from one ear, down her chin, and across her throat. "Did they do that to you?"

She nodded.

"Did it hurt?"

"No," she said without pause.

Hudson took in a gulp of air before he said, "I watched two people die."

"Oh, Hudson." She had no idea what he'd been through, and she'd been told not to push him or ask too many questions. She felt as if she were teetering at the edge of insanity. How could those people have done this to her son? He'd never been a fearful child. They had taken his innocence from him without any thought.

"It's OK, Mom. Grandpa had to see all sorts of horrible things during the war."

"Maybe so," she said, "but he wasn't nine years old. You're a very brave boy, and we're all so proud of you for finding a way to stay alive and for helping Joey. I talked to the doctor yesterday at the hospital, and he said Joey is going to be all right and that children's services have found a family for him to stay with."

"What about his foot?" Hudson asked. "On our last day in the woods, he couldn't walk."

"He might lose a big toe due to frostbite, but it was pneumonia that made it difficult for him to go on. He'll be in the hospital for at least another week."

"I'm glad he's alive."

"Me, too," Faith said.

There was a short pause before he added, "His parents sold him to those people."

She closed her eyes for a long moment, doing her best to stay strong and hold it together.

"They told me over and over again that you and Dad didn't want anything to do with me. That kids were hard work and I was a trouble-maker." His gaze had fallen downward, but he looked up at her again and said, "But I knew they were lying. They laughed when I said they were liars, but I knew you and Dad would never give us away."

She rested both hands on his small shoulders. "There was never a moment, let alone a day, that Dad and I didn't love you two so much it hurt."

She hugged him tight, glad when he lay back so she could tuck the soft blankets over his chest close to his chin. His eyelids had been drooping all day, and now, despite his attempts to stay awake, he couldn't fight sleep any longer. Within seconds of his head hitting the pillows, he was out for the count.

Faith stayed with Hudson for another twenty minutes, watching him, unable to take her eyes off him. He was alive, and he was home.

At the sound of voices downstairs, she found the energy to push herself from the bed. Her family, along with Beast and Rage, two friends who'd been at her side since she started her search for her kids, had agreed to meet to discuss plans for finding Lara. Everyone was in the living room. Jana and her husband, Steve, sat on the love seat. Colton was seated on the stone hearth, stooped over, elbows on knees. Dad was in his favorite recliner. Beast had pulled up a chair from the kitchen, leaving an empty spot on the couch next to Rage.

"How's Hudson doing?" Jana asked.

"I think he's doing OK, considering," Faith told her sister. "He wanted to know if Craig suffered."

The room grew quiet.

"He also saw two people killed while he was in the mountains," Faith added, "but he's trying to be brave like his grandpa."

"It'll take some time, but he'll get through this," Colton said. "I'll make sure of it."

Faith nodded. Her brother had been with her every step of the way. He'd sacrificed so much, and yet nothing would stop him from seeing this through to the end. She glanced around the room. If not for every single one of them, she'd never have gotten this far. Hudson wouldn't be asleep upstairs. She owed them all so much.

"About this list of yours," Jana said, her voice filled with emotion. "Steve and I have taken a look at all the names you gave us. It seems so overwhelming. It would take months to figure out who's who."

Faith's heart went out to her sister. She was seven months pregnant, and from the start her hormones had gotten the best of her. Jana could go from tearful to laughing inappropriately to extreme worry in the bat of an eye.

"What do you plan to do with the list of names anyhow?" Steve wanted to know.

The list, Faith thought. Everything now revolved around the list she'd obtained from the sister of a man who had been working for Aster Williams, the alleged trafficking ringleader in Sacramento. "Rage, Beast, Little Vinnie, and I have been using whatever means at our disposal to put faces to names, trying to find out who these people are and what they do," Faith said. "One thing we've discovered is that these are not your run-of-the-mill thugs. The list includes some very important people in the community: doctors, lawyers, and businessmen. Politicians and bankers." Faith shook her head. "Not only is it overwhelming; it's not easy to comprehend what many of them are doing out of simple greed. It's incomprehensible."

"I haven't had time to look at the list," Colton said. "Are these businessmen mostly johns?"

"No," Beast answered. "The sex industry, at least in Sacramento, seems to be run by a highly structured organization with many key players."

Faith nodded her agreement. "The names on the list include pimps, recruiters, johns, and guys like Aster Williams who keep things running smoothly."

"But what is the goal?" Jana asked. "What do you plan to accomplish here?"

Faith thought the reason was clear. "Nothing has changed," she told her sister. "My one and only goal is to find Lara. So far we've come up against nothing but dead ends. Diane Weaver is dead. Her brother and his wife were murdered. Every time we get another name, that person turns up dead . . . including Richard Price. Except in Richard's case, I was lucky enough to locate his sister, who provided me with the list of names her brother had left behind."

"I've been doing some research," Rage chimed in. "Trafficked children are often moved around to keep them from being found. Our hope is that whoever is watching Lara is afraid to move her until media attention dies down."

"Which means we need to work fast," Faith said. "If Aster Williams is hiding Lara, it seems likely someone within his hierarchy might have her."

"Instead of walking the streets with flyers," Rage said, "we figured it might be a good idea if we do some surveillance, keep an eye on as many of these people as possible to see if one of them leads us to Lara."

"Makes sense," Colton said.

"I think it's a brilliant idea," Jana said. "Maybe we should each start with five names and start going door-to-door? I am certainly capable of sitting in a car and keeping an eye on some of these men."

"Over my dead body," Steve told Jana. "Look at you. You're seven months pregnant, ready to explode. I'll help with surveillance while you continue to man the phones and keep track of social media." Before anyone could respond, Steve gestured toward Dad, who had fallen asleep in his chair. "Look at him. He's exhausted. I don't mean to be Debbie Downer," Steve told Faith, "but how are you going to take the time to watch these guys when Hudson needs you here?" He flipped a hand toward Colton. "Your brother has a plane ticket out of here first thing in the morning to go see his wife and kids."

"I canceled the trip," Colton said. "Faith needs me, and I can't leave until we've found Lara."

Afraid for her children's lives, Bri had decided to stay with her parents in Florida for a while. Although the thought of her brother being away from his family for this long seemed like too much to ask, Faith was filled with gratitude.

"I'm going to call Bri and tell her I'll come visit her and the kids when this is over," Colton said.

"I can't ask you to do that," Faith told her brother. "You've been away from your family long enough."

"Bri and the kids will understand," Colton said. "It's not your choice to make."

"Jana is pregnant," Steve went on, "so she won't be much help. And what about Rage?"

Rage narrowed her eyes. "What about me?"

"I'm merely stating the obvious," he told her. "You're not exactly feeling one hundred percent."

"Who told you that? Are you saying I don't look right?"

Jana elbowed her husband in the ribs.

"No," Steve quickly backtracked. "I wasn't saying that at all."

Rage chuckled. "Settle down. I'm only kidding. I'm dying, and I look like shit. Thanks for reminding me."

Beast grunted.

Dad's snore came out as a long rumble followed by a squeaky whistle.

Colton found a blanket and laid it gently over him. Clearly, Faith thought, during their long trek through the mountains to find Hudson, Dad and Colton had bonded. They both tended to be a little bullheaded, always testing each other. But since their return twenty-four hours ago, it was all pats on the back and friendly conversations.

"Well," Steve said, "you might as well hand me five names so I can get started. I can knock on a few doors and pretend I'm selling something so I can get a peek inside to see if anything looks suspicious."

"Nobody goes door-to-door these days, but I guess it wouldn't hurt to try," Colton said.

"Unless they're armed and dangerous," Beast said. "In which case, it's probably better if all of you stay in the car and use binoculars to watch them."

"How's your leg?" Faith asked Steve. "Jana said you were supposed to keep off it for another week or two."

"I've got my crutches if I need them. I'll be fine."

"We can only do so much research," Beast said, looking at Faith. "It's time to start checking up on these guys. At the very least, we might be able to cross a few names off the list. Or better yet, find Lara and bring her home."

"Rage mentioned earlier that you gave a copy of this list to Detective Yuhasz," Colton said. "What did he have to say about it?"

"He's still in the hospital recovering. I don't know if he's had a chance to take a look at it, but he promised to keep everything I gave him confidential until he's on his feet again."

"Why can't the police pay these guys a visit?" Jana asked.

"The police don't have the manpower or the time," Faith said. "And even if they did, they would be duty bound to tell the person the reason for their visit."

"And if Aster Williams discovers what we have in our possession," Rage added, "every trafficker within a hundred miles of the state capitol will head for the hills."

"And they'll take Lara with them," Faith said as fear and anger threatened to strangle her once more. Those two emotions had been the bane of her existence for so long she no longer remembered what it felt like to be a regular person living a normal life.

"Faith is right," Rage said. "Another reason why the people on this list should be watched from afar."

"It's as good a plan as any," Colton said. "Give me a few of those names, too. I'll get started in the morning."

Two

Patrick entered the Chinese restaurant in Granite Bay, took a quick look around, and then headed for the back room. Without a word spoken, the owner, a petite woman with straight black hair and a crooked spine, stepped out from behind the cash register and led him down a narrow hallway. Aster seldom asked him to meet in public, but he'd called a few hours ago to tell him to arrive an hour before closing.

Using arthritic fingers to open the door, the woman gestured for Patrick to enter.

Aster and three men Patrick had never seen before sat at a large round wooden table. In the center was a lazy Susan covered with food. Too busy shoving raw pinkish clumps of octopus into his mouth, trying to get the tentacles under control before he slurped it all down, Aster didn't bother greeting him or making introductions.

Watching Aster eat never failed to cause Patrick to lose his appetite.

Aster swallowed, took a swig of sake, and gestured for Patrick to take a seat in the empty chair next to him. He figured whatever it was Aster wanted to discuss had to be important.

And it couldn't be good.

Not only had Hudson McMann been found; he was alive and well, most likely snuggled in a warm bed.

Patrick sat quietly and waited as Aster used a cloth napkin to wipe his mouth. He missed a spot of green glob on his upper lip, but nobody pointed it out.

Aster motioned at the big man sitting directly across from Patrick. "I want you to meet Hansel."

Patrick half stood so he could lean forward and offer a hand, but Hansel ignored him, didn't even bother to meet his gaze.

"He's a germaphobe," Aster said with a chuckle. "He's not comfortable with *people* germs."

Unsympathetic, Patrick plopped back down into his seat. "So if my dog was here, he'd shake his paw?"

Nobody laughed.

"Yeah," Aster said. "I'm sure he would be happy to shake your dog's paw."

Awkward silence followed.

Hansel's face was fucked up. A thick scar ran diagonally through his upper lip, making him look as if he had a permanent snarl. A bulbous nose and a wart above his right eye completed the picture. Patrick figured the other goons sitting around the table were Hansel's bodyguards; all broad shouldered and young and wearing serious expressions.

"I've hired Hansel and his men," Aster said, "to take care of Faith McMann, her family members, and every person she's ever called her friend."

Patrick had to work not to clench his teeth. Once again Aster was letting him know that he and his men had failed to do their jobs, and therefore he had to find someone else to finish McMann off once and for all. "How are they going to do what all the rest of your men haven't done? The FBI is practically living with the McMann family."

Aster laughed. "Tell him, Hansel."

He shrugged. "We tail her and take her out."

"And then witnesses call in," Patrick said. "You're dragged in for questioning, and thirty minutes later, police are knocking on Aster's door and dragging him off to prison."

"We drive an unmarked car and shoot her in the head as we drive by," the man seated next to Hansel said in a tone insinuating Patrick was an idiot.

"And what about the rest of the family?" Patrick asked, annoyed Aster had brought it to this.

"Kaboom!" another man said, using his hands for full effect. "We blow up the whole damn house. Take the entire clan out all at once and send a strong message." He smiled. "Maybe we'll blow up a few of their neighbors, too. Just for fun," he added.

Hansel and Aster looked equally amused.

If Aster was hiring these guys to finish McMann off, why had he bothered to invite Patrick to this gathering? What did Aster want—congratulations and a pat on the back?

"You're going to be their go-to guy," Aster said, reading his mind. "If Hansel or his boys need anything, anything at all, Hansel's going to let you know, and you'll take care of it for him. Whatever it is. Understand?"

"Sure," Patrick said.

Aster snapped his fingers. "What's the big guy's name? You know, the giant who's been attached to McMann's hip since the beginning?"

"They call him Beast," Patrick said.

Aster finished off his sake and asked, "Want to remind me why he's still alive?"

"Last I heard Peter convinced you to leave him and his dad alone. Apparently they're bounty hunters."

"So?"

"So you decided to leave them alone in hopes that all the fuss would die down."

"And what were your thoughts on the matter?" Aster wanted to know.

Patrick didn't understand the line of questioning. What was Aster trying to prove? That he was the alpha male? Bottom line, Patrick refused to cower. "I told you Peter was an idiot, and that they should all be taken out sooner rather than later."

"Hmm." Aster wiped his mouth again, still missing the green glob of shit on his face. "Give Hansel your private number," he told Patrick. "And give him the address where he can find Beast and his dad so he can get rid of them. In fact," he said, turning his attention back to Hansel, "take the big guy out first and then McMann's nosy neighbor. I want the McMann bitch to know we're coming for her."

There was a desperate air to Aster that Patrick hadn't noticed until now. Something was going on. The only other time Aster had hired outside assassins to take care of a job was when he'd gotten a call from one of the head bosses in Los Angeles. Aster didn't like when they poked their noses into his business. He was territorial that way. But Aster also knew if he didn't do as the outsiders suggested and make it all go away, he'd appear weak. And everyone knew what happened to the weak. They were eaten alive.

Patrick watched Aster mindlessly shove piles of food into his mouth. Aster wasn't himself. His shirt was wrinkled, and he hadn't taken the time to shave.

Yep. Those LA dogs are on his ass. What would they do to Aster Williams once they realized he couldn't handle a schoolteacher?

When the waitress appeared again, Patrick asked for a pen and paper. When she returned, he wrote down his number and slid it across the table toward Hansel. He watched with amusement as the big man pulled out his tiny bottle of hand sanitizer, cleaning up before he reached for the paper and placed it neatly into his coat pocket.

"Anything else, boss?" Aster liked to be called boss when they were around people he didn't know well. He said it showed respect. No reason to piss him off now.

Aster gestured toward the food. "You're not going to eat anything?"

"I'm not hungry."

"Stay," Aster told him. "Drink your sake, and have something to eat like everyone else. Then you can go."

THREE

Another day had come and gone.

Hudson was upstairs, asleep in bed. He was home. Faith knew she should be overwhelmed with joy, but instead she felt restless as adrenaline moved continuously through her system. Seeing her son again and holding him in her arms had been so surreal, was still surreal. Talking to him and watching over him the past forty-eight hours made her feel as if she were being dragged back to life. And yet all she wanted to do was hide him away, put him somewhere safe while she continued her search for Lara.

She had work to do, and time was running out.

Until she found her daughter, her world would remain tilted on its axis. She couldn't think. She couldn't focus.

Maybe what she was feeling wasn't fair to Hudson, but there it was: she needed both her children safe at home before she would have any chance of moving forward.

Hudson had grown increasingly quiet. Yesterday he'd gobbled down three helpings of lasagna and an entire carton of chocolate chip ice cream. He had visited with family, watched his favorite shows on television, and slept.

Today Hudson did the same. Big, hearty meals followed by lots of television and video games. At first Faith worried he was moving on way too quickly. Upon closer examination, she saw something else entirely. She saw it in his eyes and heard it in every shallow breath he took. She felt it in the tightness of his body when she put her arms around him. He wasn't moving on at all. He was simply eating, walking, going through the motions, a survival tactic she knew all too well.

Clearly her son was fighting his own inner demons.

He needed help, so she picked up the phone and called Kirsten Reich, therapist and family counselor, and made an appointment for the next afternoon.

But this was tonight, and tonight she had things to do. Dad was apprehensive about Faith leaving the house, but he didn't try to stop her. They both knew what needed to be done.

There were two FBI agents and more than one media van parked at the end of the driveway, so Faith exited through the back. Dad would look after Hudson while she was gone. Her son was in good hands.

Dad locked the door after she left and watched her from the window as she crept through the yard. From Dad's workshop she could see Beast waiting in his truck. Little Vinnie sat in the passenger seat, and Rage sat in the back.

Faith climbed into the backseat and slid in next to Rage.

They were quiet until they merged onto Auburn-Folsom, and then Beast went over the night's plan as he drove: Mark Silos, one of the top twenty men on Richard Price's list, lived in Foresthill. The ride from Granite Bay to Foresthill would take about forty-five minutes.

They had decided to start with Mark Silos since he was listed as one of the men who had once worked directly under Richard. According to Richard's sister, Robyn, it had been Richard's men who'd come to the house the day Craig was killed.

If everything went as planned, Little Vinnie and Beast would enter the house first, then bind the man while Faith and Rage searched the house for Lara or, at the very least, a clue that might direct them to her location.

And if they didn't find her?

They would leave him bound and gagged. As long as he never saw Faith, there would be no reason for Mark Silos to think their visit was anything more than armed robbery.

Rage was in a talkative mood. She told them about a recent dream she had, in which Miranda, a teenage girl who had been held captive at a farmhouse and was the last person to see Lara alive, had returned, but it was all very sad because Miranda had nowhere else to go.

Beast grunted.

"You don't have to be rude," Rage told him.

"Why don't you just come out and say what you want to say?" Beast told her.

Rage crossed her arms. "I have no idea what you're talking about."

"Not now," Little Vinnie scolded. "The two of you are like children most of the time. It's exhausting."

"You know exactly what she's doing," Beast told his dad. "This is Rage's roundabout way of letting us know she wants us to go in search of Miranda and bring her home."

"It's not a bad idea," Little Vinnie said.

"It was only a dream," Rage said. "You don't need to make a big deal out of every little thing."

Faith stared out the window at the pitch-black sky.

"And what about Sandi?" Rage asked next, causing Faith to wonder who Sandi might be since she'd never heard the name mentioned before.

"What about her?" Beast asked.

"Did you ever read her letter?"

"No need. The girl was given a fair chance to make amends."

"You have got to be the most pigheaded man in the world. You drive me crazy."

"Who is Sandi?" Faith asked, unable to swallow her curiosity.

"Sandi Cameron is the eighteen-year-old who killed my wife and daughter," Beast told her. "Texting 'LOL. I'll see you soon' was more important than the two lives she took that day."

"I'm sorry. I should stay out of this."

"It's OK," Rage said. "Sandi is twenty-three, maybe twenty-four now, and Beast refuses to read her letter and see what she has to say. I'm not sure she deserves Beast's attention. But I do think he owes it to himself to at least check it out. And then maybe, just maybe, he can find it in his heart to forgive her."

Rage put a hand on Beast's large shoulder.

Faith saw him stiffen.

"I don't want to talk about this," Beast said.

"You never want to talk about anything."

"That's not true. Yesterday I listened to you talk for an hour about the importance of being grateful. The day before that it was all about living in the moment."

"All good and important subjects," Rage said.

Faith couldn't help but smile.

"And while we're on the subject," Rage went on, "forgiving someone doesn't mean you condone what they did. But it might help you let go of some of your anger and learn to trust people again. How can I possibly die in peace if I'm forced to leave an angry shell of a man all alone to grow old by himself?"

Beast merged off the highway, taking the turn a little too fast and putting an abrupt end to any more talk of forgiveness and death.

Faith held on tight.

Little Vinnie and Beast had mapped out the area. They knew what they were doing, so she didn't question Beast when he veered right instead of left, taking them down a steep driveway. He parked in front of a dilapidated one-story home. The windows were covered with plywood. The walkway was uneven and cracked, making room for tall weeds to sprout.

Rage pulled a black cap over her head. She readied her handgun, opened the car door, and stepped outside. Faith did the same.

Little Vinnie and Beast walked ahead of them.

At first Faith thought they might take a look inside the abandoned house, but the two men proceeded past the front of the house and slipped into the dark shadows of trees. It was a moonless night, and the clouds blocked any light the stars might have otherwise provided. She and Rage followed them across the bottom of the driveway and into a wet, grassy field dotted with gangly-limbed oaks. The only noise was the hoot of an owl and the sound of rustling leaves as a heavy breeze swept through. Despite Beast's and Little Vinnie's massive size, Faith could barely make out the outline of the two men as they marched ahead. Every few seconds, though, she heard the snap of a twig as they went along.

Her foot wobbled on a clod of dirt. The last thing she needed was a sprained ankle. It wasn't easy keeping this pace and watching her step. By the time she caught up, Beast, Little Vinnie, and Rage were crouched low at the edge of the field, where trees and brush met pavement. Across a narrow road was a faded yellow house similar to the one they had just left.

Faith stared at the house, focusing on trying to see through the front window. Her heart skipped a beat. She couldn't help but get her hopes up, wondering if Lara could be inside.

Beast looked at Rage. "Dad and I are going in. Give us five minutes before you join us."

"Got it," Rage said before turning toward Faith and saying, "We'll give them two."

From where they stood, they saw Beast pound his beefy knuckles on the door. Faith counted to ten, hoping it would calm her nerves. She felt anxious, wanted them to kick the door down.

Instead, when no one answered, Beast and his dad disappeared around the side of the house.

Ready to head across the road to see what was going on, Faith forced herself to stay still and be patient.

A minute later, Beast reappeared, using the glow from his flashlight to wave them over.

Nobody was home.

Faith reached the front door just as Little Vinnie opened it from the inside. She entered and gagged before quickly covering her nose and mouth with her arm. The place smelled like urine, rotted eggs, and cleaning fluids.

The house was small enough to see most of the rooms from where she stood. The kitchen was to the right and the living area to the left. She went left. The room was all wood paneling and shag carpet from the 1970s. A beat-up brownish couch was pushed against the wall. In front of the couch was a coffee table made of driftwood and glass that was covered with cigarette ash and assorted pipes.

"Meth lab," Little Vinnie said as he stepped out of the kitchen. "Small but functional."

A far wall was covered with bookshelves, only there wasn't one book to be found. Mostly odds and ends, a couple of black-and-white photographs coated with a thin layer of dust. Beneath the shelves were three cupboards. They were locked. She continued on, opening drawers as she prayed Lara had never been anywhere near this stink hole.

Swallowing her emotions, she went to the coat closet by the front entry. The shelves above were empty. She patted down the three coats inside and checked the pockets. About to shut the closet, she caught sight of the sleeve of a vintage jacket. The button on the cuff was made of metal. It was tarnished, and upon closer view she was able to see how similar it was to the button she'd found on the edge of her grass by the driveway where Craig's SUV had been parked that fateful day.

Her hands shook as she grabbed the other sleeve.

The button was missing. Mark Silos, she realized, had to have been the third attacker in her house that day, the man whose face she'd never seen. The man who had ordered their deaths and taken her children.

Heart pumping wildly, she glanced out the front window toward the driveway. All clear.

"I'll watch the front of the house while you keep looking around," Little Vinnie told her.

She nodded and headed down the hallway. In the first bedroom she found a desk and a chair. Flowery wallpaper, peeling at the edges, bordered the room. The closet was covered with mirrored sliding doors. Afraid of what she might find, her muscles tightened as she slid one side of the closet open.

Inside were piles of unwashed clothes. The smell was overbearing.

As Faith made her way down a long, narrow hallway, images flashed within her mind like a strip of film replaying every awful detail of the day Lara was taken up until the moment her husband was killed. Lara had been bound and gagged, sitting on the couch next to her brother. Instead of fear, Faith had seen determination in her eyes.

Faith walked into a small laundry room and opened cabinets and drawers with renewed resolve. Nothing there. Next she went through a door that led her to a side yard littered with trash and old tires. What sort of man dares to take a child from his or her mother? Hands fisted at her sides, she went back into the house and found Rage in the next bedroom. She was on all fours, looking under the bed. Her head popped up long enough to say, "I checked the closet and the bathroom. I didn't see anything that will help us."

Beast stepped into the room behind Faith, blocking the doorway.

"There's nothing here," he reported. "We could hit another house or two before the night's over or wait for this guy to show up and see if he has anything to say."

"We stay," Faith stated firmly. "He has to come home eventually. And if he won't talk or claims he doesn't know anything, we'll call the police and let them—"

"What the fuck is going on here?"

Beast whirled around.

The man's voice stopped her cold. Seven words. That's all it took to know she was right about Mark Silos. He was definitely the third attacker at her house. The man who had ordered Craig's death was standing a few feet away from her with a gun gripped in his hand. The tips of her fingers brushed over the scar, tracing the hard ridges from her ear, across her chin, down and across her throat.

He stood far enough away that Beast couldn't grab his gun without taking a bullet to the gut. Her attacker was tall and slender, his dark hair grungy. Other than the striking blue eyes, he looked nothing like the picture she'd found on the Internet.

"Both of you," he said, his voice gruff. "Put your hands above your head where I can see them."

Faith looked to the floor, where Rage had been minutes ago. She was gone, disappeared under the bed no doubt.

"Now!"

Beast raised his arms above his head, his fingers clasped. She noticed the hardening of Beast's jaw and the tightening of his shoulders. If Beast found the opportunity, he'd take the guy down at the first chance he got.

Faith raised her arms, too.

"Come on," Silos said. "Get a move on!"

Faith followed Beast out the door and down the narrow hallway. They walked toward the front of the house.

Silos jabbed the barrel of his gun into her back, sending a sharp pain through her body. Faith tried to think of a way out. She didn't panic until she saw Little Vinnie on the couch. He looked dazed but alive. Blood trickled down his forehead and dripped off the tip of his nose. Silos must have caught him off guard.

She turned, ready to go to Little Vinnie, but Silos grabbed her arm and pushed her toward the kitchen. She looked over her shoulder. Her gaze went from Little Vinnie to the lamp on the side table. If she could break free from Silos and grab hold of the lamp, she could swing the thick base and knock Silos over the head.

"Outside!" Silos said before she made her move. He pushed her toward Beast and gestured for them to head for the back door. Why would he want them outside unless he planned to shoot them and take care of the old man later? There was no way she was going to simply follow orders. Her heart raced as she looked around the room. Dirty utensils were stacked near the sink. A cast-iron frying pan sat on the stove.

Her thoughts spun out of control.

She needed to do something now. If she went for the pan, she'd have to act fast. She thought of Hudson. If she lunged for the stove, one of them would get shot. She'd just gotten her son back. She couldn't risk leaving him now. Frustration made it difficult to think clearly.

Beast reached for the doorknob leading outside, his movements slow and deliberate.

"Drop your gun!" Rage's voice boomed from behind them.

Silos pivoted, gun aimed, ready to fire.

Beast grabbed Faith, yanking her close to his chest before he dropped to the floor, bringing her with him.

A shot rang out.

Silos's body jerked.

Faith watched him take awkward backward steps as he tried to find his balance. He seemed to defy gravity as he fought through whatever pain he must be feeling as blood seeped through his shirt. Silos glanced her way. His forehead was covered with a light sheen, eyes wide as if he was just now realizing this might be the end.

It was no use. He was losing control. His fingers went limp; the gun dropped to the floor.

Rage lunged for it.

Silos toppled over, knocking dishes and utensils from the kitchen table on his way down. A knife clattered across the floor.

Shock swept through Faith as she watched him fall. He couldn't die. She had questions. He had answers.

Mark Silos was on his back now. Face up. Eyes wide-open.

He'd taken a clean shot through the neck. Faith scrambled across the floor to get to him. Beast grabbed her ankle to try to stop her, but she kicked his hand away and crawled under the kitchen table toward Silos, pushing a spindly wood chair out of her way.

On her knees and hands, she hovered over Silos and stared him down. Blood oozed from the side of his mouth. "Where is she?" Faith asked. "Where's my daughter?"

His eyes found hers. "McMann?" he asked in a gravelly voice before coughing up more blood.

Faith grabbed two fistfuls of his shirt and shook him. "Where's Lara? Where's my daughter?" she cried.

He said nothing.

She put a hard fist into his shoulder. "Talk to me."

The silence was deafening. He needed to talk. Instead she watched his eyelids close as he said, "I don't know."

"Bullshit. You killed my husband and took my kids! Where is she?"

"Don't know . . . nobody knows," he said, the life fading from his body and voice.

His head lolled to the left, and his body went limp.

Nobody knows. What did that mean? "Don't you dare die!" She placed both hands, one on top of the other, over the middle of his chest and began pressing and releasing, pressing and releasing, over and over again, willing him to come back to life. "You son of a bitch. Tell me where she is. What did you do with Lara?"

She felt a hand rest on her shoulder.

Silos was dead.

Faith looked at Beast. "Where's Lara?" she asked. "Where is she?"

Beast opened his mouth as if to say something, but no words came forth.

What did Silos mean when he said nobody knew? Had Lara been shipped off somewhere? Had Lara escaped? Where could she be?

Faith's despair was crippling, her grief eclipsed only by her anger as she pushed herself to her feet. Her chest rose and fell. She would not stop looking for her daughter. Not now. Not ever. This was only the beginning.

FOUR

The next morning, after getting a few hours of sleep, Faith, her dad, and Hudson drove to the FBI headquarters in Sacramento. At the long, rectangular conference table, Faith sat to her son's right, while her father sat to his left. Across from them were three FBI agents, all in suits, all asking questions. "How are you feeling?" "What have you been doing since you've been back?" "Did you recognize the men who took you and your sister?"

They had been trapped in the stuffy room for thirty minutes already, and Faith grew impatient. She wanted to take Hudson home.

Hudson, on the other hand, didn't seem afraid or annoyed or bothered in any way. If anything, he seemed normal. Like a perfectly average boy who had never been whisked from his home and enslaved by drug traffickers only to escape and end up lost in the Mendocino forest in the dead of winter.

"In the beginning," Hudson said in response to the agent's question about the men who had attacked his family, "after the men made me and my sister get into the back of my dad's car, I was scared. I remember my body shaking. I couldn't move."

Agent Burnett, a tall, dark-haired woman Faith had met a few times before, sat directly across from Hudson. Her face softened. "Did the men who took you and your sister talk to one another? Did you ever hear any names mentioned?"

"Only one."

Faith looked at her son and found herself holding her breath, as they all were.

"Patrick," he said.

"Does Patrick have a last name?"

Hudson shook his head. "Just Patrick. One of the men seemed worried about the man named Patrick getting mad about something. That's all I remember."

Patrick. This wasn't the first time Faith had heard the name. Cecelia, the woman from the hotel in San Francisco, had told Faith she worked for a man named Patrick. No last name. Just Patrick. Faith never told the FBI or Detective Yuhasz about that night in San Francisco. She'd killed a man in self-defense. Even if she could tell them the truth, it wouldn't do them any good. Cecelia was dead.

"That's very helpful," Agent Burnett told her son. "If you remember anything else, you let us know, OK?"

He nodded.

"You were scared, weren't you?"

He nodded again.

"It's OK to be frightened. It happens to all of us."

"Later I wasn't scared because I started to pretend everything that was happening was just a video game."

"Can you explain what you mean by that, Hudson?"

He perked up a bit. "No matter what game I play on Xbox," he said, "there's usually a harder level coming up. Sometimes I feel as if I'll never beat the level I'm on, but if I stick with it long enough, there's always a way to get past the obstacles and move on." He stared at his fingers as he made a steeple. "That's what I did after I was thrown into a metal box with those other boys, and when I was taken to the mountains, and again after me and Joey got lost in the woods."

Faith watched her son with growing concern. He definitely seemed to be holding in his emotions, keeping the ugly things he'd seen bottled up inside.

"If you don't give up," Hudson continued, his focus directed at Agent Burnett, "if you keep on trying, you'll figure out what you need to do next."

"That makes sense," Agent Burnett told him. "You're a very smart boy."

He *was* smart, Faith thought. And clever and brave and all the other things people had been telling him for the past two days. Faith stared at Hudson, mesmerized by his small, upturned nose, long lashes, and wispy brown hair that had grown nearly two inches past his ears. There had been too much going on to worry about his hair. Everything felt so new—watching him and having him near.

Hudson had answered all their questions about the day their family was attacked. How he and Lara were thrown into the back of his dad's SUV and told to keep their mouths shut or they would be killed. After about an hour into their drive, he said the car stopped.

"Is that when you were separated from Lara?"

He nodded and looked at the table. "She kicked and screamed. I wanted to help her, but there were too many of them. I couldn't fight them. I didn't want them to take my sister away."

"Do you have any idea at all where you were or where she was being taken?"

He shook his head.

"Where were you taken next?" Agent Burnett asked.

"I fell asleep. At the end of the day, after they took me from my dad's car to another car, I was thrown into a metal box with other boys."

Agent Burnett and Agent Jensen quickly concluded the metal box was a shipping container. Unfortunately, there were many places in the area where shipping containers were stored.

Hudson went on to tell them about the other boys and how some of them said they had been enslaved for years. Many of the boys were bullies, worse than their captors.

"Do you remember what happened when you were released from the shipping container?"

He shrugged. "Sort of."

"When they moved you from the container," Agent Jensen asked, "were you able to see any of the men's faces?"

Hudson shook his head. "We were blindfolded. I heard the engine, and the ride was bumpy so I knew we were in a car and we were moving." Long pause and then, "But I never saw their faces." He looked at Faith. "And I never got the chance to run away."

"It's OK," she told him. "You did everything right."

"Do you remember what kind of car any of these men were driving?"

"No."

"But once you were in the mountains," Agent Jensen prodded, "you saw their faces, didn't you?"

"Yes," Hudson answered. "I saw them every day. I also saw the men who took me and Lara from our house."

"That's good," Agent Burnett told him. "We have a few more questions, and then we want to show you some pictures and see if you recognize anyone, OK?"

He nodded.

"After you were brought to the woods, what were you forced to do?"

"We were chained to a worktable. We each had our own area where we would trim cannabis." Hudson looked at Faith and added, "It was better than living in a dark box without water or food."

She gave him a reassuring smile that contrasted heavily with all the emotions running through her. Faith squirmed in her seat as her son talked about a boy he was pretty sure had died in the container and another boy who'd been shot within minutes of escaping the one-room cabin in the woods. His expression didn't change when he talked about how his captors beat them on a regular basis and hardly gave them anything to eat. His tone of voice remained even and calm. In the end, Hudson claimed it wasn't the video games that got him through his ordeal in the woods, but Grandpa's wartime stories of survival. If he could find sources of water and food, like Grandpa had talked about, he'd been certain he could survive.

And he was right.

Not only had he and his new friend, Joey, fought off their captors; they'd found a way to survive in freezing temperatures until Faith's dad and brother located them.

"Thank you, Hudson. You've been a great help."

"Will you be able to find my sister?"

"That's our goal," Agent Jensen said.

"We're going to show you some pictures now," Agent Burnett cut in. "I'm going to lay out six pictures at a time. Let us know if you recognize anyone, OK?"

Once again, Hudson nodded.

Faith glanced at Dad. He gave her a look that said it was going to be all right.

Agent Jensen opened the folder in front of him and began spreading out six eight-by-ten glossies, some women, mostly men. A couple of the photos were taken from a distance, while the other photographs were close-ups.

Faith shuddered when she spotted Diane Weaver. She was hard to miss with her gaunt face and frizzy hair. A permanent scowl made her look much older, but it was her cruel eyes Faith would never forget.

After Hudson told them he didn't recognize anyone, Jensen laid out another six photos in two rows of three.

Faith recognized two of the men from the binder she had in her possession. After she found Lara, she'd hand it over, but not until then. If the wrong person found out about the list, they might very well pressure the director of the FBI to lay off, or perhaps inspire the bosses in the area to quadruple their efforts in finding a way to shut Faith down altogether.

Either way, it wasn't going to happen.

Make a phone call. Call the cops. Hand the binder over.

Faith knew what most average, everyday citizens would think about her keeping the names from authorities. But it wasn't that easy. It wasn't that she didn't trust the authorities; they just had different objectives. Their goal was to stop the criminals. Her goal was to find her daughter.

Only Detective Yuhasz knew what she had. He was still in the hospital recovering from the gunshot wound to the shoulder, which gave her some wiggle room. But no matter which way she looked at it, time was running out.

Hudson stared at the photos for a long while and then shook his head.

Another six photos. Hudson pointed to the middle picture in the second row. No hesitation whatsoever.

The man in the photo had dark hair. His eyes were—Faith drew in a breath.

Agent Burnett directed her attention to Faith. "Is something wrong?"

"No," she lied. "It just makes me sick to see all these men's faces, knowing what they do."

Agent Burnett didn't seem to be buying it, but she let Faith's reaction go.

Faith had seen that face last night. Although Mark Silos had changed his hair and lost some weight since the photo was taken, she saw the same shocking blue eyes as the man she'd watched die on the middle of his kitchen floor.

Thinking about last night made her wonder how Little Vinnie was doing. He'd been shaken up by the hit to the head. Beast, Rage, and Little Vinnie had done their best to make the scene at the house in

Foresthill look like a drug deal gone bad. Afterward they dropped Faith off far enough away from her parents' home so she'd be able to get into the house without being seen.

How long would it be before someone found Mark Silos's body? The gunshot alone should have alerted someone, but Beast assured her that shots were often heard in remote areas of the woods.

Hudson pointed at the picture as he looked at Faith. "That was the man who ordered the other two around."

Faith nodded. Hudson knew what she'd figured out last night—that Mark Silos had been the third man at their house. What her son didn't know was that Silos was the one who had ordered the other two men to kill her and Craig.

Overall, Faith thought as she studied his photo, Mark Silos had an average-looking face. The face of a killer. The face of a dead man.

FIVE

Faith took a seat in the therapist's office.

Dad had waited in the lobby to take Hudson home after Kirsten Reich finished talking with him, and now it was Faith's turn.

The therapist, a blonde with an athletic build, settled in the cushioned chair across from Faith and asked, "How is your family?"

Agitated by the question since Faith only wanted to hear about her son and how he was doing and where they went from here, she fidgeted in her seat and arched a questioning brow as if she didn't understand.

"How are your mom and dad faring?" Kirsten tried again.

Faith's mom had been attacked by three men. If Mom hadn't had the good sense to run and lock herself in her room, and if Beast and Rage hadn't shown up, she would have been killed. "Mom is supposed to be released from the hospital any time now," Faith said, trying to keep her frustrations in check. "She's a trouper. Same with Dad. He's like the Energizer Bunny. Nothing's going to stop him."

"I'm glad to hear it." Kirsten made a note, then asked, "It's been forever since I talked to Jana. Has she had her baby?"

"No, not yet," Faith said. The small talk made her feel as if she were playing a silly game to see who would break first. "She looks as if she has an entire family living inside her." Faith tapped the toe of her shoe on the floor as she tried to think of her sister's due date. She came up blank. Her gaze fell to her hands in her lap.

More and more often, she found herself playing with her wedding ring, as she was doing now, twirling it slowly around her ring finger. It was loose. She'd have to take it to a jewelry store and have it fitted when she found the time.

When she looked up, Kirsten was looking at her. "Her husband is also doing well," Faith told her before she could ask. "I'm sure he'll be returning to work any day now."

"What about your brother?"

Faith gritted her teeth. Would she be asking about her nieces, nephews, and second cousins, too? "Colton canceled his plans to fly to Florida to see his wife and daughters so he could be close by in case we get any news about Lara. And you just saw Hudson," Faith snapped, finished with what she considered an interrogation instead of a conversation. "So maybe you can tell me how that went."

"It's going to take some time," Kirsten said. She removed her dark-rimmed glasses and used a tissue from the table next to her to wipe a smudge from the lens. "But under the circumstances, I'd say he's doing well."

Faith waited for her to continue. When she didn't, Faith blew out some hot air.

"Perhaps you should tell me what's on your mind," Kirsten said.

"Oh no," Faith said. "Some thoughts are better left unspoken."

"I insist."

Faith had been in a foul mood all day. Her meeting with the FBI had not helped. "All right," she said, sitting taller. "I'm thinking eighty bucks an hour to tell me my son is doing well under the circumstances? Seriously? My nine-year-old son has been through a horrendous ordeal, held captive for nearly two months, only to return home to discover his dad will never be coming back. He's hardly shed a tear or shown any emotion at all. Clearly he's keeping his emotions bottled up inside, but that's all you've got?" Faith dropped her hands onto her lap. Once again she busied herself with twirling her ring.

The seconds ticked by, the silence gnawing away at her like some sort of horrible flesh-eating bacteria until she lifted her head and met Kirsten's gaze straight on.

"He's doing better than you," she told Faith. "I can tell you that."

Faith stared at the woman for a moment and came very close to smiling. For some reason she liked Kirsten Reich. The therapist wasn't afraid to say it as she saw it.

"Why don't you tell me how the search for your daughter is going?" Kirsten continued.

Faith leaned toward the table, grabbed the glass of water Kirsten had put there, and took giant gulps. When she was finished, she said, "The last few days have been crazier than usual. I haven't had a chance to talk to Detective Yuhasz, so I can't—"

"I'm talking about your own personal investigation."

Faith took another sip, the water crisp and cold on her tongue. Kirsten Reich couldn't possibly know what she'd been up to last night. "Hudson is home now," Faith said as she returned the glass to the table. "I can't run off looking for Lara when my son needs me. I can only hope Detective Yuhasz is up and running again soon so he and his men can stay on top of things."

"Hmm."

"What does that mean . . . 'hmm'? You don't believe me?"

"I didn't say that. But I do watch the news, and before you arrived I saw a story about a drug dealer found dead in his home late last night. I'm wondering if a certain schoolteacher and her friends went to pay someone a visit and something went horribly wrong."

Caught completely off guard by the accusation, Faith stood and reached for her coat. Although she didn't like to think they'd been reckless, Mark Silos and men like him, in her opinion, were not human. Little Vinnie was supposed to be keeping watch last night. Silos never should have been able to sneak up on them like he had. But he did. And in the end, Rage had had no choice but to shoot the man. But that didn't mean Faith could go around telling people like Kirsten Reich the truth about what happened. As far as Faith was concerned, nothing had changed. Lara was out there somewhere, and Faith needed to find her.

"You need help," Kirsten said, breaking into Faith's scattered thoughts. "You have what? Two or three friends available to help you?"

Faith had no reason to be angry at the woman, but she couldn't help herself. This was the second time Kirsten had caused her to wonder why she'd bothered to come see her. As she snapped the front buttons of her coat and tied the sash around her waist, she looked around for her purse.

"Listen," Kirsten said in her irritatingly calm voice. "My friends and I are meeting tonight. Bring your friends, too, and let's have a serious discussion about what we can all do together as a team to make a difference."

"Why would you and your friends want to help me?"

"Because you're not the only one who needs help. Hundreds of young children are forced into child labor and sex trafficking. My friends and I have been meeting for years, doing what we can to grow awareness in our communities. Although we don't usually reach out to individuals, in your case, we thought it was vital to join you in your mission. You've done a brilliant job so far keeping the media involved in your plight to find your children. But we've also noticed that you alone can only do so much. Your parents are getting up there in age. As you said a moment ago, your mom is still in the hospital. Jana is pregnant, and one of your newfound friends is ill."

Faith didn't know what to say. This wasn't the first time Kirsten had hinted at wanting to help her, but Faith hadn't taken her seriously before. Her gaze connected with the thick leather straps of her purse dangling from the couch's edge. Instead of retrieving her purse and making a quick exit, she remained where she was, taking a moment to process what Kirsten had told her. No matter how many times she went over the list in her possession, it always came down to one thing—she needed more hours in the day. Every minute that ticked by was another minute Lara could have been harmed or moved farther out of reach. Faith was running out of options. There was no denying it. The clock was ticking.

And Kirsten was right. She needed help. "What are you suggesting?" Faith asked.

"We want to help you find your daughter."

Faith crossed her arms. "How do you propose to do that?"

"My friends and I have been tracking some of the worst offenders for years now. We hit the streets whenever possible, talk to people, and take down names. It's time-consuming, and progress is slow, but we've managed to get a few of them off the streets."

"Traffickers?" Faith asked.

"Yes. Mostly recruiters, a few pimps, people involved in some form of human trafficking."

She had Faith's attention now.

"Unfortunately, we don't have to look far to find these people and yet it isn't easy to take them down. The problem has always been what to do with them once we have them on our radar." She shrugged. "Without proof of any wrongdoing, the police can't keep these guys behind bars for long, if at all."

"So what do you suggest?"

"That's what tonight's meeting is about," Kirsten told her. "We need to put our heads together and find a way to shut these guys down."

"I have a list, too," Faith told her.

"I thought you might."

"But you should know, my goal, my endgame, is to find Lara."

"I understand." Kirsten wrote the address on her notepad, tore the paper loose, and handed it to Faith. "The gym at Mesa Verde High School. Ten o'clock. You won't be sorry."

Six

Patrick held the phone to his ear as he paced the floor of the shitty little house he was renting in the town of Elverta. The landlord had assured him before moving in that the house had been freshly painted before the new carpet was installed.

Bullshit on both accounts.

The carpets were old as fuck. He hated this place. He hated this city. But none of that mattered. Because in the end he would have everything he'd ever wanted: money, power, control. That's all he thought about anymore. Sure, he might need to suffer for a while longer, but if he could keep his eye on the prize and practice patience, he would soon be the leader of one of the largest trafficking rings in the country.

Someone finally picked up his call and greeted him with "Yeah?"

"Patrick here," he said. "Put me through to Winston Wolf. Tell him it's urgent."

"Patrick who?"

He gritted his teeth. "Tell him it's Patrick. He'll know who I am. Winston and I go way back."

"And what might I tell him you're calling about?"

The guy was chewing gum. An irritating smacking came right through the line and drilled away at his brain. "Listen, you little twat.

Tell him I'm waiting for an answer. If I don't hear back by tomorrow, I'll find another buyer." He disconnected the call, his hand fisting at his side as he clenched his teeth.

He was about to make another call when he heard a knock. He sat up and listened closer. The sound was coming from the door in the hallway—the door that led up from what the landlord called a wine cellar but was actually a basement. He proceeded down the hallway and opened the door.

Blonde-haired, blue-eyed Lara McMann, the missing golden child who'd been on the news for months now, looked up at him with a curious, examining expression. There was something about the kid, especially the eyes, that made him uncomfortable every time he looked at her. He didn't have a guilty bone in his body. He'd never felt an ounce of shame or regret when it came to what he did for a living, so whatever he was feeling at the moment had nothing to do with his own inner demons.

Maybe, he thought, the uneasiness had to do with the fact that he'd never liked kids. He was an only child—after his sister had died, that was. He spent most of his time growing up reading *Newsweek* and *Money* magazines. Money was all he ever thought about. He used to spend his allowance on candy, mark it up 300 percent, and sell it to the kids who didn't care about rotted teeth and craved sugar highs. He also enjoyed ironing his stack of dollar bills. As soon as he was old enough to deliver papers, that's what he did. When he entered high school, an older kid offered to pay him one hundred dollars to deliver a package across town. He wasn't stupid. It didn't take him long to realize he was transporting drugs. He started lifting weights in case he needed to protect himself. He paid close attention to who the players were. By the age of fourteen, he was making ten times that amount, and by the age of sixteen, he had thousands of dollars stashed away. The big money, the real money, though, was made in trafficking, the fastest-growing business in the world.

He shook his head at the thought of Aster Williams.

Patrick had just turned twenty-eight when Aster came along and fucked up all his plans. Aster had killed his boss, an old man who had treated Patrick like a son. His few bad investments had not helped. Patrick suddenly found himself cash poor and working for the biggest asshole he'd ever met.

But this lovely child, he thought as he stared at Lara McMann, would change everything. "She's alive," he muttered.

Twice a day he took the time to make sure she had food and water. Other than that, he left her alone. As far as he was concerned, he needed to keep her alive until he could collect a cool million and send her off to Timbuktu. A million dollars wasn't much these days, but it would buy him power and loyalty. He'd find a way to kill Aster and take over from there. He knew the business inside and out, making him a natural to take control of the organization. Any man or woman who remained loyal to Aster would be eliminated.

"I'm hungry," she said.

"I fed you an hour ago."

"I'm tired of frozen dinners. I want something else."

"Oh, is that right? What does the little diva want?"

Her eyes narrowed. If looks could kill, he would have fallen over dead. Who did she think she was? Before he could answer his own question, she trudged past him, headed for the kitchen.

For the sake of protecting his assets, he went to the front door and latched the top lock, one too high for her to reach in case she got it in her mind to try to run off. If she decided to enter the garage through the kitchen door, he wasn't worried. The outer garage door worked only if you knew the code. He moved quickly around the rest of the house as he checked windows before making his way to the kitchen, where he found the kid going through his refrigerator and making herself right at home. She had nerve.

Lara pulled out a half-used stick of butter, a loaf of bread, a block of cheddar, and some mustard. She then began a tedious search through cabinets and drawers until she found a frying pan.

He crossed his arms, leaned his hip against the counter, and watched her work. As the butter melted in the pan, she pulled a knife from a drawer, the biggest knife he owned, and used it to cut a slice of cheese. He watched her closely, wondering if she was going to come after him. She made her sandwich with the same focus a surgeon might when cutting into someone's brain tissue. Had the kid forgotten he was standing there? Or maybe she didn't care one way or another.

By the time she finished cooking, her grilled-cheese sandwich looked like a thing of perfection—silky cheese oozing from between two golden-brown slices of sourdough bread. He considered ordering her to make him a sandwich just to see what she would do. But he wasn't hungry, so he let it go.

She used a spatula to transfer the sandwich to a plate and then poured herself a glass of cold milk. With the plate in one hand and glass in the other, she walked past him and made her way into the living room.

He followed her. When he saw Channel 10 news reporting on the McMann kidnapping, he grabbed the remote and clicked off the TV.

"That was my grandparents' house on the news," she told him. "I thought you said they'd stopped looking for me."

He could tell by the tone of her voice and the fact that she'd already taken a seat and bit into her sandwich that she'd never believed a word he'd said in the first place. So why was the brat questioning him?

Because she wanted him to know she knew her family was looking for her, and that she never doubted it for one minute. She knew there were people out there who loved her and wanted her home. He lifted an eyebrow. The kid was wise beyond her years. For a second, he wondered if he should be worried. That made him laugh.

His thoughts turned to Hansel and his men. Although he hadn't been thrilled by the idea of Aster hiring strangers to do what should have been done weeks ago, he was curious how long it might be before they obliterated every member of the McMann woman's family.

The thought cheered him. He never wanted to hear her name uttered again. Faith McMann had been a thorn in his side for too long. He would take great pleasure in knowing she was dead. Although he didn't hate women the way Aster did, he abhorred people like McMann, people who thought they could take a stand and wreak havoc on a thriving billion-dollar business.

Faith McMann and her family had had their fifteen minutes of fame. It was time for every one of them to be silenced so he could move on to more important matters, like getting rid of Aster.

SEVEN

The next day, Faith was at home when she heard Dad's truck pull up outside. She left Hudson in the family room and headed to the front, where she found Dad assisting Mom from the car. Figuring he could use some help, she headed their way.

One of the media van doors squeaked open. *Damn.* Every time she walked out the front door, someone popped out of a news van. The reporters had become permanent fixtures in their lives. It was getting old, but her entire family had decided to be as cordial as possible since they needed the media to keep Lara in the forefront of people's minds. The nonstop media coverage kept Faith's story alive.

She had a love-hate relationship with every reporter and cameraperson. Although everyone knew they weren't supposed to come onto the property without permission, they did it anyhow.

Out of the corner of her eye, she saw a reporter hurrying up the driveway. A tall boy with curly hair and sticks for arms held his microphone an inch from Faith's nose. "How does it feel to have your son back?"

"It's nice," she said, forcing a smile as she walked past him and headed for Mom and Dad.

"How is he doing? Is he sleeping well?"

He'd only been home a short time. It was a ridiculous question, so she ignored the reporter. Faith said hi to Dad and gave Mom a kiss on the cheek. "You look good."

Mom rolled her eyes. "I'm a mess. Everything hurts, but I'm home and I want to see my grandson."

"You two get inside," Faith said. "I'll get the rest of Mom's things." She opened the door to the backseat, where she could see Mom's purse and a small carry-on.

"Has there been any word about your daughter?" the reporter asked from behind her, hovering so close she kept waiting for him to step on her toes.

Once again, she gritted her teeth and held in her frustration, reminding herself she needed the media more than they needed her. Whether they realized it or not, their presence was more than likely helping keep the trafficking ringleaders at bay.

"No," Faith answered him before leaning into the backseat of the car and reaching for Mom's things. "We've had no word from anyone concerning my daughter. But we haven't lost hope."

"First, you and your friends raided the farmhouse," the reporter persisted. "Next was the bowling alley incident in Rocklin, where dozens of arrests were made after you and acquaintances took it upon yourselves to do some investigating. Are the rumors true? Are you and your friends playing vigilantes?"

Arms filled, Faith straightened and used her foot to shut the car door. Her parents hadn't made much progress. Dad held on to Mom's elbow as they worked their way slowly toward the house. Mom had a bruised hip and fractured tibia, which made for a tedious pace.

In the blink of an eye, two more reporters and a cameraperson appeared. Faith pretended not to hear the last question. She just kept moving.

"Mark Silos was found dead at his house," a female reporter stated, pushing ahead of everyone else as Faith headed across the driveway.

"Silos was believed to have been an integral part of the trafficking ring in Sacramento."

"We're busy here," Dad said over his shoulder. "A little privacy would—"

"Grandma!" Hudson ran out of the house and into his grandma's arms.

Faith watched the reunion between her mother and her son. Seeing the joy on both their faces tugged at her heart. The two had always been close, and they held on to each other as if they'd never let go. Mom's eyes were squeezed tight.

In an unexpected rush of activity, another reporter showed up with a cameraman and assistant in tow. Faith could hardly believe how quickly the scene turned from joy to chaos. Everyone was talking at once, more than one journalist shouting questions at Hudson in rapid succession.

Someone rushed past Faith and knocked her forward. Unable to catch her balance, she fell to the ground, her knees scraping against pavement. Mom's bag dropped from her grasp. A pen, lipstick, and other assorted items rolled around on the ground. "Get into the house," Faith told Hudson. "Now!"

One of the reporters helped her from the ground. Another quickly gathered her mom's belongings.

Red-hot anger flashed through Faith's body, heating her face. Her heart raced as the original reporter, the same asshole who'd been throwing questions at her since she walked outside, continued on, unfazed by her being pushed to the ground.

"Mark Silos is said to have been part of the human-trafficking epidemic in the area," he said as if she might not have heard the first time. "Anything you'd like to say about his death?"

Faith thanked the woman who helped her to her feet as she brushed dirt from her jeans. Lifting her chin, she set her steely gaze on the man. It took some effort not to tell him to get off their property before she called the police. She glanced at her dad, who was standing near the door, waiting. *Don't say anything you might regret*; that's what he was trying to tell her with one look.

As much as they all hated having cameras and microphones shoved in front of their faces 24-7, they needed the media. Shifting her weight from one foot to the other, she said, "There is something I'd like to say."

The reporter gestured toward the cameraman, who quickly hoisted the heavy camera onto his shoulder. A tiny red light came on.

"On a beautiful Friday afternoon in November, my family was attacked by a group of people who have no regard for mankind. Traffickers like Mark Silos need to be stopped. Human trafficking," Faith said, her voice even, "is horrifying and morally unacceptable. Traffickers prey on the vulnerable and the defenseless. Many of their victims have suffered domestic violence before they find themselves recruited by traffickers, who make false promises for a better life. These victims include runaways, homeless youths, and teenagers hanging out with their friends at malls. No one is immune. Young girls are being sold into prostitution; young boys are forced into long days of labor. Men, women, and children of all ages are abused and enslaved right here in the United States. It's time we take a stand and work together to put a stop to this atrocity. Not a year or a month from now, but today. It must stop now. Thank you." Before the reporter could say anything else, she turned and walked into the house, shutting the door behind her.

Later that night, Faith peeked through the window to take a look outside. There he was. The FBI agent had returned and was parked in the driveway, the light from his cell phone washing over the bottom half of his face. She left the window and headed for her bedroom upstairs, where she quickly began gathering her things piled on top of the bed.

Dressed in dark jeans, dark shoes, and a dark wool coat, she made sure the Taser was charged before shoving it inside her coat pocket. Next came the canister of pepper spray and finally the 9mm she was getting all too used to carrying.

In the hallway she stopped to listen, making sure everyone was fast asleep. The wood floor creaked in a couple of spots as she made her way down the stairs and across the kitchen floor. She stepped outside into the cool air, locked the back door, and headed off.

Beast was waiting for her near the small building that used to be her dad's workshop but was now known as the command post. "There's no reason for you to stand out here in the dark," Faith said. "I'm fully armed, and I can see your truck from here."

He merely grunted, a familiar sound she knew meant he wasn't listening to a word she was saying, and he would continue to do things his way. As they trudged along through trees and past thick brush, she saw that the truck was empty. "Where are Rage and Little Vinnie?"

"Rage isn't feeling well."

"How bad?"

"Never good."

Over the weeks Faith had done some research about Rage's diagnosis, stage four astrocytoma. Rage had refused treatment, which meant less time on this earth, but also less time sitting in bed suffering long bouts of nausea, headaches, and bloating that would ultimately have the same results. When the time came, she assured Beast and Little Vinnie, she would use nurses to help her with pain, nausea, and breathlessness.

It wasn't until they were driving down the main road toward Mesa Verde High School in Citrus Heights that Beast asked, "How's your boy doing?"

"He keeps to himself mostly."

"Understandable since he's only been home for a couple of days. You'll need to be patient. Let him know you're there for him when he's ready to talk."

"Good advice," she said. "And I know I shouldn't stick my nose in your business, but don't you think it's time to have a heart-to-heart with Rage?"

"About what?"

"About life and death. About what she means to you and how much you'll miss her when she's gone."

"She knows I care about her."

"Yes, I suppose she does, but it's always nice to hear."

"Have you talked to her about these things?" he asked.

"A little. She thinks you're holding back. She's worried about you."

"She's worried about me?" He shook his head in wonder.

"I think she's afraid."

"Of dying?"

"No," Faith said. "She's accepted the inevitable, and she's doing her best to seize every moment left on this earth. But I think she's afraid of leaving you behind. Afraid of what might happen to you when she's gone." Faith thought of Craig, wishing she could have told him how much she loved him before he died.

"I'll be fine," he said.

"Will you?"

He didn't answer, and the silence weighed heavily on her shoulders, causing her to wonder if this was how Rage felt when she was confined in a small space with a man like Beast, who could not be cracked.

Not another word was spoken until they arrived at the high school and Beast pulled up next to a long row of cars. "Looks like your therapist wasn't kidding about having friends who want to help," he said.

"Kirsten mentioned the first time we met that she and some friends had formed a group. It all sounded a bit mysterious, like some sort of neighborhood watch gang but more hard core."

"So you really have no idea what we're walking into here?"

"Not a clue."

Beast shut off the engine.

"I don't know if Detective Yuhasz has had much time to look at the information I gave him," Faith said before either one of them made a move to leave the truck. "Once the detective knows what he has in his possession, I don't think he'll be able to hold off very long before handing it all over to the FBI."

"I figured that's why we've bothered coming here tonight. We need help getting through these names before the suits get involved."

Faith nodded her agreement. "Once that happens, we won't be able to get anywhere near those people." She looked at Beast. "I can't bear the thought of having to sit at home all day waiting for updates."

"It's not going to come down to that," Beast said. "We're doing the right thing by coming here tonight and getting help. It would be almost impossible for those sleazeballs to move Lara out of the country without someone recognizing her. The faster we can check out the names on this list, the faster we can bring Lara home."

A shiver coursed through Faith, causing the tiny hairs at the back of her neck to stand on end. The idea of any one of those men keeping Lara locked away made her crazy. And if they ever found out that Richard Price's list of names was in Faith's possession, Lara would be in more danger than ever. The risk of keeping her alive or trying to smuggle her out of the country would be too great.

Faith reached for the door handle and jumped down from the seat of the truck. If Kirsten Reich and her friends wanted to help her find Lara, who was she to turn them down?

The night was dark and starless, the air crisp and cool. Icy fingertips skittered up her arms as she followed Beast toward the main building.

"Are you planning on handing over the entire list?" he asked her before they reached the building.

"Not every name. I don't know Kirsten very well, and I have no idea what to expect tonight." She patted her bag. "I left Aster and the men directly under him off the list I plan to give them, since we've already discussed saving those scumbags for us."

"Rage mentioned having an idea of how we might get into Aster Williams's house to have a look around."

"Great," Faith said. "We'll talk about that tomorrow when we meet."

He nodded.

Beast opened the double doors leading into the gym.

Faith stepped inside. There had to be close to fifty people sitting in row after row of folding chairs facing a small stage. For the first time since the attack on her family, she thought about her life as a teacher. She used to feel such pride walking into her classroom. The kids saying "Good morning, Mrs. McMann" never failed to make her heart grow a little bigger. She always liked to start the day feeling as if she was making a difference in children's lives.

"This could be interesting," Beast said as he followed her inside.

Kirsten Reich made her way from the front of the crowd to the back. "Glad you could make it."

"Rage couldn't come," Faith told her. "She's not feeling well."

Kirsten stopped in the middle of the aisle. "I'm sorry."

"She'll be fine," Beast said.

Kirsten nudged them toward the front of the room. "If it's all right with you two, we'll take the empty seats in front and face the group. Since I like to keep things moving along, I'll make introductions, and then we'll discuss our plans to help find Lara."

"Sounds good," Faith said.

Kirsten didn't waste any time. The second Faith and Beast were seated, she turned toward the audience and said, "My name is Kirsten Reich." She waited a few seconds while the murmuring and private talks came to a hush. "For those who have not met me, I'm a therapist and counselor and one of the founders of CAW, Crimes Against Women. I'm going to introduce you to a few of our founders and our special guests, and then we'll move right along since I know many of you came here tonight on short notice and have families to get back to." Kirsten gestured toward a woman sitting in the front row.

The woman wore a brace around her left leg and used a cane to push herself from her seat.

"This is Lyssa Falcao. Her résumé is long, but she's best known for her work with Lawyers Against Human Trafficking. She works tirelessly to bring awareness by hosting events and panel discussions all over the US.

"Next to Lyssa we have Caralea Batts, our newest CAW member. Caralea works closely with antitrafficking advocates in Sacramento County. She makes her way around the country teaching teens and their parents how to be safe on social media. You may be surprised to know that seven out of ten kids post their name, age, and town where they live, making them easy targets for online predators."

Kirsten waited for the murmurs to subside. "We're glad to have Victoria Mitchell in attendance tonight. She's a women's bantamweight titleholder, a jujitsu blue belt, and a kung fu purple belt. When she's not at the gym, Victoria can often be found with a camera in hand, all in the name of bringing awareness to our various causes."

Kirsten turned toward Faith and Beast. "The gentleman sitting here next to me is known as Beast, bounty hunter and friend of Faith McMann, the subject of many recent late-night meetings."

More murmurs from the audience.

"As most of you know, with the help of friends and family," Kirsten continued, "Faith has managed to successfully track down one of her two missing children."

People cheered and clapped.

Faith was impressed by the turnout and by the résumés of the women already mentioned. She had no clue groups like this existed. There was a certain kind of energy in the room, energy filled with hope and excitement, the kind that bounced off walls and made people pay attention.

After the room quieted, Kirsten went on. "Faith's daughter, Lara, is still missing. I think it's safe to say, based on what we've read in the papers and seen on the news, that Faith won't slow down until her daughter is home where she belongs.

"Thanks to Faith's vigilance, these traffickers are being exposed, one at a time. They broke into Faith's parents' home and attacked her mother. They're feeling the heat, and they're only going to get bolder." Kirsten paused before adding, "What Faith needs now are reinforcements. We need to find Lara before they have a chance to regroup. That's why we need to move swiftly. As of tonight, all CAW members will be added to a shared app on our cell phones. Let me know if you don't want to be added. Over the months, thanks to many of you, we've compiled a list of twenty-five names of some of the worst offenders in and about Sacramento."

More applause.

"I feel for Faith," a woman in the back row said, "but human trafficking is a widespread problem. So why focus on finding *one* child?"

"Because finding Lara could be the blow that takes the wind out of these traffickers' sails. Finding Lara would inspire everyday citizens to get involved. Of course, there is no perfect solution to this ever-growing problem. The only answer up until now has been to stop one john or pimp at a time. But if we join together, imagine what we can accomplish. Right now, because of Hudson's return, the media is in a frenzy. They want more, and I believe we should give them what they want."

Everyone began to talk at once.

Faith reached into her bag, pulled out the names and addresses she'd brought, and quickly explained what she knew as she handed the list to Kirsten, who then passed the names on to her friends in the front row. They talked among themselves as Kirsten said to Faith in a low voice, "There has to be close to a hundred names here. That's a lot of information you gathered in a very short time. Do you want to share where you got your information from?"

"I can only assure you my resources are legit."

"Looks like we have our work cut out for us," Kirsten said. The room had grown quiet again, so she turned to face the audience. "Our main objective is to locate the people on these lists and watch them closely, track them when possible, see if anyone might lead us to Lara's whereabouts."

"I don't know how your group does business," Beast said, "but I don't think it would be in your best interest to approach any of these people directly. They're dangerous and should be watched from afar."

"We've got the basics covered," Kirsten said. "This isn't our first hurrah."

But Beast was a protector, Faith thought. It's what he did. It's who he was.

"I suggest anyone doing surveillance do it in pairs," Beast said.

"Every member of CAW has had basic training," Kirsten assured him. "They carry a weapon at all times and are well protected. Mo Heedles sitting in the second row there was trained by her two brothers, both SEALs, Special Forces." Kirsten gestured toward another woman. "Eva Malone, middle row, spent a decade with the US Marine Corps. In the back we have Shannon Trickett, champion in women's combat sports."

"Point taken," Beast said.

With every passing moment, Faith felt sure she'd done the right thing by coming tonight. Knowing that these women might be able to help her get through a long list, knowing that every time they could cross someone off that list, they would possibly be one name closer to finding her daughter, made her sit up a little taller and caused her heart to beat a little louder.

"If you learn anything at all that you think might help us locate Faith's daughter," Kirsten went on, "let us know ASAP."

Faith nodded her agreement, thankful to have their support.

Victoria was the next to speak. "I know there are some of you who might wonder why we don't simply hand these names over to the police." She paused. "Unfortunately the police don't have the resources to go door-to-door, let alone keep an eye on every person we believe is up to no good. Without solid proof there's not a whole lot they can do. But if you believe someone you've been watching is dangerous or has anything to do with victimizing young children, do not hesitate to call the police."

"That's it," Kirsten said. "I'm going to give Faith the floor, and then this meeting will be adjourned."

Faith got to her feet, unsure of what to say to these people. "In the beginning," she began, "after recovering from my injuries, I didn't want anyone's help. But then my family got involved, and Beast and Rage approached me, and I realized that sometimes it really does take a village, a community, maybe an entire city, to get results." She swallowed. Exhaustion was setting in, her emotions getting the best of her as she thought about all the people who had gone out of their way to help her. "Without help from so many, I never would have found my son. We came close to finding Lara, too, but our group was small and we could only do so much." She paused to think. "What I'm trying to say is thank you for being here tonight. There are no words to express the gratitude I feel at this moment. Thank you."

"One house at a time," Kirsten added. "One criminal at a time until we find Lara. That's our goal." She raised her hands to let them know she wasn't finished. "Many of you in this room have been working tirelessly for years to fight against human trafficking. This is our chance to use our resources to help Faith find her daughter and use the media attention to our advantage. Thank you for coming. Meeting adjourned."

EIGHT

Beast returned to his home in Roseville to find his dad and Rage watching television, which wasn't a surprise since Rage seldom slept, claiming she had insomnia. But Beast knew it was more than that. She'd never had trouble sleeping until recently. He had a hunch it had more to do with her illness than anything else. Little Vinnie had a soft heart and stayed up with her most nights, taking naps during the day.

After filling them in on what happened at the meeting, he left them to watch the news while he went to his bedroom to change his shirt and brush his teeth. It was late, and he was tired. Hudson McMann's return was being played on every news station across the country. He was happy for Faith. She had her son back.

He tossed his shirt in the basket and then slipped on a clean one. As he did most nights, he glanced at the framed picture of his wife and daughter. Five years since the accident, but it still felt as if it had all happened last week. On more than one occasion he'd been certain he saw his wife from a distance, only to lose sight of her as he rushed to have a closer look. His wife's close friends and relatives had reached out over the years, but keeping in touch with them only made him feel worse.

He'd read about the stages of grief.

Denial and isolation. Check.

Anger. Check.

And that's as far as he'd made it.

He opened the top dresser drawer, pulled his keys and wallet from his pants pocket, and placed them there next to the envelope. The letter from Sandi Cameron, the young woman who'd been texting while driving, crossed the divide, and hit his wife's car head-on. Everyone told him he should be thankful his wife and child had died instantly. *Sorry, people.* That didn't help. He'd prefer it if they hadn't died at all, thank you very much.

He picked up the envelope, examined the return address. It was handwritten, big loopy letters. Sandi had been living at her parents' house in Roseville at the time of the accident. This particular letter had come all the way from Texas. Rage had said she was twenty-three or twenty-four. He didn't care. After the accident, before her court date, he'd given Sandi a chance to make things right by talking to other teenagers about texting and driving, and she'd turned his offer down. She'd done her six months' probation or whatever and went on with her life. Good for her. His thumb flicked across the part of the envelope that had been sealed but was now lifted slightly from age. When he'd first received the letter, Rage had been all over him to open it and see what she had to say. She was convinced Sandi Cameron was probably riddled with guilt and was now asking for forgiveness. Even if that was true, he could never find it inside himself to forgive her for what she'd done. A text message in exchange for two lives. *Nope.* It would never happen.

As he dropped the envelope back into the drawer, movement out of the corner of his eye caused him to turn slowly toward the window and then remain perfectly still.

Most of the light in the room was coming from the bathroom, leaving him standing in the shadows. Through the window he saw what he'd been seeing a lot of this winter. Raindrops hitting the glass and tree branches swaying. And one more thing: a dark shadow hunched forward as the figure ran past.

Beast didn't panic. He never panicked. Slowly, inch by inch, he reached back and opened the same drawer he'd just closed, slid his hand inside, and grabbed hold of his pistol. He knew it was loaded and ready to go because his gun was always loaded and ready to go.

Not wanting to take any chances that whoever was outside might see him, he dropped to the ground and crawled across the floor to the other room.

Little Vinnie saw him first.

Beast put one finger over his lips right as Rage realized something was going on and met his gaze. She started to get up, but Beast shook his head.

Both Rage and Little Vinnie dropped to the floor as if they had been waiting for this moment for a while now.

Low to the ground on his belly, Beast crawled to the kitchen, where he reached a drawer, opened it. He found Rage's gun, made his way back to the other room, and slid it across the wood floor toward her.

With everything going on of late, Little Vinnie had been keeping his rifle close by. At the moment he had it tucked under his arm. He tilted his chin, letting Beast know they were ready for whatever happened next.

Again Beast crawled to the kitchen.

He stopped. Listened. Didn't hear a thing. As he passed the kitchen table, the back door was kicked in.

Splinters of wood rained down around him as he jumped to his feet.

A large man, more fat than muscle, stepped inside.

Using both his fist and his handgun, Beast knocked the guy over the head.

No sooner had the man dropped to the floor than a second man clad in dark clothes rushed through the back door and into the house. Beast jabbed an elbow into the man's jaw, laying him flat, then glanced over his shoulder. He saw his dad and Rage standing a few feet away.

Little Vinnie had the barrel of his rifle aimed at the open door. "How many are there?"

"No idea."

One of the men squirmed. A swift kick of Beast's boot to the guy's head quieted him.

Beast waited to see if anyone else would join them before he stepped outside to have a look. A voice he didn't recognize said, "Nice and slow, so I can see—"

Beast didn't do nice and slow. He spun around, knocked the man's gun from his hands, and took him out with a left hook.

A few seconds later, Rage stepped outside. "Don't shoot your dad," she told him. "He went around the side of the house."

Sure enough Little Vinnie came around the corner and said, "It's all clear."

"Should we call the police?" Rage asked.

"No. I have a better idea."

After Beast relayed his plans, the three of them made quick work of pulling off the men's clothes. They used zip ties to fasten their wrists and duct tape to bind their ankles and cover their mouths. Beast and Little Vinnie tossed them into the back of the truck and took the men for a drive.

Hours later Beast was finally able to drag himself to bed after driving around town and depositing the men at various locations. All three of them had been questioned about Lara's whereabouts, and each of them had denied knowing anything about the girl.

Worried about someone being harmed, Rage had used a marker to leave messages on their bodies and faces to let people know the men were dangerous. That way, any Good Samaritan who happened by might think twice before letting them loose.

Faith hadn't been asleep for very long when she sensed someone inside her room and quickly came awake. She looked around in the dark, stopping at a shadowy figure standing perfectly still near the door. Groggy from sleep, she reached slowly for the gun she kept in the top drawer of her bedside table.

"Mom. Are you awake?"

Her shoulders relaxed. "Hudson?"

"I couldn't sleep."

She patted the empty space next to her. "Come here. Get under the covers and get warm."

The mattress dipped slightly as he climbed in. She moved toward him, wrapped her arms around his shoulders, and kissed the top of his head. He smelled like her mom, hints of lavender and soap. "I love you," she whispered.

"I want to go home."

She didn't respond right away. She knew sooner or later he would make mention of their home on Rolling Greens Lane. She'd just hoped it wouldn't be this soon. "I want to go home, too, but we can't. Not yet."

"Why not?"

"Because I did something I shouldn't have. I let my anger get the best of me, and, because of that, I've been ordered by the court to live here with Grandma and Grandpa."

"Forever?"

"No. Not forever."

"My stuff is at home. Can we at least go there for a little while?"

She thought about his request for a moment, wondered if he could handle seeing the house. Would it bring back bad memories for Hudson, or would it help him deal with all the horrible things that had taken place? She would call Kirsten tomorrow and see if she would mind meeting them at the house.

"Can we?"

"Of course," she said. "We'll go after breakfast. But only for a short time." She wanted to ask him how he was feeling, but she knew these things couldn't be rushed. "If you ever want to talk about anything, Hudson, I'm here to listen."

"I know."

He fidgeted but didn't leave the comfort of her arms, so she stayed still and concentrated on the beat of his heart against her chest.

Minutes passed before he fell asleep.

Since he'd returned home, she couldn't help but stare at him, watch his every move. It took everything she had within her to find the strength to leave him be and give him his space. She breathed in his scent, his soapy-clean hair. Hudson was home. It wasn't a dream. He was here with her now, in the flesh. She wanted to stay like this forever, keep her son wrapped tightly in her arms, safe and sound.

But people didn't always get what they wished for.

───────

Faith pulled up to the house on Rolling Greens Lane and shut off the engine. She looked at Hudson. "Well, here we are."

He turned toward her. His face was still gaunt from his ordeal. Had they starved him? He was pale, too, and his eyes had lost their usual rascally spark.

She wondered if he was thinking the same thing about her. She was merely a shell of the mother he once knew—inside and outside. She looked wiped out most days. She used to have a nightly ritual of washing, scrubbing, lathering on creams and lotions. Showers were now taken for the sole purpose of waking her up. Makeup and lotions, blow-dryers and curling irons were all things of the past.

"Are you scared, Mom?"

The question surprised her. She reached for his hand, to comfort him as much as herself, but then stopped. If she touched him right now, she would lose it. She was certain of it. The emotions had been building like a volcano ready to spew lava and destroy everything in its path. She needed to be strong for her son. And yet she also knew she needed to be truthful. "I am," she said, those two words strained and heavy. "Not in the way you might think, though." She was thinking of the last time Hudson was here. Like his parents, he'd been bound and gagged. He might have seen the man with the knife lean down close to Craig and slice his throat. She wasn't sure.

"What do you mean?" he asked.

She swallowed the lump in her throat. "I'm not afraid of those men." Her voice became a whisper. "But I am afraid for my family, and for my children."

His chin came up a notch. "You don't need to be afraid for me, Mom."

A sob nearly escaped, but she held back. She took his hand in hers, and gave his small fingers a gentle squeeze, something she used to do all the time when the kids were younger. She would walk them to class or to the library if she needed to stay after school for a teachers' meeting or to talk to a parent. She would squeeze Hudson's hand and then Lara's, and they would squeeze her hand, too. But not this time. Hudson was preoccupied with worry.

"I remember what woke me up last night," Hudson said.

She waited for him to go on.

"The men who took us. The ones who talked about a man named Patrick."

"What did they do?"

"I saw the car in my dream. I was asleep when they pulled me from Dad's car and carried me to another car."

He paused.

"What did you see?"

"It was dark, but I heard them say, 'There's Patrick.' One of them went to talk to him. The man named Patrick was driving the same kind of car the principal at our school drives."

She tried to think, couldn't remember what sort of car Mrs. Forbes drove.

"You know, the kind with the letters on the front of the hood."

It hit her then. Mrs. Forbes drove a black BMW. "A BMW?" she asked.

His head bobbed. "Yeah, that's it. He drove a black BMW. That's what he drove, and there's more," Hudson said. "I saw his face."

"You did?" Her pulse raced.

Hudson nodded again. "He stepped out of his car to talk to the guy, and I saw white skin and black hair."

"How old do you think he was?"

He shrugged. "I don't know."

"If you had to guess, would you say he was younger than your uncle Colton?"

"Umm. Maybe Colton's age."

In the rearview mirror, she saw Kirsten pull up behind her. She gave Hudson a warm smile. "You did good. I'm so proud of you."

He glanced at the other car. His shoulders hunched downward as if he was trying to make himself smaller. "Somebody's here."

"Kirsten Reich thought it would be a good idea if she came inside the house with us. Do you mind?"

He shook his head. "I like her."

"I do, too. Are you ready?"

He nodded.

"OK, then. Let's say hello and then go get your things."

Hudson turned away from her to open the car door. His movements were slow, guarded, as if he was taking in his surroundings before he took another step. She'd noticed the same thing at her parents' house. He appeared to be always on the alert, always ready. Ready for what, she didn't know, didn't like to think about it.

Faith watched him shut the car door and then make his way to Kirsten, who was greeting him with a warm smile. Faith grabbed her purse and joined them. She and Kirsten acknowledged each other with a nod.

Kirsten led the way, following the path around the front of the house to the main door. The lawn had grown weedy and long. The maple tree and decorative bushes were overgrown and misshapen from neglect.

Faith nudged ahead and unlocked the front door. Hudson was at her side. She stiffened as she remembered the wall on which she'd painted images of the men who had attacked her family. Her chest tightened, and she stopped short. She couldn't allow Hudson to see such a horrible reminder of that day. She reached out to grab his arm to keep him from going inside, but he rushed across the main living area toward the sliding glass door leading to the pool in the backyard.

"It smells like paint," Kirsten said.

She was right. Faith stepped inside and turned toward the wall—the drawings and notes, the detailed painting, every brushstroke . . . gone.

"Are you all right?" Kirsten asked.

She nodded, grateful to her sister for taking care of the wall. Jana thought of everything. Faith followed Hudson outside and through the gate leading into the pool area.

"The pool is dirty," Hudson said.

"Yes," she agreed. "I'll have to call someone."

Faith looked past the fence surrounding the pool, to the trees bordering the property. Once spindly and sparse, the trees looked tall and thick as if she'd been gone for years instead of weeks. She remembered clearly the day Craig had planted the trees so many years before. She'd watched him dig the holes from the kitchen window, could still see the sweat on his brow and the appreciation in his eyes when she'd brought him iced tea. His eyes. Beautiful, loving, caring eyes. She'd been staring into those eyes when he was killed. Murdered. How would she ever go on without him?

A noise caught her attention. She turned and saw Hudson's shoes slap against the pavement as he walked back into the house. Once again she followed him. She would have stayed on his heels if Kirsten hadn't stopped her in the living room.

"I think we should give him some time alone," Kirsten said. "Just a few moments to himself."

Faith wasn't so sure, but she didn't follow after him.

"You did the right thing by bringing him here. He needs to see his home."

"I'm surprised he would want to come back so soon," Faith said. "After everything that happened."

"He has more good memories here than bad," Kirsten reminded her.

There was a knock at the door. It was her neighbor Beth Tanner. Faith greeted Beth with a warm embrace.

"I heard about your son. I'm so glad he's safe," Beth said.

"Thanks."

"No word yet about Lara?"

"Nothing yet." Faith gestured toward Kirsten. "This is Kirsten Reich, a friend of the family. Actually," she added, "she's a therapist."

Kirsten and Beth shook hands. "You look familiar," Kirsten said. "Have we met before?"

"She was an ER nurse," Faith explained. "She saved my life."

Beth harrumphed. "I did what anyone would have done under the circumstance." She touched Faith's shoulder. "Have you seen the news this morning?"

"No. Why? What's going on?"

Beth walked to the large-screen TV and picked up the remote. "Do you mind?"

"Be my guest."

Beth scrolled through various channels. "Here we go," Beth said. "They've been replaying the story all morning."

Tammi Clark with Channel 10 news stood in front of a two-story house. According to the news ticker at the bottom of the screen, ten arrests had been made. A couple had been running a sex-trafficking operation out of an apartment building in Davis. The pair used social media to find clients. Their arrests led authorities to four other locations—Elk Grove, Woodland, Vacaville, and Folsom.

"We recently got word," Tammi said, "that one of the arrests included an alleged leader of a sophisticated sex-trafficking ring. As we hear more, we'll keep you updated. Back to you, Stacey."

"If you're just tuning in," Stacey told viewers from behind a podium at the station, "it's been a busy morning for the police and the FBI." She reached for the piece of paper someone handed her. "Human trafficking, also referred to as modern-day slavery, is a growing problem in the United States. Many of these youths are recruited or lured by false promises and then forced into trafficking through violence, compelled drug use, and ongoing threats and intimidation. Sex exploitation has reached epidemic proportions in the United States. But in the past few days alone, dozens of arrests have been made. A citizen in Elk Grove, and others like her, are speaking up when they see suspicious activity. The word out in the street seems to be 'If you see something, say something.' I'm going to turn this over to Barb Moore, who is standing by, reporting live in Elk Grove."

The next shot was of Barb standing next to a woman in front of a home in a quiet neighborhood. "This is Nicky Beechler, who lives across the street from where a half-dozen arrests were made in the past hour. Nicky, if you don't mind, could you tell our viewers exactly what happened?"

"Well," Nicky said nervously, seemingly not quite sure whether to look into the camera or at the reporter. "I've got three kids I need to watch after. And for months now I've seen a lot of activity over there." She pointed across the street. "People, mostly men, visited the house at odd hours. That wouldn't have struck me as strange, but one time I saw a young girl in the upstairs window looking right at me, and I swear to God she mouthed the words *help me*. So I called the police. But nothing came of it." She shrugged. "There wasn't nothing else I could do. But earlier today I got an anonymous call. The person told me the people across the street were part of a sex-trafficking ring."

"Who do you think called you?"

Nicky Beechler shook her head. "No idea."

"What did you do after you got the call?"

"I was upset, very upset. So this time I decided I'd go ahead and call everyone I could think of: the FBI, the police, and you people in the media."

"Well, it looks like you did the right thing."

"I hope so. I'm tired of this sh—oops, sorry, this crap going down right in front of my eyes and nobody doing nothing about it."

"As you can see," Barb said as she looked into the lens of the camera, "everyday citizens like Nicky Beechler have had enough—"

Beth hit the "Power" button, and the screen went black. "There was also news of three men duct taped to various telephone poles on Cavitt Stallman Road in Granite Bay. Each of the men had been stripped naked and had the words *sex trafficker* written on their chests and foreheads." She looked at Faith. "I think you're helping to get the word out," Beth went on, "by bringing awareness and giving citizens the courage to make phone calls and let people know what's going on."

Faith looked at Kirsten. "Do you think there could be a connection to last night's meeting?"

Beth frowned. "Did I miss something?"

"We can trust her," Faith told Kirsten before returning her attention to Beth. "In my search for answers, I was able to get my hands on a long list of names, people in Sacramento said to be involved in trafficking."

"So I gathered my friends," Kirsten chimed in, "and we met last night. The plan is to watch these people to see if any of them might lead us to Lara."

"And the connection between the arrest and your list?" Beth asked.

Faith's and Kirsten's cell phones beeped at the same time.

Kirsten smiled. "It's a text from Caralea Batts. Nicky, who we saw on TV, happened to be the neighbor of one of the men who appeared on both our lists. Caralea was our anonymous tipster."

Faith smiled, too. Twenty-four hours hadn't yet passed since their talk, and yet they'd already managed to take a known trafficker off the street. And the best part was Aster Williams and his men would never be able to make a connection to Faith.

Beth's eyes brightened. "I want to help."

Nobody said a word.

"I'm a firearms expert," Beth went on. "I've spent hours volunteering my time, teaching women of all ages about pistol packing and personal safety."

"I had no idea," Faith said.

"Between your friend Beast and your dad, I figured you were taken care of in that regard. I should have said something when you came to visit on Thanksgiving Day."

"I think Faith would agree we could use all the help we can get," Kirsten said. She then proceeded to explain to Beth how to download the app so she could add her name to the list.

Faith nodded. "We would love your help," she said before gesturing toward the bedroom at the end of the hallway. "I'm going to go check on Hudson. I'll be right back."

She found Hudson in Lara's room, sitting on the bed and holding his sister's favorite stuffed animal, a German shepherd named Frisky. She was about to go to him, try to comfort him, when he said, "You won't find her."

"What did you say?" she asked, unsure if she'd heard him correctly.

"You won't find Lara. She's gone."

"No," Faith said, her heart breaking from the sad picture he made. "We will find your sister. We have lots of people helping us, and we'll never stop looking."

"It won't matter."

Faith's brow furrowed as she watched him, waiting for him to look at her. Instead he continued to study the stuffed animal, intently, his fingers brushing through old, wiry fur.

"You don't know these people the way I do," he said. "I've lived with them. I've heard stories about what they do with girls like Lara. You don't know the bad things they can do."

There was a long pause before Faith said, "You don't know the bad things I can do. We found you, and we *will* find your sister."

He looked at her then, really looked at her, and for the first time since he'd returned home, she felt as if he saw her.

NINE

"Are you sure you want to do this?" Faith asked Rage.

Faith had just arrived at the house in Roseville where Rage lived with Beast and Little Vinnie. Rage was sick. Very sick. When they first met, it was easy to forget that Rage had terminal brain cancer; mostly because she did everything with such confidence and determination. How could anyone who was dying walk with a swagger and talk with such bravado, she used to wonder. But now Faith knew it was 100 percent stubbornness that kept the girl up and moving day and night.

"I'm only going to say this once." Rage pointed her index finger at Faith, and then at Beast, and finally at Little Vinnie. "In case you didn't hear me one of the hundred times I told you all, I'm *not* going to be around very much longer. Until I take my last breath, though, I refuse to lie in bed like a worthless corpse. I'm not quitting until I've done all I can to help find Lara."

When Faith opened her mouth to speak, Rage shook her hand at her and said, "I'm not finished."

Faith waited patiently for her to do just that; they all did.

"I like to think I played a hand in helping you find your son," she said to Faith, "but that's neither here nor there because we're not finished. Hell, we've hardly got this party started. And none of you are continuing on this mad search for Lara without me." She plunked her hands on bony hips. "Understand?"

Faith nodded. Beast grunted, and Little Vinnie stood there in his faded denim overalls and rubbed his chin.

"Can we talk about those men you three deposited around the city?" Faith asked.

"Sure."

"What were you thinking, leaving those men naked and fastened to telephone poles?"

"What did you want us to do?" Rage asked. "Call the police?"

Faith nodded. "That might have been a good idea."

"Listen," Beast said matter-of-factly. "The last thing I wanted to do was spend hours at the police station filling out paperwork. Besides, I wanted to send a message."

"A message?" Faith asked.

"Yeah, don't fuck with us, or else." Rage smiled. "Any more questions?"

Faith frowned. Rage, Beast, and Little Vinnie made quite a trio. All for one and one for all. Like it or not, they were going to do things their way. She wasn't looking forward to being interrogated by Detective Yuhasz. If he did question her, she would just have to play dumb.

"All righty then. Time to move on." Rage reached into a brown paper bag and pulled out a beige utility shirt and matching beige slacks that she held up for their perusal. On the front shirt pocket was embroidered "West Coast Gas," and beneath the fake organization was the name "Jim." "I ordered one for each of us." With a wink she added, "Names were changed to protect the innocent."

Beast crooked his neck.

"What's all that for?" Faith asked Rage.

"After you brought over that binder of yours, I got an idea and went ahead and ordered these uniforms. I think it's time we pay Aster Williams a visit. I would love to have a look inside his house and see what we might find there."

Beast crossed his arms. "And how do you propose we do that?"

"I thought you'd never ask. We dress up like the local utility guys—the same people you would most likely call if you were afraid you had a gas leak. We park outside Aster Williams's mansion at the top of the hill. I used the satellite feature on the Internet to get a good look at the property. The place overlooks Folsom Lake. We wait for him to leave. When he's gone, we go to the door and talk to his wife, tell her it's urgent and how calls have been flooding in about a suspicious odor at the end of their road. We'll tell her officials believe there's a natural gas leak in one of the underground pipes, and we need to take a quick look around inside and outside the residence to make sure there are no signs of a gas leak inside her house."

"What sort of signs?" Faith asked.

"Has she noticed any hissing or blowing sounds coming from any of her appliances," Rage said. "Stuff like that."

Beast crossed his arms. "All four of us are going to walk up to Aster Williams's house and knock on the door?"

"Of course not. Little Vinnie and I will be the utility people. We both have a certain air of innocence about us."

Beast released a ponderous sigh, but he kept his thoughts to himself. "What?"

"Nothing," he said. "Go on."

"You and Faith will sit in the car, and if anyone shows up unexpectedly, you shoot me a text."

Nobody said a word.

"I'm finished," Rage said. "That's all I've got. This is our chance to get information from the big guy."

"This is crazy talk," Beast said.

Rage smiled. "And that's why we need to strike fast. Men like Aster believe they're untouchable. I bet you he'd never believe for a second that Faith would be foolish enough to attempt such a crazy scheme."

"Never," Faith agreed.

"No telling what we'll find," Rage said. "But no matter what, it's worth a shot. Might as well start at the top and work our way down. If we find nothing, we strike him from our list and move on. One by one," she said as she pretended to cross names off an invisible list in the air, "until we find her."

"Going inside Aster Williams's home is risky and much too dangerous," Beast said.

"I think it's a brilliant idea," Faith said.

Rage smiled. "Thanks."

"When do we go?" Little Vinnie asked.

"Tomorrow morning. Any objections?"

"We'll need a truck or a van," Beast said, clearly not happy.

"That won't be a problem," Faith said. "I can pick one up from my brother's work tonight."

"Great. Looks like Project Gas Leak will go into effect first thing tomorrow morning." Rage turned around and began shuffling through the top drawer in the kitchen where she stored her gun. She pulled out a pistol, then rifled through another drawer for a cartridge. When she was done, she looked back at the three of them standing in various positions in the living area. "Ready to go?"

"Where to?" Little Vinnie asked.

"There's a certain bar in East Sac owned by two cousins, both of whom are on the list," Rage said matter-of-factly. "I thought we could hit them up tonight."

Beast frowned. "I thought we were focusing on Aster?"

Rage snorted. "Why are you questioning all my plans? We can't hit up Aster Williams's place until the morning, so I figured we might as well pay these two guys a visit tonight."

"Why them?" Faith asked.

"Because they own a bar, and I need a drink."

Little Vinnie shook his head. "You are going to be the death of me. You know that, don't you?"

"Sure, yeah," Rage said. "I'm the grim reaper's best friend. Are we going to stand here all night or actually get something done and pay a few of these dirtbags a visit?"

"I agree," Faith said. "I'm going."

Rage smiled. "Let's go, then."

Rage was absolutely right. What were they supposed to do, sit here and twiddle their thumbs? They needed to take advantage of every single second. She watched her newfound friends gather their things and couldn't help but wonder where she would be without them.

———

Patrick turned up the TV and did his best to ignore the knocking on the door. He never should have opened the door the first time the kid had knocked. She was becoming an annoyance. Winston Wolf had yet to return his call, which probably meant he was afraid Aster would find out about their little business deal.

Fuck Wolf.

He'd just have to find another buyer.

More knocking. Rap, rap, rap. Louder this time.

For Christ's sake. He dropped the remote on the seat next to him and headed for the hallway. He grabbed his keys from the dining room table, unlocked the door, and pulled it wide-open. "What do you want?"

She jumped and then teetered on the edge of the step, arms flailing.

He grabbed a fistful of her cotton shirt to stop her from falling backward down the stairs. Pissed at the thought of losing her in such a way, he pulled her into the hallway and shut the door.

She was breathing hard. Her eyes looked all big and glossy.

He pointed a finger at her. "Don't you dare cry."

"Or what will you do—hit me?"

He raised a fist, ready to clobber her, but something more than good sense stopped him, and he dropped his hand to his side. "What do you want?" The little shit hadn't the decency to look afraid.

"You asked me once if I wanted to come upstairs and watch TV."

"Yeah, so? That was before. This is now."

"I'm bored."

"Too bad. Read another book. I gave you a whole pile of them."

"I can hear the TV in the other room. Can't I watch it with you? Just for a little while?"

He narrowed his eyes, wondering what she was up to.

"How come you're not married?" she asked.

Yeah, he thought. She was definitely up to something. Trying to get him to open up and become her pal. "Because I like being alone," he answered.

"Why?"

"Because when you live alone you don't have anyone talking in your ear. Constant gibberish gives me a headache."

He proceeded to the living room.

The kid followed.

He plunked down on the couch and continued to watch his show. "Who's this?"

He glanced to his right where she was standing. She was looking at a framed black-and-white photo on a bookshelf. He ignored her, even went so far as to turn up the volume again.

"Is this a picture of you when you were little?" she asked, her voice loud enough to be heard over his show.

"Yeah."

"Is that your sister?"

Fuck. He turned the volume down. "Yep. She drowned about a year after the picture was taken."

"Oh."

He returned his attention to his show. Out of the corner of his eye he watched her examine the photo closer. She wasn't playing games. He couldn't help but wonder what it was about the photo that intrigued her. He considered asking her, but then inwardly scolded himself and tried to forget she was in the room. He wasn't worried about her getting away. Every door in the place, and there weren't many, was bolted shut. He didn't have a landline, and he kept his cell phone on him at all times. That didn't mean he was stupid enough to let her run willy-nilly alone in the house all day. But it also didn't hurt to let the kid stretch her legs a bit since the basement was basically a ten-by-ten space surrounded by four cement walls. He'd be rid of her soon enough.

———

Clearly, Lara thought, Patrick had gotten used to having her around. He wasn't a friendly person, but neither was he especially cruel. Every time he let her out of the basement and into his own personal space, he seemed to relax a little bit more. If she made her way into the kitchen for a glass of water or something to eat, though, he always followed her.

He didn't trust her. And that was too bad because she knew which knife was the sharpest, and she wanted to hide it in her waistband. Once she had the knife in her possession, she figured she could pretend she was sleeping the next time he came down the stairs to check on her. When he got close enough she would pounce, stab the knife into his throat, and then run. Once she reached the top of the stairs, she would lock him in the basement and then use a chair to reach the higher locks on the front door. Or toss the chair through the window, at the very least.

She set the picture of him and his sister back on the table and then slid open the tiny drawer.

"Shut the drawer," he said without looking at her. "And stop being so nosy."

She sighed. "I'm hungry. Can I make cookies?"

"No."

"Why not?"

"I don't have the ingredients. Sit down and shut up, or you're going back to the basement."

"You have sugar, flour, eggs, and butter," she said. "That's all I need."

He looked at her then. "What are you up to, kid?"

"I'm bored, and when I'm bored I like to eat cookies."

He shook his head. "Go ahead. Have fun."

"Really?"

"I'm not going to say it again."

She ran off, couldn't believe he'd agreed to let her bake cookies. Her plan might work. The thought of escaping, of seeing her family again, made her feel happier than she'd felt in a very long time. She wanted to bake in her own kitchen with her mom, watch her brother's face light up when Mom gave him cold milk and a plate of cookies. Dad would make a joke about how he didn't get enough chocolate chips in his cookies, and then he would chase Hudson around, fighting for the "good" cookie. Her heart swelled at the thought of seeing them again. She missed her family so much.

It took Lara a while to find everything except the vanilla extract. She preheated the stove and then found a mixing bowl and began measuring flour. In one of the drawers she found a metal utensil she thought might be long enough for her to reach the lock at the top of the door. She walked toward the front entry, worrying her bottom lip as she went. She eyed the top of the main entry door. If she stood on a chair, she was pretty sure she could unlatch the lock. *Yes.* She could do it. She was sure of it.

Excitement stirred within as she walked back into the kitchen. What if this was her best chance at escaping? What if this was her *only* chance?

She picked up a chair, surprised by how light it was. Slowly, quietly, she carried the chair and the utensil to the front door. She took her time setting the chair on the floor, careful not to make even one tiny sound. Her stomach lurched as she looked toward the living room, where Patrick was watching TV. She could hear TV voices but nothing else. She was scared, but she forced herself to remain calm.

The wood creaked as she placed a foot on the seat and stood tall. Standing on the chair, she raised the metal object high above her head until it touched the lock. There was no chain on this particular lock. She needed only to push the lever to the right.

Almost there. Every muscle in her arm was on fire as she strained to push the lever to the side. Her brow wrinkled. She could do this. Just a little farther. The tip of the utensil slipped off the metal latch and made a clunky noise.

Her attention was back on the living area. Her heart was beating so fast she thought he might be able to hear the pounding against her chest. She waited to see if there was any movement, any sound at all. Nothing.

She reached for the lock again, determined to make it work. Again she strained, standing on tiptoes as she made contact with the latch. When the lever moved half an inch, excitement rushed through her body. She could do this!

But then she heard movement in the other room, heard the TV volume turn down and then the rattle of his cup. She glanced that way, saw movement in the shadows near the window. He was coming!

She hopped down from the chair, picked it up, and hurried back to the kitchen. The second she put the chair back where it belonged he stepped into the kitchen and gave her a funny look. "What are you doing?"

"I was just going to come in and ask you what this is." She held up the utensil for him to see.

He had an odd look on his face. He knew. She swallowed.

"That's called a microplane."

She wrinkled her brow in confusion.

He shook his head as if she were a lost cause as he crossed the room to refill his glass with ice and water. "It's used for grating citrus or cheese. You don't need it to bake cookies." He looked around. "Doesn't look like you've gotten very far."

"I couldn't find a mixer," she said, although she hadn't looked.

"You'll have to mix by hand," he told her. He was about to exit the kitchen when he angled his head and gave her a long look. "Hurry it up," he said, "or you can forget baking cookies altogether."

After he left, Lara put the metal gadget back in the drawer. The look in his eyes told her he was suspicious, which meant she would have to wait for another time before she attempted to unlock the door. If he caught her before she escaped, he'd never let her out of the basement again.

With a heavy heart she went back to her search for vanilla extract.

———

Patrick was impressed. The sugar cookies were crispy on the edges and soft and chewy in the center. The kid could actually cook.

"So who taught you to bake, your mom?"

She finished chewing and then swallowed before shaking her head. "Grandma Lilly. My mom can't cook at all. Dad usually makes dinner, and I make dessert."

"Now that your dad is gone, I guess your mom will have to learn to cook."

She tossed her half-eaten cookie in the sink.

"What's wrong with you?"

"My dad isn't gone."

He hadn't realized she didn't know. "Hate to be the one to break it to you, but he's dead and won't be coming back."

"You're all liars. Mother told us all that we weren't loved or wanted, but I've seen my mom on television twice, begging for my return. Why are all you people so mean?"

He shrugged. "Not everyone grows up with a roof over their head surrounded by loving parents."

"I want to go home. Let me go. I won't tell anyone about you, I promise."

"Sorry, kid. Not going to happen."

"I hate you."

"The feeling is mutual."

She stormed past him, made her way to the door leading to the basement before he said, "Hold on a minute."

She stood still.

"Turn around and face me."

"I don't want to."

"I don't care." He grabbed hold of her shoulders and yanked her around. Then he lifted her shirt high enough so he could see the handle of a knife. He removed it. "What else do you have hidden away?"

She said nothing. A tear escaped and slid slowly down the side of her face.

"I don't know why you're crying," he said as he leaned over and patted her down, making sure she was clean. "You should be happy I'm not going to use this knife to slice your throat wide-open like they did to your father."

"You're a liar. My dad is alive. He's looking for me right now."

"Yeah, whatever, kid." He found no other weapons on her. "What were you going to do with that knife?" he asked, curiosity getting the better of him.

She lifted her chin in defiance. "I was going to pretend I was sleeping," she told him. "And when you got close enough, I was going to stab the knife into your neck."

Her brutal honesty took him by surprise. The serious tone of her voice and the fire in her eyes told him she meant every word. "And then what would you have done?" he asked.

"I would have locked you in the basement and run away, far, far away."

He laughed and then backhanded her so hard the back of her head smacked against the door.

She was sobbing now, and he was glad for it. When she looked up at him with big watery eyes, he didn't see a scared little kid. He saw his own weaknesses. It didn't matter how old she was. He'd let his guard down. For the first time in years, he realized it had been bad choices on his part that had gotten him nowhere. Trusting the McMann kid and letting her roam around the house had been a mistake—one that wouldn't happen again.

She sniffled and said, "You're evil."

He slapped her again, practically felt her teeth rattle. He liked the way hitting her felt, and it took some control to stop from pummeling her to death. His heart raced as he flexed his fingers. "And here I was beginning to think you liked me," he said. The fact that she'd called him evil didn't bother him. Sticks and stones and all that, but her defiance did irk him. She reeked of disrespect, and she needed to be put in her place.

He opened the door. As he watched her walk down the stairs, he said, "I wouldn't knock on this door again if I were you. Not unless you want to see how I punish people much bigger than you for disobeying my orders." With that said, he shut the door and locked it tight.

The kid had gumption. Like her mother.

He felt deceived. Hoodwinked. Betrayed. And that bothered him because he'd never been one for emotions and feelings. The notion that the little brat could unnerve him made him want to march down those stairs and beat her to a pulp, finish her off, and be done with it. At the very least he wanted to teach her a lesson she wouldn't soon forget. But harming the girl more than he had might leave a permanent mark, which would bring the price down when he found a buyer.

He continued to flex his fingers as he walked back to the living room. From here on out, he needed to stay disciplined and focused.

TEN

Russell Gray was inside the command post in his backyard, taking inventory of guns and ammunition, when he felt a spasm. He reached for his lower back and rubbed the kinks out as best he could. His journey up the mountains to find his grandson had been a tough reminder that his old bones could take only so much. Stress wasn't helping, either. He was worried about Faith. Hell, he was worried about Colton and Jana, too. The stress had taken a toll on all of them. And yet he knew it would be impossible for any of them to give up on looking for Lara.

He'd always had a special spot in his heart for his granddaughter. She was the sweetest little girl he'd ever had the pleasure of being around. Lara was a cloud watcher, a flower picker, a seeker of answers. She'd always been quiet, but you could almost see her brain working overtime inside that head of hers if you watched her long enough.

A noise outside the door caused a jolt within, waking him from his meandering thoughts. He grabbed a pistol, made sure it was loaded, then took careful steps that way.

"Russell. Are you in there?"

His shoulders relaxed. It was his wife. He opened the door to let Lilly in. She stepped inside, no easy feat considering the damage done by her attackers. He looked around outside, past acres of grassy fields and trees, before locking the door behind her.

"What are you doing out here?" he asked. "It's late."

"I was going to ask you the same thing." She swung her arms wide, then winced from the pain it caused her. He stepped toward her, but she raised a hand, stopping him from getting too close. "Everything hurts right now."

He nodded in understanding.

"You can't disappear like that in the middle of the night. Even if you're just coming out here to"—she looked about—"what *are* you doing out here?" She walked toward the two folding tables covered with guns and ammunition.

"I'm taking inventory."

"It looks like you're getting ready to go to war."

"In a way, I guess you could say I am."

She turned back to face her husband. "Russell. I couldn't bear to lose you. There's no possible way I could go on if something happened to you."

He set his gun down, rested a gentle hand on her good shoulder. Then he kissed her forehead. "You're not going to lose me. Everything's going to be all right. I promise."

"You can't make those kinds of promises, especially at a time like this—we both know that."

There was nothing he could say to appease her.

She walked to the door. "I need to get back to Hudson. I wanted to see if Faith was here with you since she isn't in her room. I don't know where she went this time, but it's a miracle she hasn't dropped dead from exhaustion."

Russell glanced at the clock. It was one in the morning. "Come on," he said. "I'm finished here. Let's go inside."

The command post was two hundred feet from the house. As Lilly walked ahead, Russell focused on the darker areas of their property, every part of him on alert. A cool breeze rattled brittle leaves overhead. A squirrel or some other critter skittered off to his right.

A loud crack sounded in the distance. Lilly stopped walking. "What was that?"

"Sounded like a branch breaking free. Come on." With his hand on her back, he nudged her onward, careful not to hurry her so much that she tripped and lost her balance. Her attackers had left her bruised and battered, body and mind. Her gait was off-kilter, would be for a while, maybe forever. She had a long way to go before she'd get to her new normal, whatever that might be.

It killed him to think of her being alone and scared, fighting for her life. The thought always took him back to the day he'd found out Faith and her family had been attacked. He'd always sworn to protect his loved ones, and once again he'd failed.

He'd fought in wars, been captured by the enemy, escaped, and made it home to his family. He thought he'd done a decent job of putting the horrors of that time behind him. But the fighting and violence weren't over, after all. Knowing the enemy was right here on his home turf caused all the little fragments of fury he'd spent years burying to claw their way back to life.

By the time they stepped into the house, every muscle in his body felt tight. His hands had curled into fists at his sides. Something niggled at him, and he rushed up the stairs, forgetting all about his bad hip as he went.

The door to Hudson's room was ajar.

He was about to flick on the light switch when he saw movement in the bed. As his eyes adjusted to the dark, he saw Hudson tucked away for the night. Everything was fine.

Russell checked the entire house, made sure nobody was hiding in a closet or under a bed. When he was finished, he went downstairs, where Lilly found him looking out the window, staring into the night.

"What is it?" she asked in a concerned voice.

He said nothing.

"Talk to me, Russell."

"I promised to love and protect you, and look where it's gotten us."

"You're the reason we're still a family. You used your contacts to help Faith get out of jail, and you've stuck by her side every step of the way."

He looked at her. She was still as beautiful as the day he'd spotted her at a dance hall and asked her to dance.

"You found Hudson and brought him home," she continued. "Colton told me you saved his life up there in the mountains." Her eyes watered. "Most important, you came home to me. So stop this nonsense."

She was right. He'd always prided himself on his ability to remain calm under fire. By letting his emotions get the better of him, he'd forgotten some of the most important lessons he'd learned during his years in the military. *Gather a trusted group of people. Stay focused on the long-term goal. Stay positive, and never give up.* "I love you," he said.

"I love you, too. I'm going to bed. I suggest you do the same because tomorrow will be another long day."

"Why? What's happening tomorrow?"

She had turned to walk away, but she stopped at the door and glanced over her shoulder at him. "They're all long days. Haven't you noticed?"

Peanut shells crunched beneath Faith's shoes as she stepped into the bar. The place was a dive—dark, seedy, and small. The air, filled with smoke and sweat, stuck to her lungs. The wood tables were scarred. Music played in the background: "Crazy Train," by Ozzy Osbourne, bringing to mind the 1980s and the singer who bit the head off a bat.

The three of them, Faith, Rage, and Beast, walked single file through the bar until they found an empty table next to a graffiti-covered wall.

Beast sat facing the bar. Rage sat to his right, and Faith took a seat across from her, which gave her a view of a man and woman dancing in a dark corner. Not really dancing but hanging on to each other and swaying back and forth.

Beast, Faith noticed, was on the prowl, taking it all in, sizing up everybody in the place. The couple in the corner was oblivious to everyone else. Beast seemed uncharacteristically anxious, as if looking for a fight.

The guy standing at the bar waiting for his drink looked like a younger version of Willie Nelson. His beard was long, the lines in his face beginning to deepen. Faith glanced over her shoulder to see who or what Beast was looking at. Three rough-looking men and a redheaded female sat at a table nearby. The woman sported a welt along with a string of bruises around her throat. When she laughed, a loud, cringe-worthy cackle, it was easy to see she was missing a few teeth.

"That's Eddie Harlan behind the counter serving that guy a beer," Rage said.

Faith looked that way. There was only one person behind the counter. He was tall and thin as a pole. His eyes were round and glossy like marbles. He looked familiar. She'd looked at so many people over the past few days it was sometimes difficult to put names with faces. The ringleaders, johns, and pimps were quickly becoming a blur swirling around inside her mind. Faith trusted no one outside her family and a few friends. She was becoming paranoid to the point that it seemed everyone was involved in human trafficking.

Despite the bone-chilling cold, Eddie wore a sleeveless shirt, revealing long, skinny arms covered with colorful tattoos.

"What was the deal with Eddie?" Faith asked, her voice low, knowing Rage would have the answer. "Are he and his cousin pimps?"

Rage nodded. "According to Richard Price's notes, these two started out as recruiters. They made enough money to buy this bar, making it easier for them to find a steady flow of clientele."

"What do you think?" Faith asked Beast.

"About what?"

"Any ideas about what to do with these guys?"

"I have lots of ideas."

"Want to share?" Rage asked.

"Not really."

"The place closes in another hour," Faith said. "Maybe we should wait until some of these people clear out before we approach Eddie and question him."

But Beast was pushing himself to his feet. "I'll be right back."

They watched him walk toward the bathrooms and disappear.

"He's in one of his moods," Rage said.

"Why? What happened?"

She shrugged. "Sometimes he wakes up like this—all moody and pissy for no apparent reason. It's annoying as hell."

"How's Little Vinnie doing?" Faith asked since she wasn't around him 24-7 like Rage and Beast. "Is he still forgetful?"

"Not too bad," Rage said. "His short-term memory seems to come and go."

It was quiet for a moment before Faith said, "Remember what I told you about the Cecelia woman who Miranda and I talked to in San Francisco?"

"The woman who worked at the hotel?"

Faith nodded.

"She's the one who mentioned the name Patrick," Rage said. "Isn't that right?"

Faith nodded again.

"She wasn't the first person to mention that name," Rage told Faith. "Fin, the tattoo artist, also mentioned a Patrick, but then Fin got blown to pieces, and we never had the chance to question him—remember?" Rage didn't wait for a response. "Without a surname it all seemed a bit useless." Rage shrugged and added, "Since we didn't have anything else to go by, I made a list of every Patrick I could find within a fifty-mile radius of Sacramento." Rage scratched the side of her head. "I had no idea there were that many people with the same name. Without a social security number, or a last name, it's like looking for a needle in a haystack. We need more information; otherwise it's wasted time."

"Well, earlier today," Faith said, leaning closer, "Hudson told me he had a dream where he saw the car, a black BMW, and he also caught a glimpse of Patrick's face."

"This is huge!"

Faith nodded. "After I got off the phone, I made some calls and did some research. Hundreds of thousands of BMWs are sold every year in the United States alone. I also talked to a local BMW dealer, and he said it would be impossible to track down a particular black BMW sold to a man without a last name."

Rage rubbed her forehead. "Yeah, it doesn't help much, does it? What else did Hudson say about him?"

"He's a white man with black hair. He guessed his age to be the same as my brother, which would mean he could be in his midthirties."

"White man, midthirties, dark hair. Drives a BMW. I'll see what I can do."

"Thanks," Faith said. "I called Agent Burnett with the FBI to let her know."

"What did she say?"

"She'll let me know if anything comes of it."

There was a commotion outside the entrance to the bar. The door flew open. A young woman stumbled inside, nearly falling to the floor before she was able to put a hand to the wall and catch her balance. Brown, stringy hair framed a thin, pale face.

A short, stocky fellow walked in behind her and gave her a push, sending her forward on wobbly legs. This time she did fall on her knees and hands. She looked strung out. Eyes wide, pupils dilated.

Faith was about to go to her and try to help, but Rage shook her head and mouthed the words, *Not yet.*

Eddie came forward and helped the girl to her feet. "What the fuck do you think you're doing?" he asked the man standing behind her.

The man pulled a cigarette from his pocket and lit up. He looked around, his gaze stopping on Rage and then settling on Faith.

There he was. Eddie's cousin, Gage. Faith recognized this particular face right away. He had a scar resembling the one Faith was left with after the attack. His deep, craggy mark began below his left earlobe and then curved over and down his chin. It was the other scar that had left him disfigured, though. Thick and wide, the scar ran straight down from his hairline and across his right eye, stopping at the top of his cheekbone. It was safe to say he'd been in a few scuffles over the past forty or so years. He wore heavy work boots, and the floorboards rattled with each step he took their way.

Rage looked at him. "What do you want?"

"Think I don't recognize you?" he asked Faith, blowing a thick stream of cigarette smoke into her face.

"Think she cares?" Rage asked.

His gaze moved to Rage. "You're the sick one, aren't you?" He didn't wait for an answer. "The newspeople love a good story, and they sure like talking about the girl with brain cancer. Funny you two happened to show up here at my establishment out of the blue." He looked at his cousin. "Isn't that funny, Eddie?"

The two people sitting near the door left some money on the table and headed out, careful not to draw any attention their way. The three men and one woman sitting at the table were all smiles, as if they'd been waiting for the entertainment to begin.

Eddie shook his head at Gage and tried to warn him. "They're not alone."

Beast appeared just then. He stood a foot taller and at least a foot wider than Eddie. Faith waited for Beast to say something, but he simply stood there, quiet as a mouse.

"It's time for you three to move on outta here," Gage said, loud enough for everyone in the bar to hear.

"You heard the man," the toothless female shouted.

By the time Faith reached into her purse and got to her feet, Beast had Eddie by the throat. A chair crashed to the floor. Beast dragged him to the wall and held him there; Eddie's feet dangled in midair.

Mötley Crüe's "Shout at the Devil" had replaced Ozzy's song.

"Where's the girl?" Beast asked, the veins in his neck bulging, his face crimson.

Unsure of what to do, Faith looked at Rage.

Rage pointed her way. "Behind you!"

Faith pivoted on her feet. At the same time Gage hooked an arm around her waist, Faith jabbed his arm with her Taser and pressed the button.

Gage groaned in protest, stumbled backward, and fell to the ground, his arms and legs quivering.

A beer bottle flew past Faith, barely missing her head before it struck the wall and shattered. It was the redhead from the other table who had thrown the bottle. She stood in the middle of the room, her hands curled into fists at her sides.

Rage lunged for the woman, wrapping her arms and legs around her thick middle to stop her from going after Faith.

Beast dropped Eddie and came after the redhead, who was now punching Rage in an attempt to get her off. The redhead's three male friends all stood at once, blocking Beast's path.

Big mistake.

Beast went ballistic. He took hold of the closest man's arm and snapped it in half. Bone crunched. The man screeched, an ear-piercing sound that made Faith wince.

Without hesitation Beast picked up the next guy in line and tossed him across the room. He slid across the floor, headfirst, striking a row of stools lined up at the bar.

The third man, having the benefit of a few seconds to think, grabbed a wooden chair and held it above his head, ready to defend himself. Before Beast could get to him, Faith stepped up from behind and jabbed the Taser into the man's side, giving him a jolt of electricity. He went down. The chair toppled to the side.

The couple dancing in the corner had disappeared through the back.

The redhead Rage was riding liking a bull was now shouting obscenities and going round and round like a dog chasing its tail. Rage hung on tight until Beast got a hold of the woman and picked her up off the ground, allowing Faith to help Rage off the roller-coaster ride.

"Are you OK?" Faith asked.

"Just a little dizzy. Don't let go of me."

Faith helped her get to a chair.

Rage rested the palm of her hand on her forehead. "I told you he was in one of his moods."

Rage wasn't kidding.

When the woman refused to shut her mouth, Beast wrapped an arm around her throat and squeezed until she passed out. She dropped to the floor.

Eddie had managed to crawl halfway across the room by the time Beast grabbed a fistful of his hair and pulled him back to where his cousin lay on the ground. Beast placed a booted foot on Gage's throat and pressed down.

Gage coughed as he tried to get the boot off his throat, but it was no use.

Beast pressed harder until Gage's face turned blue. "Where's the girl?" Beast asked.

"Let him go," Eddie said. "You're gonna kill him."

"Where's the girl?"

"OK. OK. Let up on him, will ya?"

Beast took some pressure off the man's throat. "Talk."

Eddie was bent over at an awkward angle, his hair still wrapped in Beast's grasp. "I d-don't know where the g-girl is," Eddie stuttered. "Nobody does."

"Did she run away?" Faith asked.

"I don't know. I told you. Nobody knows!"

Beast gave Eddie's hair a good yank, then looked around the room. "Everybody out. Now!"

The young woman Gage had pushed through the door when he first entered made a quick exit. So did the Willie Nelson look-alike sitting at the bar.

Beast used his free hand to pull out a pistol. He waved it at the guy who had been thrown into the bar stools and said, "Grab your friends, and get out of here!"

This time they got the message. Two of them ran out the front entrance, leaving the third guy to drag the redhead out onto the sidewalk.

Rage shut the door and locked it.

Beast aimed his gun at Gage's head. Judging by the wild look in his eyes, Faith knew he was done talking.

"Don't kill him," Eddie pleaded, no doubt sensing Beast's frustration.

And Eddie wasn't the only one who sensed a change in the air. Faith could smell the two cousins' vulnerability. These guys knew something, and they were scared. "Shoot him," Faith said. "I'm tired of all these tight-lipped creeps protecting one another and getting away with abusing young girls. It has to stop."

"I don't know," Rage said. "What would we do with their bodies?"

"I don't care," Faith said, hoping to scare Eddie enough to make him talk. "We need to set an example right here, right now."

"There's gonna be a meeting tomorrow night," Eddie sputtered.

Faith angled her head, surprised by his admission. "That's very interesting," she told Eddie, trying to play tough. "Now, was that so difficult?"

"Who is going to be at this meeting?" Rage asked.

"Shut up!" Gage told his cousin, prompting Beast to press hard on his throat again.

"Jesus. You're gonna kill him," Eddie wailed.

"You know what you have to do if you want to save your cousin," Rage said.

"All the important people are going to be there," Eddie blurted. "A couple of la-di-da district attorneys, and that lawyer, Max something or other. You know, the one from Los Angeles who used to be on that celebrity show. And some young girls will be there, too."

Beast let up some, allowing Gage to catch his breath.

As soon as the last few words came out of Eddie's mouth, Gage closed his eyes and cursed.

Faith pointed a finger at Eddie. "What did you say?"

Eddie's gaze darted around the room as if he was searching for the answer.

"You said some 'young girls' were going to be there," Faith reminded him.

"Yeah, yeah, that's what I said."

"What girls?"

"I don't know. Just girls."

"How many?" Rage asked. "And how old?"

"A few," Eddie said. "Mostly between the age of ten and fifteen is my guess."

"This is ridiculous," Faith told Beast. "Taser him! Shoot him in the leg. Make him talk!"

Eddie's eyes widened. "I only know what Jimmy told me the other day."

"They're going to kill you for talking," Gage said. "We're both fucked."

Beast slapped Eddie across the back of the head. "Who's bringing the girls?"

"I swear I have no idea."

"So all these men are coming to Sacramento to meet with whom?" Faith asked, doing her best to keep her cool.

"With Aster Williams and his men," Eddie said. "Who do you think?"

Another slap across the head.

"Ouch." Eddie rubbed his head. "The mayor's brother is supposed to be there, too. They're trying to figure out a way to make sure you and that kid of yours are taken care of once and for all."

Beast kicked him in the shin.

"Fuck! What did you do that for?"

Beast ignored the question. "Who told you about this meeting?"

"I already told you. Jimmy did. He was bragging about moving on up. Yap yap yap. It's all I ever hear."

"Shut the fuck up," Gage told Eddie.

"Keep Eddie here," Beast said as he let go of his hair and grabbed Gage instead, then dragged him across the wood floor and into an alleyway located behind the kitchen.

"You said a mayor's brother would be at the meeting," Rage told Eddie. "What mayor are you talking about?"

"I've said enough."

"Seriously?" Rage asked. "You don't think I'll shoot your ass?" She pressed her gun against the side of his head.

Faith readied her Taser. "We'll start with a little jolt to his system," Faith told Rage, "and see if it will help his memory."

Eddie raised his hands in surrender. "The mayor of Sacramento," he said. "The mayor's brother is the reason most of these guys get a get-out-of-jail-free card. They've got links to judges and lawyers, too. Nobody can stop them."

They heard a scream, followed by Gage begging for his life. Next came a muffled curse, a clang as if two cymbals had been banged together, and then a couple of grunts were followed by the sound of the door coming open.

Beast walked back into the room. "We got what we need," he told Faith and Rage. Then he grabbed hold of Eddie's arm and pulled him close. "You and your cousin may want to get out of town," he told him. "The sooner the better, because if anyone gets word I was here and that you told me when and where the meeting is being held, you and your cousin are dead."

"We can't just up and leave!"

Beast pushed him away. Eddie stumbled backward and fell to the ground. "Have it your way. But if and when they find out you talked, they'll probably kill you. And if they don't kill you, I will."

ELEVEN

When Faith came downstairs the next morning, Hudson was eating pancakes as fast as Lilly could make them. Faith ruffled her son's hair, kissed the side of his head, then found a large mug and filled it with coffee. Mom didn't have to say anything at all for Faith to see that she wasn't pleased with her. Mom didn't appreciate Faith sneaking out every night; she didn't like worrying about her. But they both knew Faith would do the same thing if push came to shove.

Faith didn't bother with cream and sugar any longer. Too much work. She dragged herself to the family room, where Dad was flipping through channels. He was quiet.

"Are you angry with me, too?"

"Nobody's upset with you."

She didn't believe it, but that didn't stop her from taking a seat. She drank her coffee and stared at the television screen as he flipped through the channels. She sat up a little taller when she recognized Detective O'Sullivan. "Wait. Don't change the channel. What's going on?"

He turned up the volume.

O'Sullivan was standing in front of a three-story office building in Rancho Cordova. A long line of people, mostly men, were being led out of the building and into police cars. Some of them tried to hide their faces from the cameras. Others didn't seem to care.

"More than fifty johns were arrested early this morning," the reporter said. "Many are calling it entrapment since advertisements were arranged by undercover cops on the Internet. The suspects face up to a year on misdemeanor promotion of prostitution charges. The men's ages range from twenty-five to seventy-six."

The camera zoomed in for a close-up of O'Sullivan. "We're sending a strong message," he told the reporter. "Letting citizens know that people who pay for sex will be treated as criminals."

"What do you say to the people who believe johns are victims?"

He shook his head. "These men are exploiting and victimizing trafficked females and males. They are not victims."

"All suspects so far have professed their innocence," the reporter went on once the camera panned back to her. "Legal experts are saying they don't expect any of the people arrested to face jail time. According to Detective O'Sullivan, though, the message has been sent. Johns will continue to be targeted since they are the people funding the trade that supports violence against women. The sheer number of arrests has sent shock waves through the state, upsetting marriages and law offices alike as these men and their lawyers set out to prove their innocence."

Dad turned down the volume, looked over his shoulder to make sure Hudson was preoccupied, then looked at Faith. "What's going on?"

"What do you mean?"

"You've been out every night since Hudson has been home. You're not getting enough sleep, and we hardly ever see you eat. You can't keep up like this for too much longer. You'll crash and burn."

She raked a hand through dirty, unkempt hair and then scooted closer to him and lowered her voice. "There's a lot going on. I've been waiting for the right time to tell you about a meeting I attended. I've found a group of people to help us."

"I've been right here, Faith. Why haven't you told me about this?"

She raised her hands in frustration. "When have we had time to talk?"

"If you were home for more than five minutes, we could have squeezed it in. Don't shut me out, Faith."

She sighed. "Let's not fight about this. We're both tired."

"I'm fine," he said. "I've been getting plenty of sleep. Where were you last night?"

The truth was Faith had been worried about her dad. The long days and nights spent searching for Hudson had taken a toll, but he was stubborn and wouldn't back off. She needed to come clean. "Two of the people on the list are cousins who happen to own a bar in the area," she told him. "Beast managed to get them to talk last night. If they are to be believed, Aster Williams will be meeting at a warehouse in East Sacramento with some very important people."

"We should call the FBI," Dad said.

She shook her head. "We can't do that. There might be young girls brought to the meeting." Faith placed a hand on Russell's arm. "What if Lara is one of them?" The thought made her heart swell. "If that's the case, I can't risk having this meeting shut down."

"If Lara is brought to this warehouse," Dad said, his voice also low, "it seems even more of a reason to get the FBI involved."

"You're not listening to a word I'm telling you. The traffickers in the upper hierarchy are related to mayors. They are judges and lawyers and district attorneys. If word gets out, any one of these men could shut the meeting down so fast our heads would spin." She released a heavy sigh. "We could end up right back where we started. Knocking on one pedophile's door at a time, searching for a needle in a haystack."

"I don't like it," he said.

"I don't like it, either, but it's the way it has to be. If we call the FBI, Aster Williams and every other man involved will scatter, and you know it."

"Are you saying the FBI is corrupt?"

"I'm saying I don't trust anyone. Somebody has Lara." She rubbed her temple, her frustration palpable. "The moment these guys find out about the list of names Richard Price left behind, our chances of ever seeing her again will grow slimmer. If we handle this right, we can trap them while they're all together in one building. Once we have Lara, we'll call the cops and the FBI and anybody else you can think of. But not a minute before."

"You said you had help. Who?"

"The therapist you met the other day. Kirsten Reich. She and a group of women have been keeping an eye on some of these guys for quite a while. These women come from all walks of life. They've been trained. Many of them are fighters. They're the reason for many of the arrests being made."

"And they've agreed to join you when this meeting takes place?"

"I only learned about the meeting last night. I'll be talking to Kirsten soon. I'm certain they will want to help. If everything goes as planned, nobody will get hurt."

"I want to help," Dad said.

Her shoulders fell. "The truth is I was hoping you would stay out of this one. You've done enough, Dad. Mom needs you here. Hudson needs you, too. He needs stability. He needs one of us, and you know as well as I do it can't be me right now."

Dad looked over his shoulder to make sure Mom wasn't within earshot. "I know you want what's best for everyone and that you think it's your decision to make. But you're wrong. That isn't how things work around here. I'm not ready to sit back and watch things unfold, and neither is your mother. We're family, and families stick together. Go eat and take your shower. I'm going to give Colton a call."

———

Faith took a quick shower, grabbed a bite to eat, and then, with the help of her dad, she snuck out of the house. Beast, Rage, and Little Vinnie were waiting for her in one of her brother's utility vans.

Twenty-five minutes later, they parked on the side of a private road in Folsom, where they had a decent view of a mansion sitting at the top of a hill overlooking Folsom Lake.

It was still early. The sky was gray, and the air was brisk.

Rage used a comb to brush gel into Little Vinnie's silver hair until it was slicked back away from his face.

Rage smiled at the older man and said, "Ready, Jim?"

Little Vinnie grinned, too.

Faith was pretty sure there wasn't anything Little Vinnie or Beast wouldn't do for Rage. She had them both wrapped around her finger.

Aster Williams, driving a Mercedes, had left the property a few minutes ago. He'd been alone. From what little she'd seen, he looked like his picture online. He wore a suit; his dark, silver-tipped hair had been slicked back much like Little Vinnie's was now.

Faith could see the worry in Beast's face as he watched his dad and Rage, dressed in the uniforms Rage had purchased, climb out of the van. They lost sight of the two of them a few feet before they reached the front door.

"This is a crazy idea," Beast said. "We have absolutely no idea if the place is crawling with security. His house could be surrounded by bigger men than me, men with guns."

The panic in his voice prompted Faith to reach out and squeeze his arm. She wanted to tell him everything would be OK, but she didn't because she was worried, too, even having second thoughts. She thought about Mark Silos and how she'd regretted being reckless. Any of them could have been killed that night.

"At the very least they should be wired. This," Beast said with a wave of his hand, "is a suicide mission. We can't hear a thing. We have no idea what the hell's going on."

Faith never should have let Rage talk her out of being the one to knock on the door. Rage had been afraid Aster's wife might recognize Faith from all the media attention she'd received. Faith looked at Beast.

She wasn't sure what to do or say to calm him. "Do you want me to go knock on the door, tell whoever is inside that Jim has a call, an emergency?"

"No. We'll wait. Stick with the plan."

———

Despite the frigid air, Rage could see a light sheen of sweat on Little Vinnie's brow as they approached the front entrance. Suddenly she felt sort of bad about coming up with such a crazy, harebrained idea. Sure, she might have nothing to lose, but what about the rest of them? Faith's son was home. He needed her. And Beast would never be able to live with himself if something happened to Little Vinnie. She was about to tell Little Vinnie she'd changed her mind about the whole thing and wanted to leave when the door opened. The woman standing before them was tall and elegant. Her nails were painted a light pink to match her lipstick. She looked as though she'd stepped out of one of those popular glossy magazines. "Can I help you?"

Rage had a speech prepared, but her mind went blank.

Thankfully, Little Vinnie took over. Not only did he appear confident; he was convincing. He'd obviously done his homework because he said his spiel with little effort, telling Aster's wife all about the problem with the gas lines. He went on and on, and Rage simply followed along without a word spoken. Next thing she knew, they were walking through the house.

Aster's wife's name was Rae. The woman seemed more worried about the idea of her house blowing up than letting strangers in.

While Little Vinnie kept Rae occupied, Rage walked deeper into the house, down long hallways with ceilings so high she had to crook her neck to see them. Still within earshot, she heard Rae tell Little Vinnie that she was going to call her husband.

Rage's stomach dropped as she stepped up her pace. If Aster returned, it was over. She examined every room as she went along. A laundry room bigger than her bedroom. A sewing room, which appeared to be used solely for wrapping gifts, shelves lined with every color of ribbon imaginable. *Nothing here. Time to move on.*

She peeked inside every closet and built-in cupboard along the way, keeping quiet but working fast. The house was as big as any hotel she'd ever seen. Every time she opened or closed a door, the sound echoed off the walls.

She felt as if she were making her way through a maze and wondered if she'd ever find her way back to the front entry. The floors were a light-colored stone, and the cream-colored walls were adorned with paintings framed in gold, every picture lit up by its own personal light fixture. The next room she walked into was the largest yet. A library lined with rich mahogany shelving that gleamed wherever the light coming through the high windows hit. There were so many books. And so little time. No reason to linger.

Back in the hallway, she made a left and spotted a grandfather clock at the very end of the corridor. She could go right or left. Both hallways led to a closed door. She went to the right. As her fingers nestled around the knob, she flinched when the clock chimed. Her insides flip-flopped as she wondered how Little Vinnie was handling Aster's wife. Had he been able to find a way to stop her from calling her husband?

If Aster was coming, Rage figured she had five minutes, maybe six. Tops.

The room she found herself in was large and majestic, with a wood-beamed ceiling. This had to be Aster's office. A rich cherrywood desk and cabinets, floor-to-ceiling windows showing off views of the pool and the glistening lake beyond.

Rage moved in front of the leather desk chair and attempted to open the drawers, but they were all locked. She reached beneath the middle of the desk, her fingers brushing over the smooth wood, where she found a key on a small hook. She used the key to try to unlock the drawers, but it was too small. Frustrated, she looked around the room, her gaze settling on a screen where she could see images of the entire house.

Her heart raced with excitement as she headed that way.

It appeared he'd installed a camera in nearly every room. Rage played with the buttons, sweeping through images of the library and kitchen and finally the bedrooms upstairs. Her heart sank when she realized there was no sign of life anywhere. She'd gotten her hopes up. The thought of telling Faith she'd wasted their time weighed heavily on her shoulders.

Her legs wobbled, forcing her to hang on to the shelving for support.

She'd been growing weaker by the day but had been doing everything she could to hide her quickly deteriorating health from Beast and Little Vinnie. Sometimes, like now, she felt disoriented. Her stomach turned, and her head throbbed.

Her time was running out.

Most times she talked tough in hopes of appearing stronger than she felt. But she knew she was dying. Sooner rather than later. That was her truth, and all the wishing and hoping in the world wouldn't stop it from happening.

The idea of leaving this world without being able to see Faith reunited with *both* of her children left a gaping hole inside her. Why she cared so damn much, she wasn't sure. She liked Faith, and for some reason that surprised her. They came from two different worlds.

Seeing Faith get the best of Aster Williams and his gang wasn't the only reason she wanted to hang on. It was something else altogether. She'd made too many bad choices in her lifetime, but using her time and energy to help Faith find her little girl was meaningful and made Rage feel useful. Helping Faith find her daughter was the right thing to do; it gave Rage purpose. And even though it was a good choice, Rage realized it was also a selfish one.

As the pain in her head subsided, she straightened and looked away from the images on the screen. Half-hidden behind a row of books and framed pictures of family, she spotted a keyhole to a safe that blended in with the wood shelving. Unwilling to get overly excited this time, she moved two picture frames to the side, slid the key into the slot, and turned.

Voilà!

The twelve-by-twelve-inch door opened.

Inside the safe were stacks of hundred-dollar bills, a few coins, a Luminor Submersible 1950, and a Smith & Wesson 9mm.

She heard voices. They were coming this way.

She shut the safe, locked it, then rushed back to the desk and quickly returned the key to its hook. Her gaze fell on a notepad, where she could still see the indents from a note written on the previous piece of paper. Using the oldest trick in the book, she grabbed a pencil and slid the lead tip back and forth across the indentations until the note appeared: "1354 Stone River Drive, Elverta" The voices grew louder. She was out of time. Her pulse raced as she tore the page from the notepad and slid it into her pants pocket. Then she ran to the door, escaping the room just as Little Vinnie and Rae appeared from around the other corner.

"Please don't go in there," Rae called out.

Rage lifted both hands, making it look as if she had yet to open the door.

"Found anything so far?" Little Vinnie asked.

"Everything has checked out. The place is clean. How about on your end?"

"It's all good. Her husband's on his way to check out the rest of the house."

"OK," Rage said. "Why don't we wait outside until he arrives?"

Rage led the way. She kept up a good pace, and yet she didn't want to appear as if she was in a rush to escape. She pulled out the phone, pretended to key in a telephone number, and then held it to her ear. "Number five-oh-seven-six checking in," she said. "Yes, everything's clear . . . Got it. We're on our way."

As soon as she stepped outside, she inhaled. Turning toward Rae and Little Vinnie, she said, "Looks like we have another emergency across town. We've got to go."

Little Vinnie handed Rae a business card and told her to have her husband call if he had any questions or concerns. Then he shook her hand and followed Rage down the stone walkway, across the driveway, and to the other side of the street, where the van was parked.

Rage jumped into the back and slid onto the seat next to Faith.

Little Vinnie climbed into the front and sat on the passenger side next to Beast. "No time to explain," he said. "Aster is on his way home. We need to—there he is now."

Beast turned on the engine. As soon as Aster drove past them, he headed slowly down the road. The moment they were through the gate leading to the property, he sped away.

TWELVE

Beast, Rage, and Little Vinnie had been home for about an hour when Beast knocked on Rage's bedroom door before entering. On the drive home, he'd noticed how pale she looked when he glanced in the rearview mirror. He didn't like seeing the dark circles under her eyes. "What are you doing?" he asked.

"The same thing I've been doing every time I get a free moment . . . looking for the mysterious Patrick everyone seems to be talking about."

"Patrick?" Beast asked as he walked to the side of the bed and took a peek at her laptop screen.

"Yep. You were standing right next to me when Faith first mentioned his name. Sometimes I don't think you listen very well."

Beast scratched his chin, knowing she was probably right.

"When Faith and Miranda were in San Francisco, they talked to a woman who worked in the spa, a woman Miranda recognized. When Faith questioned her, asking for names that might lead to Lara's whereabouts, the woman mentioned the name Patrick." Rage's finger clacked against the keys as she worked.

He remembered now. Faith had mentioned the name on the same night Faith's mom had been attacked. A lot had been going on at the time, and he vaguely recalled thinking there wasn't much he could do without more information. "So what do you have there? Every Patrick living in the United States?"

"Pretty much," she said with a laugh. "The first thing I did was use social media and a telephone book to start gathering a list of people with the same name. I think it's safe to say I've written down every Patrick I could find who lives within a fifty-mile radius of the California state capitol."

Beast inwardly winced.

"I know it's a wild-goose chase and there's not much to go on, but it keeps my mind off the whole dying thing, so it's a win-win."

He hated when she talked that way, but he also knew it was her way of fighting the emotions that surely came with knowing you didn't have much time left. She used humor and sarcasm to fight depression and despair. "If this Patrick was or is involved in trafficking," Beast said, "why wouldn't he be on Richard Price's list of names?"

She shrugged. "I'm not sure. I've looked over Price's list so many times I have every name on the list memorized." She smirked. "I'm exaggerating, of course, since my brain isn't what it used to be."

"OK," he said. "Enough with the jokes."

"Anyhow," she went on, "there's nobody in Richard Price's binder named Patrick. But," she added, lifting a finger for emphasis, "there are fifteen guys on the list who are still unaccounted for." She narrowed her eyes. "Why would Richard Price take the time to make note of people who didn't exist?"

"It's been my experience in the bounty-hunting business," Beast told her, "that some people are simply better than others at keeping their information private. It has nothing to do with Richard Price. Maybe Richard Price's list was outdated by the time he sent it to his sister." He scratched his ear. "It could be any number of things."

"Well, what would you say if I told you Patrick is a white man, about thirty-five years old with dark hair, who drives a black BMW? Would that be enough information to track him down?"

"No."

"You're such a buzzkill."

He didn't like seeing her look so frail. He wanted to ask her if there was anything he could do to make her more comfortable, but she hated when he pitied her. She'd told him and Little Vinnie from the start that she didn't want to be babied in any way. "You've been working on this for how long?" he asked.

"Obviously not long enough. But I've crossed off anyone on the list who is under twenty-five and older than forty-five, which eliminated fifty Patricks."

She was putting everything into this search for Patrick. Since it would be cruel to make fun or tell her she was wasting her time, he decided to go along with the whole thing, even went so far as to feign an interest in her investigation. He and Little Vinnie looked for people for a living. Looking for a man named Patrick, a man with no last name, no date of birth, and no social security number was like looking for a needle in a haystack. "So how many Patricks do you have left?"

"Why don't you pull up a chair and help me?"

"No, thanks."

"Oh, come on. It's sort of fun."

"Fun is overrated."

Rage rolled her eyes. "I've got thirty-two Patricks left."

He cracked his knuckles and then shifted his weight from one foot to the other.

"What?" she asked.

"Nothing."

"No. Tell me. What?" She put her laptop to the side. "You never come in here to talk to me. You came in here for a reason. What is it?"

"I wanted to see how you were doing. That's all."

She smiled one of her half smiles that made a slight dimple appear and said, "I'm good. Thank you very much."

He didn't believe her. "Nothing hurts?"

"Just my head," she told him. "It sort of feels like there are a large group of mountain climbers inside using pickaxes to climb my skull. But other than that, I'm good."

He stared at her.

She stared back.

"Just say it, Beast."

He said nothing.

"You love me, and you're going to miss me."

His bottom lip twitched, but no words came forth.

"I love you, too," she said.

He stood there, his chest tight, his insides crumbling, unsure of what to do next.

"Will you do me a favor when I'm gone?"

"Anything."

"Will you take Little Vinnie on a long drive on the back roads of Dixon until you find a never-ending field of sunflowers? It's hard to miss."

"And then what?"

"And then pull over, sit still, and enjoy."

Thirteen

Lara wished Patrick hadn't found the knife she'd tucked away. It was sharp and deadly. Instead she would have to make do with the nail. Lara used the cement wall to keep the tip of the nail sharp. Patrick, she decided, wasn't as smart as he thought he was.

Before Patrick had caught her trying to get away with one of his knives, he'd allowed her upstairs into the main part of the house many times. On those occasions, Lara had gotten at least a glance at every door leading outside. Two of them had bolts and chains that were too high for her to reach.

No matter which door she tried to escape through, she would need a chair.

If she tried to hurt him with the nail, she was pretty sure it wouldn't do enough damage to give her time to escape. She needed to wait for just the right moment. When she was trapped in the trailer park, she'd waited too long to make her move. Next time Patrick let her inside the main part of the house, if ever, she would be ready. She had to be.

Although Patrick had never touched her or been creepy in that way, he was scary. And now she knew he was violent, too. The slap to her jaw had caught her off guard. Her mouth still felt bruised. But that's not what frightened her the most. It was the way he looked at her sometimes . . . as if he wanted to get rid of her for good, maybe even kill her. She knew he was only keeping her alive because she was worth a large amount of money. She'd heard what men paid for young, untouched girls like her when she was at the farmhouse. Miranda had hinted at what these men did to girls like her. Lara had been too disgusted to think about it.

When she'd first been brought to Patrick's house, she'd hoped to find a way to make him feel sorry for her, maybe let her go, but now she knew that would never happen. He didn't have a heart. He was a horrible man, and she needed to do whatever she could to get away. Sometimes, when he let her watch TV with him, she'd hear him muttering about the dingy furniture or how much he hated the house. How he deserved better.

She wondered if he had a split personality. He could go from quiet to shouting at the top of his lungs in seconds. Whenever she heard his phone ring, she would run to the top of the stairs and listen at the door. That's how she found out he was trying to sell her to the highest bidder. He spent hours every day trying to make a sale. His boss, whoever that was, seemed to be the problem. From what she'd overheard, the people Patrick was dealing with were afraid of what the boss would do if they made a deal with him.

Patrick, it seemed, had managed to hide her away without anyone else knowing. That's why he kept her locked in the basement. During the last phone conversation she'd overheard, he'd sounded hopeful. Although she heard only one side of the conversation, he'd said something about meeting at a shipping yard and putting her on a boat. She didn't like the sound of that, but if it ended up being her only chance at getting out of this house, then she would take it.

She was using a nail to scrape another letter into the wall when she heard him talking on his phone. Again she hid the nail away and tiptoed up the stairs to listen.

Patrick was about to open the door to the basement, check on the kid, and see what she was up to, when his phone rang.

"Hey," the caller said, "it's Eddie. Gage and I need to talk to you."

Exasperated, Patrick said, "I'm busy. I'll stop by the bar at the end of the week."

"It has to be now. Today. Something happened last night. We need money."

Patrick groaned. "How much?"

"A hundred thousand."

Patrick held back a laugh. The good news was he had them all fooled. Morons like Eddie and his cousin, Gage, thought he had money, which gave him power. He looked around at the place he was renting. Peeling wallpaper and a cracked front window, drafty doors and a heating unit that could wake the dead. The place wasn't fit for a fucking dog, let alone a human being. But he drove a sleek new BMW and he dressed in Armani, so they all thought he was rolling in dough.

"We'll give you the deed to the place in exchange for cash," Eddie went on.

The fucker was serious, Patrick realized. It was Patrick's job to take care of guys like Eddie and Gage since Aster didn't have time to deal with this sort of crap. What the hell had the two idiots gotten themselves into? He didn't have to ask the question before Eddie told him.

"Faith McMann and friends stopped by the bar late last night," Eddie said. "The giant who follows her around nearly killed Gage."

Patrick shut his eyes and used his free hand to rub the throbbing ache at the back of his neck. "So, what did they want?" Patrick asked.

"They wanted information about the girl—what do you think?"

Patrick didn't like his tone, leaning toward disrespectful, but he let it go for now. Nobody knew Patrick had the girl hidden away in the basement, so he wasn't worried. Yet. "Why don't you tell me what happened to make you think you need a hundred thousand dollars in cash? Are you two planning on running away?"

"Just need to hide out for a while until things calm down."

Did he detect a stutter in Eddie's voice? "That's a lot of money," Patrick told him.

"If you can't manage it, we'll have no choice but to pay Aster a visit and talk to him directly about getting some money and hiding out for a while."

The boy had gumption. He'd give him that. "Is that a threat?"

There was a long pause before Eddie said, "No. It's just that we don't have too many options."

Fucking liar. "I'll need to run to the bank," Patrick said to ease Eddie's mind. "Why don't the three of us meet at the construction site off Florin Road between Hedge and Bradshaw exactly two hours from now?" The site had been abandoned in 2009 after the builder went bankrupt. Foundations and partially built structures still dotted hundreds of acres, making the place look like a ghost town.

"We'll be there," Eddie assured him.

"Good." Patrick disconnected the call. Forgetting all about the kid in the basement, he went to the closet in his bedroom and rifled through his things until he found a small bag to use to carry the money. He put a towel inside to give the bag some weight. He would go to the bank, withdraw everything he had in his account, which wasn't much, and put the cash on top. He hurried to the bedside table and grabbed his gun. Then he looked in the mirror and frowned. The shabby weekend look wouldn't do. He needed to shave, comb his hair, and put on his best suit.

Fourteen

Faith was in the family room playing cards with Hudson and Dad when Mom appeared with Detective Yuhasz in tow.

"Look who came to visit," Mom said in her usual cheery tone.

Faith stood, surprised to see the detective out and about. She smiled at Yuhasz and said, "You're looking pretty good. When did they let you out of the hospital?"

Dad stood, too, and shook the detective's hand.

"I was released the other day," Yuhasz said. "So this is Hudson, I gather?"

"Hudson," Faith said, "this is Detective Yuhasz. He played a big part in helping find you."

Hudson stood and offered his hand as his grandpa had done. "Thanks," Hudson said.

Detective Yuhasz smiled. "You're welcome." He glanced at Faith. "Can I have a word with you in private?"

"Why don't we take a walk outside?" Faith suggested. "I don't believe you've ever seen the command post my family set up."

The detective nodded, apologized for interrupting their card game, and then followed Faith through the sliding glass doors.

Once they were inside the garage-size room now referred to as the command post, she locked the double doors behind them, then watched Detective Yuhasz make his way around the room as he checked things out. Although he had a sling strapped to his shoulder, his color was good. He looked healthy, as if the hospital stay had provided some much-needed rest.

He stopped to take a closer look at the maps on the wall and the list of names and places on the whiteboard. He looked from the pictures of suspects to the table covered with handguns and rifles.

She gestured for him to have a seat on one of the folding chairs scattered around the long, rectangular table in the middle of the room.

"So this is your headquarters," he said.

She nodded. "My family thought we could use a place to meet and throw out ideas. It's come in handy."

He continued to look around.

"What's going on, Detective?"

Neither of them bothered to take a seat.

"It's about the information you gave me when I was in the hospital."

She sort of figured that was what this was about.

"I think you know what has to be done," he said.

"I understand, but is there any way you can hold off for a little while longer?"

"Why? Give me one good reason?"

"Lara."

He scratched the back of his head. "Do you have any idea what you're asking me to risk?"

"I think I do. Your job, probably your reputation."

He rapped his knuckles against the table. "What exactly are you doing with this information?"

"I just need a little more time to watch some of these people. Once you hand the list over to the FBI or the chief of police, word will get out. You know it will. And once these guys find out authorities have the names of every john, pimp, and trafficker in the area, they'll run."

The tension hovered thick and heavy like rain clouds ready to burst. He closed his eyes, exhaled.

"If you've looked over the list of names, you know there are very important people on it, including the mayor's brother, a high-profile lawyer, and your son-in-law. Shit will hit the fan. And once that happens, Detective, it'll be over. And what will happen to Lara? Can you tell me that?"

"I can't keep this from them. And to tell you the truth, I don't see what good another day or two is going to do you."

"Please," she begged. "I'm trying to get information to help me find my daughter."

"You seem to think everyone else is sitting on the sidelines, twiddling their thumbs."

"I never said that."

"I have been gathering evidence," Yuhasz told her. "But you know when it comes to entering any of these men's homes or places of business, my hands are tied unless there is proof of any wrongdoing. Laws are put in place for a reason."

"That's the difference between you and me. I don't have time for warrants. I can't let the system slow me down, but I do understand you need to work within the law. I'm not looking for a conviction," Faith told him. "I'm looking for my daughter."

A hush fell around them before Yuhasz said, "There has been a string of arrests made lately—most having to do with persons linked to trafficking. Do you know anything about what's going on?"

"Not a thing," she lied. The truth was, Kirsten Reich and friends were out in full force, following the men on the list and calling in anything from a broken taillight to tinted windows.

He rubbed his chin thoughtfully.

She said nothing. Just waited him out.

"Twenty-four hours," he told her. "Not a minute longer."

Twenty-four hours could very well be the difference between finding Lara dead or alive. The men in charge of this trafficking business had to be getting nervous. The recent arrests were no fluke. In twenty-four hours there would be no doubt in anyone's mind that Faith and her friends were just getting started.

———

The moment he heard a knock on the door, Beast grabbed his gun. They didn't get too many visitors. And after the bar episode last night, he figured it couldn't be good. A peek through the window revealed he'd been wrong. There was no reason for worry. It was Faith's sister, Jana.

He opened the door.

Her gaze fell to the gun in his hand.

"Don't worry. I'm not going to shoot you."

She put a hand over her heart. "That's good to hear. I was in the area and wanted to stop by to talk with Rage. Is she here?"

"She's in her room," Little Vinnie said from the kitchen.

"Should I come back another time?"

Little Vinnie came forward, the same ugly apron he always wore tied around his neck and waist. He used the spatula to wave her inside.

"Put the gun away," he told Beast. "Come on in," he said to Jana. "Rage is awake. She's doing some research on her computer."

"Next time it might be a good idea if you call first and give us a warning." Beast locked the door behind her and then set the gun on the table next to the door.

"I'll do that," Jana said as she made her way through the kitchen. "What are you cooking? It smells good."

"Spaghetti with mushrooms. Rage's favorite. Are you hungry?"

"Spaghetti is not my favorite meal," Rage said as she stepped into the kitchen.

Jana looked as if she might weep as she wrapped her arms around Rage and held her tight.

Beast held back a laugh at the expression on Rage's face. She looked annoyed as the very pregnant and too-friendly-for-her-liking mother-to-be held her close. The friendship the two of them had formed was thoroughly perplexing, and Beast had a feeling they both knew it.

"Why don't you all sit down?" Little Vinnie said. "You might as well eat while you talk about whatever it is you came to talk about."

"Oh no, I couldn't possibly intrude."

Beast took Jana's purse and set it aside while Little Vinnie ushered her into a chair before she could protest further.

"It's no use fighting them," Rage said. "It's easier if you just pick up your fork and enjoy whatever Little Vinnie puts in front of you."

Jana blushed but did as she was told.

Once everyone had a plate of spaghetti, they ate in silence.

Except Jana, who couldn't seem to keep her mouth shut.

Beast assumed she was one of those people who wasn't comfortable with too much quiet. After each bite, she wiped her mouth, sipped her water, and then rambled on about one thing or another. She told them what her mom was up to and all about Steve's recovery and about watching her neighbor's two-year-old for forty-five minutes, just long enough for the toddler to get into the pantry. And then she began to sob.

Beast kept his eyes on his plate, tried to pretend he didn't see her crying.

"What's wrong?" Rage asked Jana with what sounded like genuine concern.

"I'm going to be a horrible mother. My neighbor's child could have died."

"How? Did he get a hold of cleaning supplies?"

"No, but he could have if I hadn't found him in time."

Rage put down her fork. "Did you want to talk to me about something?"

Jana sniffled, wiped her nose with the tissue Little Vinnie handed her. "The reason I came," she barely managed, "is because your son's parents, Sue and Danny, have been asking about you." Jana got up from her chair, which seemed to be a struggle, and went to where Beast had put her purse. She pulled out an envelope.

"Go ahead and leave it all there on the table," Rage said. "Thanks."

Beast watched the exchange and wondered why Rage seemed so obviously disinterested.

Jana did as she requested and set the envelope on the coffee table. "There are letters and pictures," Jana told Rage. "They've been trying to call you, but thought maybe you weren't feeling well and therefore sent everything to my address and asked me to get it all to you. They would love to visit again if you're up to it."

Rage didn't respond. Instead she made eating spaghetti look like a time-consuming and complicated process. She picked up her fork, poked it into the center of her plate, and began turning the fork, winding the noodles in the tines.

Jana, Beast noticed, hadn't moved from the spot where she'd found her purse. She simply stood as if frozen in place. For a moment Beast wondered if something was wrong. And then he noticed water gushing down both legs.

"Jana?" Beast said.

Rage narrowed her eyes. "What's going on?"

Little Vinnie jumped to his feet. "I think her water broke."

Rage dropped her fork onto her plate. "What the hell?"

Jana hadn't moved a muscle. Either she was in shock or she was in pain. It was hard to tell. "What should we do?" Beast asked nobody in particular.

"I can't do this," Jana said.

"Umm, you don't actually have too much of a choice," Rage told her as she rushed to her side, took her arm, and slowly escorted her to the couch. "I'm going to call your sister," Rage said calmly. "She will call your husband, and then someone will talk to the doctor, and we'll take it from there."

"No," Jana said. "Really. I mean it. I can't do this."

Rage made a face at Beast right before he went to grab a pile of clean towels.

When he returned, Little Vinnie picked up the phone, dialed, and then hung up. Beast had no idea who he'd been calling.

Little Vinnie scrambled around the kitchen next, filled a pot with water, and put it on the stove.

"What are you doing now?" Beast asked, more concerned about his dad than Jana.

"Boiling water. The first thing everyone does is boil water."

Jana cried out in pain, a piercing screech that made Beast clench his teeth.

"You must know what to do," Little Vinnie told Rage. "You've had a baby before."

"Someone needs to call my husband," Jana wailed. "I can't have this baby without my husband."

"I was in a hospital," Rage told Little Vinnie. "I was in a lot of pain. I let the nurses and doctors handle it all."

"Stop!" Beast shouted. "Everyone stop!"

They all looked at him with wary eyes, everyone silent for the first time in twenty minutes. "What is wrong with all of you?"

Nobody said a word.

"Her water broke. It's not a big deal. It could be hours before she has the baby, so let's all stay calm." He looked at Jana. "Everything is going to be fine. I'm going to grab the keys to my truck, and we're going to take you to the hospital. Rage is going to call Steve right now, aren't you, Rage?"

"Yes, sir."

Despite Jana's low tolerance for pain and his dad's inability to calm down, Beast somehow managed to get Jana in the truck and to the hospital in record time. Although Rage had wanted to go along for the ride, she'd offered to stay home and watch over his dad.

FIFTEEN

Faith stood in front of the window, peering in at Jana and Steve's baby boy. Although he had been born six weeks early, he looked healthy.

Steve kept patting Beast on the back, thanking him for helping Jana get to the hospital. According to Rage, when they'd first arrived, Jana had been dizzy and had a rapid pulse. The doctors were afraid she was going into shock. But everything turned out fine, which was a good thing because Faith didn't think they could take any more bad news.

Faith looked around for Hudson and noticed him sitting on the bench nearby, watching people walk by. She couldn't look at her son without wondering what was going through his mind. Was he afraid, she wondered, that he might recognize someone from his time away from home? Or was he merely people watching, and she was the paranoid one?

Seeing Steve's excitement over his firstborn, Faith found herself reflecting on the last time she'd been at the hospital with Hudson after Colton's youngest daughter was born. Hudson had been so excited. He'd wanted to hold his new cousin and feed her a bottle. That was the very same day he'd told Faith and Craig that more than anything he wanted a baby brother.

Her insides tightened.

The kids and Craig had never known she'd been pregnant before the attack. Boy or girl, she would never know. She'd lost a baby, her baby, their baby, and yet she hadn't had time to think about the loss of that tiny life. She and Craig had never gotten the chance to talk, late at night after the kids were asleep, about the child she'd been carrying. They never got to choose a name. Never had the chance to feel giddy with excitement over their baby's future and all the endless possibilities.

Faith walked to the bench where Hudson sat and plopped down in the empty spot next to him. "Are you OK?"

He nodded, but it was so subtle she wasn't sure he'd heard her.

"Do you want to see your brand-new cousin?"

"Does he have a name?"

"Not yet, but I'm sure Jana and Steve would give serious consideration to any name you might want to throw out there."

He said nothing.

They had another appointment with Kirsten Reich set up for tomorrow morning. She watched Hudson closely, praying she'd be able to help him get through this. When his eyes brightened, she followed his gaze and smiled when she saw her brother come around the corner. Seeing Colton made her heart swell. He'd been her rock since the beginning of her ordeal. His wife and kids were on the other side of the country, and yet he'd decided to stay close by until Lara was found.

Although she'd seen Colton more than once since he'd brought Hudson down from the mountains, she didn't notice until now how long his hair had grown. His jaw was covered with stubble. He looked different.

Colton's eyes lit up when he saw them. He rushed to where Faith sat with Hudson.

Her brother didn't say a word. He just leaned down and took Hudson into his arms. Colton was tall and strong, and he had no problem holding him as he talked.

"Have you talked to Bri?" Faith asked.

He nodded.

"How is everyone doing?"

"They're all good. The girls like their new school. They sounded happy."

"I'm glad."

"We'll talk more later," he said. "Stop looking so serious," he told her, chucking her under the chin.

Faith had heard from Mom that Colton wasn't ready to make any decisions about whether he would be moving to Florida in the near future. He and Bri had a lot to work out.

"Come on, buddy," Colton told Hudson. "Let's go see your new cousin." With Hudson still in his arms, Colton made the rounds, embracing Mom and Dad, Beast and Steve. He then pointed his finger at the new baby, and Faith knew the exact moment when Hudson saw his cousin for the first time. His mouth fell open, and his eyes grew a smidgeon bigger. It was a while before Colton put Hudson down. Then he pulled a small wooden box from his coat pocket and passed out cigars.

She watched everyone celebrate, and for a moment in time, she felt something other than anger within. She felt an outpouring of love for her family. Faith and Hudson were lucky to have each and every one of them. But the thought, along with the feeling, exploded into tiny particles and disappeared as quickly as it had come. Because it always came back to the fact that Lara and Craig should be there, too.

———

After leaving the hospital, Faith and Hudson returned to her parents' house.

It wasn't long before Hudson fell asleep and Faith went to the command post to wait for Beast, Colton, and Dad to join her for a quick meeting.

Beast had gone home to check on Rage since she wasn't feeling well.

Colton and Dad had decided to drive by the warehouse in East Sacramento where Aster Williams was supposed to hold his meeting tomorrow night.

An hour later, Faith and Beast were on the computers set up in the command post. Just as she had done last night before going to bed, Faith pulled up satellite maps of the warehouse. She could see every building and street.

Beast was quieter than usual, which prompted her to try to get him to talk about anything. "Were you nervous when Jana's water broke?"

"No."

"Really?" she said, surprised. "Have you delivered a baby before?"

"No," he said, and she thought that would be the end of it, but then he added thoughtfully, "There was a time when I did worry I might have to deliver my daughter. My wife was doing the breathing thing all the way to the hospital, but we made it in time. She ended up needing a C-section." There was a long pause before he added, "Your little nephew obviously couldn't wait to come into the world."

Faith put her hand on top of his. "Thank you for everything you've done for me and my family. It makes me wonder how I ever got along without you."

"You're a good woman, Faith." He angled his head just so. "No matter what happens. You and Hudson are going to be fine."

Beast was strong and bigger than life, and yet when she looked into his eyes she always saw sadness there. She was about to tell him how she wished there was some way she could repay him for all he'd done for her. She also wanted him to know that he was part of the family now, but then Faith heard talking outside the door right before it opened. It was Colton and Dad, and Faith jumped to her feet. "How did it go?"

Colton shook his head, letting her know they hadn't seen Lara. "The place was empty."

Faith couldn't hide her disappointment. It was a warehouse, and she knew it would most likely be empty, but she'd held out hope that maybe, just maybe, they would find Lara there.

"It's not in a great area," Colton said. "A few kids hanging out on street corners."

"What were they up to?" she asked. "Did you talk to any of them?"

Dad settled a hand on Faith's shoulder, letting her know it might help if she slowed down.

"We talked to one guy, asked him if he ever saw anyone entering or leaving the warehouse, but he had nothing to say."

"It was clear he and his pals were up to no good," Dad said.

Faith noticed how wiped out Dad looked. His hair was disheveled, and he had dark circles under his eyes. "While you two were out," Faith said, "we took another look at the area using satellite maps online. Mostly warehouses and empty lots."

"Yeah, that's what we saw," Colton said, focused on the weaponry laid out on the table in the center of the room. "Where did you get all this stuff?"

"Mom told me Dad has been busy getting ready for war," Faith said. "I thought she was exaggerating, but obviously she wasn't."

Russell rubbed his hands over his face. "Just about anyone can get their hands on a variety of military-grade weapons these days. Rifles, grenades, whatever you need. A click of a button and you can have it mailed to your house. I figured it was time to add to the stockpile."

Colton took a seat. "It's getting late, so we better get to it. Dad told me everyone has been working on gathering volunteers. I know we haven't had much time to plan, but what have you all come up with so far?"

"I have four men, ex-military, joining me tomorrow," Beast said, turning toward Colton. "I was hoping we could use one of your trucks if you have any available."

"Not a problem," Colton said. "Dad told me what was going on. I'll have two trucks ready to go."

Dad went to stand next to the whiteboard. He picked up a blue pen and made a square in the middle of the board, then filled it in with an *X*. "I've made a few calls, gathered a couple of retired military friends myself." He drew a street around the building and then made more squares with *X*s on every corner. "As you saw on your map, there's a street on every side of the building," he said. "If the meeting is to be held at nine o'clock tomorrow night, I suggest we get there early. It'll be dark by six. According to the weather report, we should also be prepared for rain."

"Do we have any idea at all how many men will be at the meeting?" Colton asked.

"No," Beast answered. "But we've been over and over the list of names. If Eddie was right about this being a VIP gathering, I think it's safe to say there could be anywhere from ten to twenty men. We know nothing about the gang from Los Angeles, so we need to be ready for anything."

"The warehouse is two stories and about twenty-five thousand square feet," Dad said. "They could definitely fit a hundred men inside. Even ten men, armed and dangerous, would be enough to cause worry."

He drew another square next to the warehouse on the whiteboard. "This represents the chain-link fence at the back of the building. Inside the fenced area are two empty semitrailers. Colton was able to climb over the fence right about here."

He pointed at the two small rectangles he'd made at the back of the building. "These are fire exits. The doors were chained and bolted, but we were able to use wire cutters to get inside."

"Won't they notice the cut chains?" Faith asked.

"Not a chance," Colton said. "They would have to climb the fence to check it out, and even close up the chains look as if they've never been touched. Besides, the back door hadn't been used in years. There's an unpaved parking lot and a loading dock on the premise, but my guess is that they'll be entering through the double doors at the front of the building."

"What was inside?" Beast asked.

"Other than a few rats, the place was empty," Colton said. "There are stairs leading to two large offices. The main floor is mostly empty warehouse space. It looks as if it's been abandoned for a while. No shelving. Just dirt and a few boxes. To the right I saw a desk and some folding chairs, which led me to believe that's where they handle business."

"We need someone posted outside every corner of the building," Dad said, "so we can see the warehouse at every angle when they start showing up."

Faith pointed to her computer screen at one of the buildings across the street. "Can we put someone on the rooftop? They could keep an eye on the place using binoculars."

"That shouldn't be a problem," Beast said.

"Who will call the police?" Dad asked. "And when?"

"The second I see Lara, I'll call the police," Faith said.

"Sounds good," Colton said.

Dad nodded. "Colton is going to hide inside the building just in case."

Faith looked at her brother.

"I'll be fine. I've already picked out a couple of places inside where I'll be able to stay out of sight."

"You're sure you don't want to bring Detective Yuhasz in on this?" Dad asked Faith.

"I'm sure," Faith said. "I've told you the names of the people involved. We can't risk it. If the police or the FBI shows up, this meeting won't happen, and we'll never find Lara."

"OK," Dad said. "It's OK. We won't call anyone until we've seen Lara with our own eyes."

Faith nodded.

"I could set up a surveillance camera inside the warehouse tonight," Beast said. "We'll be able to hear what they're saying. At least this way we might have a chance at convicting one or two of them after all is said and done."

"Good idea," Colton said.

"I have all the equipment needed. I'll take care of that once we're done here."

"I'll go with you," Colton said.

"I don't like the idea of Colton being trapped inside a building, especially when we have no idea how many men with guns will be inside," Faith said.

"I'll be wearing a vest, and I'll be armed," Colton said.

Beast crossed his arms and waited for them to finish.

"Between my men and Beast's," Dad added, "we'll be able to cover the loading dock area, fire exits, and the entrance. We'll have one or two heavily armed individuals at every corner of the property to keep them from going anywhere."

"I'm meeting with Kirsten in the morning," Faith said. "I'll fill her in and make sure everyone in her group knows what's going on."

"Any update from her yet?" Beast asked.

Faith nodded. "Five sex-trafficking suspects were arrested in Elk Grove. They were stopped and found traveling with a sixteen-year-old girl. Three more adults were arrested near Auburn. Her group is responsible for more than a dozen arrests in just a few days. That's more than we hoped for. At least two dozen of Kirsten's members are keeping surveillance on as many of these guys as possible, but so far there have been no sightings of young children."

"This is good news," Colton said.

"If we're done here," Beast said as he stood, "I'm going to go set up the cameras and get home. It's been a long day."

Colton stood.

After Colton and Beast left, Faith looked at her dad. "Detective Yuhasz will be turning the list over in the next twenty-four hours," Faith told him.

He raised an eyebrow.

"If we don't find her," Faith said, "I don't know what I'll do."

"You'll do what you've done from the start. You'll keep talking to the media. You'll do everything you can to make sure nobody forgets Lara's out there. If we don't find her tomorrow, then we'll find her the next day, or the day after that."

Sixteen

Boom. Boom. Boom.

Patrick jumped out of bed, half-dressed, arms spread wide in defense mode. It took him a moment to realize he wasn't in any imminent danger. Thinking he'd heard the girl in the basement, once again banging on the door, he headed that way without bothering to get his gun or his shirt.

As he marched down the hallway, a square of block glass in the center of the front door revealed a shadowed figure outside. And then again, boom, boom, boom.

About to turn around and head back for his gun, he heard a voice. "Patrick! It's me, Aster!"

The familiar sound of Aster's voice made his stomach roll. *Shit.*

How the hell did he know where he lived? He'd been using an address in another part of town for years. If Aster discovered he had the McMann kid in his basement, it was over. One of them would have to die right here, right now. And it sure as hell wasn't going to be Patrick.

"Open the door!"

Every muscle tensed as Patrick headed that way. It took him a few seconds to undo the chain and metal bar at the top of the door.

Aster entered the house uninvited. The boss didn't look like himself. Everything from his hair to his overcoat was wrinkled and disheveled. Colorless and drab, he did not resemble the man who made most men quake in their shiny wing-tipped shoes.

Patrick glanced outside at the car parked at the curb. Nobody else appeared to be inside the vehicle. But the windows were tinted, and he couldn't be sure.

"What the hell took you so long to let me in?" Aster bellowed.

Patrick shut the door and turned back toward him. "It's four in the morning."

Aster looked about, his gaze fixed on the door leading to the basement for a few seconds too long before he continued on to the main living area.

"What the hell is this place?" He took a couple of sniffs. "Smells like old shoes."

"It's where I live," Patrick said, his jaw tightening. "Mind telling me how you knew where to find me?"

Aster snorted. "You've got a lot to learn, kid. I know where every fucking whore, pimp, and asshole who works for me lives. And that includes you." He took off his coat and tossed it on the back of the ugly green couch. The last person on earth Patrick wanted to see standing inside his own personal shit hole was right in front of him.

"Coffee," Aster said with a wave of his hand. "I need coffee. But put on a shirt first, would you?"

Patrick didn't like leaving the man alone, not even for a minute, but he didn't have much of a choice. He went to the bedroom, slipped a T-shirt over his head, then grabbed a robe from the closet and shoved his gun into the front pocket. As he proceeded to the kitchen, he ignored the tingling in his chest as he passed the door to the basement.

Patrick set about making coffee as quickly as he could, didn't bother cleaning out the pot before filling it with water. He then shoved a coffee filter in place and filled it with ground coffee beans.

But he still wasn't fast enough.

"What's with all the locks on your doors?" Aster wanted to know as he joined him in the kitchen. "Afraid the boogeyman is gonna get you?" His guffaw made Patrick cringe. The man thought he was a fucking comedian.

Patrick hit the "On" button and then grabbed two mugs from the cupboard. "I'm not afraid of anything," he answered, daring the asshole to refute his statement.

Aster did nothing of the sort. Instead his expression turned pensive. An unnatural stillness floated between them as they looked at each other. Aster swept a hand over his forehead and through his hair. "I came here because I need your help."

Patrick pulled out a chair and gestured for him to take a seat at the beat-up table.

"Fucking incompetence has brought me here this morning."

Patrick said nothing as he gathered creamer and sugar and put everything Aster might need on the table in front of him.

"It's impossible to find good help," Aster went on. "Stupidity rules the day. There's no other way to explain what brought Faith McMann, a fucking schoolteacher, into my life." He shook his head. "My entire life is turning to shit." His hand fisted before he used it to pound the table.

Patrick went to stand by the coffeemaker. He reached into his pocket, felt a whole lot better with the weight of his gun nestled in his palm.

"Is that coffee ready yet?"

"Almost."

"I promised myself I would remain calm," Aster said.

Patrick looked over his shoulder and watched the man with distrusting, narrowed eyes.

"Three men go to the McMann house and fuck everything up." Aster held up three stubby fingers. "Number one: they don't find the two million dollars, which was the reason I sent them there. Number two: they don't kill the kids or the McMann woman. Number three: they take the fucking kids with them."

Aster shook his head in disgust. "And then what happens? Richard Price has a sudden change of heart. He comes to *my* house where my family lives and tells me he wants out of the business."

Patrick had been there. He'd killed Richard Price himself. Why was Aster telling him this? Here he was in the middle of the night looking like hell. Was he having a fucking meltdown?

"And now suddenly everyone's getting arrested or going missing."

"What are you talking about?" Patrick asked.

"I got a call. Eddie and Gage shut down their bar and disappeared. The same bar I loaned them the money to get, and now they've run off." He looked at Patrick then, unblinking. "You don't happen to know anything about what might have happened to those two, do you?"

"First I heard of it," Patrick lied as he carried the coffee to the table and filled up their mugs. "Who else went missing?"

"Randy Price. Haven't heard from him in weeks. And what about all those arrests of late? I can't turn on the television without seeing a bunch of doctors and lawyers loaded into police cars, named and shamed for hiring an underage prostitute. Those girls want it. They beg for it. They're being fed and housed." He flexed his fingers. "Fucking whores. All of them."

Patrick put the coffeepot back on the burner and took a seat across from Aster.

"It wouldn't surprise me if McMann was behind the recent string of arrests," Aster told him. "The apartments in Davis, the bowling alley in Rocklin, and now quiet neighborhoods in Elk Grove and every other fucking town." Aster added a spoonful of sugar to his coffee, stirred, and then took a gulp and wrinkled his nose.

Asshole.

"McMann has gotten the whole fucking city of Sacramento taking up arms."

"And what do you propose?" Patrick asked, hoping to get to the bottom of this so he could get the man out of his house.

"The only way to tackle the problem will be to bring in some new blood, and I'm not talking about a dozen new men. I'm talking a hundred, maybe more." Aster's bloodshot eyes grew round and he snapped his fingers as something came to him. "What was the name of that guy who came to us a few months ago? He was from Fresno or—"

"Bakersfield. Joe Santos. What about him?"

"He wanted to join forces."

"If I remember correctly," Patrick said, "you told him to fuck off. And that's being kind."

"Talk to him, would you? Call him after I leave and tell him I've had a change of heart. Put some of that charm of yours to good use."

Patrick got up and went to refill their mugs. "What happened to Hansel, the answer to all your problems?"

"You getting smart with me?"

"Nope. Just wondering if the big guy did what he said he was going to do."

Aster popped up from his chair and came at him so fast Patrick didn't know what hit him until he had all ten of Aster's fingers wrapped around his neck.

"Don't you watch the news?" Aster asked him, squeezing hard. "Maybe you didn't see Hansel's men with the words *sex trafficker* scrawled across their foreheads. All three of them were found taped to fucking telephone poles on a well-traveled road."

As the life was choked out of him, Patrick strained to reach inside his pocket for his gun.

"McMann's sidekick Beast made fools of us—you and me—and if the McMann situation isn't taken care of soon, if you don't find that kid of hers before the meeting tomorrow night, the gang from Los Angeles has promised to pay us a visit." He let go of Patrick, and just like that it was over.

Patrick held on to the counter for support as he gasped for breath. He wheezed and coughed. It took a moment for his vision to clear. He reached for his gun, thought about killing Aster right now. It would be over in a second. But neighbors would hear the gunshot, and the last thing he needed was the police to show up and find Lara in the basement. He needed to be patient, meet him at the same construction site where he'd taken out Eddie and Gage. There was plenty of open space. A perfect burial ground for Aster and friends when the time came.

Aster filled his own mug and headed back to the table, where he took a seat as if nothing had happened.

"I've decided I need a partner," Aster said between gulps. "Whoever I choose is going to get a piece of the action."

"What does that mean?" Patrick asked, his throat still sore.

"A percentage of the business. Eighty-twenty. I'm being generous."

Patrick didn't trust him. After all these years, Aster was going to give up a big chunk of change? Either he was lying or things were worse than he was letting on, Patrick realized. McMann had gotten to him. It must hurt bad to know a schoolteacher and mother of two might very well bring him to his knees.

"Do you think Hansel's men will talk?"

"No. If they do, they'll be dead within an hour of being released. But I do need to get control of this situation."

"I'll take care of it," Patrick told him.

Aster's eyes lit up. "Oh yeah?"

"Yeah. I'll do what Hansel proposed. I'll make sure the McMann household is blown to smithereens."

Aster let out a belly laugh. "See. This is why I need you, kid. You have a way of reminding me of how things used to be. Pow!" he said, spittle flying, his expression suddenly bright and merry. "Blow the fucking place up." He guzzled the rest of his coffee, then pushed himself to his feet. "That partner I was talking about," he said, his ugly gaze on Patrick's. "I want it to be you."

Patrick forced the corners of his mouth to turn upward, but he wasn't falling for it. Aster was a greedy son of a bitch. No way, no how would he give up power, let alone a percentage of the business.

"Speechless, kid?" Aster laughed again, an irritating wheezing sound. "Don't tell me you have to fucking think about it."

"No," Patrick said, forcing himself to continue to stare at Aster's jowly face. "You caught me off guard, that's all. It's early and—"

"OK. OK," Aster cut him off. "Calm the fuck down."

Fucking asshole.

"I should get going. Just wanted to share the news, so you could start gathering an army." He pulled an envelope from his pocket and plopped it on top of the table.

"What's that?"

"Some up-front money, a goodwill gesture, to show you I'm serious about this." Aster looked around. "Maybe you should use the money to find a new house, for crying out loud."

Patrick followed the asshole down the hallway and back to the living area, where Aster grabbed his coat and handed it to Patrick so he could help him with the sleeves. The man was a fucking invalid.

"I like the idea you came up with, too," Aster said. "Set that in motion, would you?"

"Which idea was that?"

"Bomb the McMann place. Kill them all!"

"Got it," Patrick said. Then he ushered the old man toward the front door.

Aster stopped at the basement door, even rested a hand on the knob.

Patrick stiffened.

"What's with all the locks? What are you hiding in there?"

"Why don't you have a look for yourself?" Patrick said with as much bravado as he could muster.

Aster smiled. "Nah. I've spent enough time in this dump. Rae is going to make me waffles and bacon when I return. She makes the sweetest fucking waffles you've ever tasted." Aster winked, then headed out.

Yeah, I know, Patrick wanted to say, but he kept quiet. *Move along, Aster. Move along.*

"See you tonight."

"Yeah," Patrick said as he watched the prickly son of a bitch waddle down the walkway, climb into his car, and drive off.

He didn't believe one damn word of the whole let's-be-partners bullshit. Aster didn't get up early and drive himself to anyone's house for nothing. He was up to no good. He knew something, and he was testing him. *This is it,* Patrick thought. *Time to make one last call and get rid of the girl.*

———

The second Lara heard the main door shut and the car engine start up, she sat upright on her cot. She could hear Patrick's footsteps above. When she had first heard the gravelly tone of the visitor, she'd been unable to move. She recognized his voice and his laughter from the times he came to visit Mother at the farmhouse. According to the other girls, he was the boss of all the other bad guys. He was the one who told everyone else what to do. He was scary and mean. Everybody used to hide when he came around.

Shivers prickled her skin as she thought about what he'd said about blowing up the McMann house and killing them all. She felt under the mattress for the nail she kept hidden away and reminded herself that she needed to stay strong.

If and when the time came for her to use the nail, whether it was sharp enough or not, she would plunge it hard and fast into Patrick's neck, and then she would run and never look back.

SEVENTEEN

"I've got bad news and good news. The good news," Kirsten told Faith, "is that I think we might have actually made a dent in that list of yours over the past few days. Just this morning one of the men arrested was charged with seven counts of trafficking and prostitution."

"And the bad news?" Faith asked after a long pause.

"Only twelve of the fifty women who showed up at our last meeting have volunteered to join us tonight."

"Understandable," Faith said. "I'm sure many of them have families, and we have no idea what to expect. It's not the same as watching these men from the safety of our cars."

Kirsten tapped her fingertips on her desk, making a galloping noise.

"I also understand," Faith said, "if you'd rather stay out of this fight. I never meant for you to get involved in the first place."

Kirsten crossed her arms. "I've always made a point of not doing anything I don't want to do. And this isn't just your fight. Trafficking isn't going away. We both know it's growing every day. It's gotten out of hand, and it needs to stop."

"Yes, but—"

"It starts tonight. And it starts with us. You. Me. Your neighbor . . . whoever shows up. If we can't stand up to these scumbags, who can? More importantly, who will?"

She was right, Faith thought. But she also wondered selfishly if she, personally, would continue to fight the fight once she had Lara back. She didn't have an answer.

"You said you and your friends had a plan," Kirsten went on. "Why don't you share the specifics with me, and then I'll get the word out? We can go from there."

For the next twenty minutes Faith laid out everything that had been discussed last night: Faith, Beast, her dad, Colton, and any other volunteers who were willing would arrive early. Colton would hide inside. As soon as children were spotted or the meeting began, Faith would call the police and the FBI. Thanks to Beast, the meeting would be recorded. Hopefully the audio and video would provide authorities the ammunition they needed to have the men brought in for questioning.

Kirsten asked a lot of the same questions brought up last night.

Once all the details were ironed out and Kirsten was satisfied, she sat back in her leather recliner and casually asked about Jana and the baby.

"Jana and Steve are doing well," Faith said stiffly. She hadn't realized that talking about Jana and her new baby would be so difficult, but there it was. "Their baby boy is healthy," she went on, forcing her shoulders to relax. Faith smiled. "What more can they ask for?"

"What is the emotion I'm sensing?" Kirsten asked.

Faith put a hand on her chest. "From me?"

Kirsten nodded.

"Ah, it must be that body-language-detection thing you're so good at."

Kirsten said nothing. Merely waited patiently for an answer to her question.

The truth was Faith had been feeling out of sorts ever since Jana's baby was born. She wasn't jealous or any of that kind of nonsense. But seeing the baby, being surrounded by such innocence and sweet new beginnings, had made her think of her own loss. "No one besides my parents and Jana know I lost a baby in the attack," Faith told Kirsten. "I was going to tell Craig that weekend, but I never had the chance." Faith swept stray hairs from her forehead. Her insides twisted and turned as if their baby were still growing inside her. Ghost pains. Faith's chest ached. "I haven't had time to think about Craig or the baby," she said. "I miss my husband. I'm not ready to let him go."

Kirsten sat quietly and didn't say anything.

"Sometimes I wonder if I'll ever be able to truly mourn my husband," Faith found herself saying. "People you love should be properly mourned. And yet a part of me expects Craig to walk through the door when this madness ends . . . if it ever ends."

"I'm sorry for your loss," Kirsten told her. "Losing someone you love is painful. Your situation has forced you to put your emotions on the back burner, which can't be easy. Once you get a chance to breathe, the pain and sadness you're experiencing will most likely begin to feel as if it'll never let up, and that's normal."

Faith wondered if that was true. At the moment, she felt empty, soulless. Her heart had been broken into so many pieces, trampled on, and swept aside. Her newfound emotion—anger—came in waves: massive, cold, dark swells that threatened to wipe out the person she used to be.

But at the moment, she felt nothing. She met Kirsten's gaze and said, "Most days I feel hollow inside."

Kirsten nodded.

"I know my family and you and Hudson will help ease my pain. I'm sure the passing of time will do what it does best as I find a way to move on, but that's what scares me most," Faith said. "I don't want to get used to a new normal. I don't want to think about what the future holds without Craig. Most people are afraid of dying. I'm afraid of living."

———

At seven o'clock sharp, Aster grabbed the key from beneath his desk. He walked across his office and unlocked the safe, retrieved his handgun, and then peeled more than a few hundred-dollar bills off the top of the stack of money inside. He found himself staring inside the small, dark space for a second longer than necessary.

He frowned, then shuffled around the items inside.

Walking slowly from one side of his office to the other, he looked at the familiar space, sniffing and examining. The door opened, and Rae walked inside.

She knew better than to enter without warning, and yet she gave him a haughty look as if she didn't have a care in the world. He'd grown tired of people's inability to follow orders. His jaw hardened as he walked toward her. "What have I told you about knocking?"

"I knew you didn't have any visitors."

He slapped her across the cheek, enjoyed the look of shock on her face. He liked the way it made him feel—in control. He raised his hand, ready to strike again.

"I'm sorry," she cried, cowering as she should have done from the start. "I should have made my presence known before I entered."

Her apologies didn't quell his anger. "Who has been inside this room?"

Her eyes widened. "Nobody, I assure you."

He pointed to the open safe. "One of my coins is missing. My 1943 copper cent. Where is it?"

"I have no idea. Please settle down, Aster. The kids are home. They'll hear you."

He clasped his fingers around her slender white throat as he had done to Patrick earlier today.

She grabbed his arm and struggled to pull free.

"Who was in here?" he asked again. "Did Patrick pay you another visit?"

She hesitated a few seconds too long. Although he hadn't been serious about her and Patrick, the fearful expression on her face told him there was some truth to what he'd said. The first time he'd asked her about Patrick's unexpected visit, he'd been preoccupied with business. Rae had played it cool. But not this time. It shocked him to think he'd been duped. The heat inside his belly sizzled and crackled. "Tell me the truth about Patrick, or I will choke you until your last breath is squeezed from your lungs and you fall at my feet."

Her bottom lip trembled. "I don't know what you're talking about."

"Did Patrick ever come here when I was away?"

She remained silent.

"Answer me," he said.

"Yes," she said, trying to retain her usual confidence. "But nothing happened."

"Did he touch you?"

The door opened. Their younger child peeked inside. "Mom, are you OK?"

"Get out, you fucking brat!"

The door clicked shut.

Rae's beautiful features hardened. Her shoulders stiffened. "Patrick was here, and he did touch me," she said boldly. "He carried me in his arms, laid me on the marble island in the kitchen, and fucked me, hard and deep, like nothing I had ever experienced before. I think about him all the time. Your man Patrick is exquisite in every sense of the word. I hope you keep him around for a long, long time."

The thought of her making a fool of him went beyond his wildest imagination. He dug his thumbs into her throat. Women were monsters. Had he forgotten? Clenching his teeth, he squeezed until she turned blue.

She fell to his feet just as he said she would, but she was alive, choking and wheezing on the floor while their older child called out worriedly from the hallway, asking if everything was all right.

No. Nothing was all right.

Patrick had lied to him. Was the kid really that stupid? Or had Aster truly been the fool all along? Most men had a difficult time taking their eyes off his wife, but he'd never believed Patrick would dare make a move on her, let alone fuck her in Aster's own house. Sadly, he didn't have to talk to Patrick to know it was true. Every conversation, every look, every move Patrick had made over the past few weeks suddenly made sense. The kid wanted what Aster had, including his wife. How he'd become blinded to it all, he didn't know. Neither did he care, since it wasn't too late to remedy the situation. He thought about his visit with Patrick, recalled the panicked look on the kid's face when he'd first opened the door. Patrick had been worried about something. Clammy hands and a pale face should have been Aster's first clue something was going on.

"Don't you go anywhere while I'm gone," he said to Rae. "I'll deal with you later." He used the tip of his shoe to nudge her body out of his way.

He peeked through the door and told the worried children in the hallway that their precious mother would be right there, and then he shut it tight again and went about locking his safe and gathering his things.

He wasn't angry, he thought as he crooked his neck and heard it creak. He was fucking livid.

He grabbed two handguns before setting out for his meeting, relishing the moment when he would see Patrick again. Because this time he wouldn't give the kid a chance to say a word. He'd simply meet his gaze straight on and shoot him dead.

Eighteen

Beth Tanner searched through the guest room she used to store miscellaneous items, looking for the night-vision binoculars she'd bought years ago. She figured they might help Faith and the others keep an eye on the warehouse in East Sacramento. Instead, she happened upon an old scrapbook filled with memories of her daughter, Rose.

She took a seat on the edge of the cushioned futon and began turning the pages. She smiled at the expression on her daughter's face as Rose devoured a cupcake on her first birthday. The ribbons glued on the pages surrounding the Polaroid pictures had grown brittle and yellow, but every precious memory squeezed at her heart: Rose on the teeter-totter at the park; Rose standing on a large rock in the middle of a field of high grasses, waving, happy; Rose proudly showing off the team leader award she'd been presented in the fifth grade. Rose. Rose. Rose.

Beth shut the book, hugged it to her breast, and closed her eyes.

She missed her daughter so much.

She was about to resume her search for the binoculars when she heard what sounded like the clanking of metal coming from her garage.

Slowly she put the scrapbook aside and came to her feet. Her first thought was of her guns locked in the master bedroom at the other end of the one-story house. She stood silently, listening, before stepping into the hallway.

At the end of the hall was a dark figure—a massive, broad-shouldered man, his eyes hidden beneath the hood of his sweatshirt, his lip deformed by a scar. He stood in place, unmoving, staring her way.

She whipped about, ran back into the spare room, and slammed the door shut. The second she turned the lock, the door handle jiggled.

Her gaze darted from one side of the room to the other. She needed something to defend herself with. She ran to the desk, rifled through the drawer, and grabbed the scissors.

A loud thud made her jump. The hinges rattled as her attacker threw his body at the door, again and again until the wood cracked down the middle. She rushed to the closet, slid open the mirrored door. On the floor were ten-pound weights she'd purchased but never used. With a weight in one hand and the scissors in the other, she went back to the cracked door and flattened herself against the wall.

Silence.

Where did he go? She prayed he'd left.

His leg smashed through the cracked wood. She cried out in surprise.

His booted foot was only inches away.

Without hesitating, she lunged, stabbing the scissors into his shin more than once. Blood spurted. He cursed and pulled his leg away.

Once again, all was quiet.

She remained still, her chest rising and falling. The adrenaline pumping through her blood made it difficult to think. The next few seconds felt like minutes. She was tempted to peek through the gaping hole he'd left in the door but didn't dare move.

"I see you in there," came a voice.

"I've already called the police," she said.

"Funny, because I heard your cell phone ringing in the other room. Nice ringtone. Come out now, and I won't hurt you. I promise."

Through the window, she saw her neighbor Mr. Hawkins carrying a box. Pastries no doubt. He was a baker. The last time she'd run into him, he'd mentioned paying her a visit. *Not now,* she said inwardly. *Not now, for God's sake.*

Hoping Mr. Hawkins would go away, she didn't move a muscle. The doorbell sounded. Her shoulders fell. Not long after, she heard the front door open.

It was now or never.

Still holding the barbell and the scissors, she pushed through the splintered wood, scraping her legs and arms as she went.

"Run!" she shouted to Mr. Hawkins as she ran past the front entry toward her bedroom. But it was too late for her neighbor, she realized, as he fell forward in a bloody heap.

As she rushed past the kitchen, she considered escaping through the sliding door, but where would she run? How far would she get? Figuring her chances were better if she could get a hold of a gun, she continued toward her bedroom. She got as far as the bedroom door when he lunged for her, grabbed hold of her leg, and brought her to the ground with him.

Her head smacked against the floor. The scissors fell from her grasp. He held tight to her left ankle.

Dazed from the hit to the head, she felt the barbell beneath her stomach. When he rolled to one side, he let go of her ankle long enough for her to thrust the heel of her boot into his head.

He cried out. She landed another kick to his shoulder.

This time he grunted but hardly slowed. As he came to his feet, she pushed herself to her knees and swung the barbell hard, swiping the left side of his face and hitting him in the nose and mouth. He stumbled forward, blood flowing from his nose, blocking her path to her gun case. She pushed herself to her feet, ran from the room, and headed for the sliding door.

A shot rang out.

She ducked as she ran to the kitchen for cover instead. Before hiding behind the center island, she grabbed the turning fork from the pan she'd used to cook a pot roast. She didn't realize she'd been shot until she noticed a thin trickle of blood trailing across the floor.

With her back to the wood cabinet, her knees bent high in front of her chest, she waited. Her heart raced as she concentrated on listening to the man's every movement.

He was taking slow, careful steps into the kitchen.

He was close.

The second she saw the tips of his boots, she sprang from her hiding place. Another shot rang out a split second before the sharp tips of the three-pronged fork sank deeply into his right eye. She grunted as she pushed hard, her body sagging fully against him as they fell to the floor together.

He was screaming, his body twisting in pain, but she used every muscle, all she had left to hold tight to the handle, gouging and prodding, refusing to give up until he fell silent.

Long moments passed before she found the strength to crawl from the kitchen, her fingers reaching, her legs pushing. Only last week she'd canceled her landline. Just as her attacker had said, her cell phone was in her bedroom. *You can do it.* She thought of Rose as she crawled on her belly, making her way across the floor, inch by inch. In her mind's eye she saw her daughter, heard Rose's voice encouraging her to keep moving.

At the door she saw her phone on the table by the bed.

She could make it. She could do this.

Beth wasn't sure how long she'd lost consciousness, but when her eyes fluttered open, she was lying on her back on the floor. The phone was in her hand, pressed close to her chest. She heard a voice on the other end. "I need help," she said. Her tongue felt numb, every word heavy as she gave her name and address. The woman told her to hang on, they would be there soon. Beth closed her eyes and smiled.

Nineteen

Rage woke up in bed surrounded by pictures of her son, Callan. She'd been looking through the contents of the envelope Jana had brought when she'd dozed off, something she tended to do more and more often these days.

On the bed next to her were dozens of three-by-four glossy pictures of Callan along with two letters from his adoptive parents, Sue and Danny. According to Sue, Callan loved the *Goodnight Moon* book Rage had given him when she'd met her son. And he insisted Sue and Danny read him the book every night before bed. They had taken a picture of Callan asleep in his bed. Next to the nightstand was a picture of Rage and Callan playing. Rage had a fire truck and Callan had a police car, and they had both turned toward the camera and smiled when the picture was taken.

He really did look like her.

The same little bump in the nose and the same large, deep-set eyes. Sue mentioned in the letter that Callan referred to her as Aunt Sally and asked about her all the time.

Rage brought the picture closer and kissed his paper cheek. He was an incredibly sweet boy, and she felt lucky for having had the chance to meet him. He was in a good home. His parents loved him. She'd done the right thing. She wiped her eyes, sat up, and called, "Little Vinnie! Beast?"

There was no answer.

She pushed herself out of bed and made her way into the kitchen on wobbly legs. The counters were wiped clean, everything put away and in its place. Ninety-nine percent of the time, Little Vinnie could be found wearing an apron and cooking something at the stove.

Rarely left alone, she realized in that moment that she didn't like the sound of silence. She looked at the clock above the sink. It was eight o'clock, already dark outside.

It took her a second to remember where they'd gone off to.

The warehouse. Aster Williams and his men were having a meeting tonight.

Panic welled inside of her.

Why didn't they wake her before they left? What were they thinking? She wanted to be angry with them both, but she knew why they'd snuck out without her. She was sick, growing sicker every day, and they knew it. Her attempts to be strong 24-7 had not fooled them one iota. For the past few days, she'd forced herself to sing in the shower and keep her bedroom neat. She'd held her head high and her back as straight as possible when she walked. She'd been doing all she could to keep her food down.

And it had been for nothing, simply wasted effort.

She stood silently in the middle of the kitchen, wearing ragged sweatpants and a T-shirt a size too large. Her reflection in the stove top revealed a shell of a girl with hollowed eyes and a thinning face. She thought of Faith and how close they'd grown in such a short amount of time. Faith McMann, a fourth-grade schoolteacher, of all things, had become her friend and confidante. More than anything, Rage wanted to see her reunited with both of her children.

How could Beast and Little Vinnie have left her here when they knew how important tonight was to her? Her heart raced as she looked about the room. Her gaze settled on the key ring, especially on a particular key. The old Volkswagen Bug she used to drive was parked at the side of the house. Every once in a while Beast would start the engine, but she hardly ever drove it. Her doctors advised against it.

Screw that.

She refused to be left behind. She went back to her room. She slipped on a pair of old sneakers, put on her warmest hoodie, and grabbed the keys from the hook on her way out.

Rage opened the door, surprised to see Miranda standing on the other side. It took her a second to realize she wasn't seeing things. It was Miranda, the young girl who had spent more than a year as a captive sex slave before escaping. Rage took in the greasy hair and dirty smudges on her face. Her shirt was torn, and overall she looked like shit. "I can't believe you're here."

"I'm sorry. I had nowhere else to go."

"There's nothing to be sorry for." Rage pulled her into her arms. When she took a step back she said, "We looked everywhere for you. You should have told us you were leaving, or at the very least let us know you were all right."

"I never should have left without saying goodbye." Miranda examined Rage with a keen eye before she asked, "Are you OK?"

"I've been better." Rage wished she'd had more time to spend with Miranda when she'd been living with them. Rage should have paid more attention to the girl. Miranda had no one. Rage would have liked to have been a big sister to her. But time was a luxury she didn't have.

Miranda looked at the keys in Rage's hand. "Were you going somewhere?"

"I am. In fact, maybe you can help me start the car at the side of the house."

Miranda nodded, then took a step in that direction before Rage stopped her. "Hold on," Rage said. "I don't want to be preachy or anything, but in the future don't run away from the people who care about you."

Miranda said nothing.

"Trust me," Rage went on. "I know what I'm talking about. It's not easy to find people who are willing to take you in and love you unconditionally. Beast and Little Vinnie . . . they care about you."

"I didn't want to be a burden to anyone. And, besides, I had a few things to take care of."

Rage knew she'd been up to no good, but lecturing the girl seemed pointless.

"When I was living at the farmhouse, I promised Lara I would help her," Miranda said. "I've let her down. I came back to apologize to all of you."

"Like I said before, no reason to apologize. Don't let it eat you up inside." Mistakes. Rage had made her fair share of them. Most people did. But mistakes only served a purpose if people learned from them and made better choices the next time.

"I've seen the news," Miranda said. "It looked to me as if people are taking a stand against these guys. I don't want to be a bystander. I need to get involved."

"Well, you came to the right person at the right time." Rage put a hand on her shoulder. "Come on."

Rage shut the door and locked it.

Miranda followed her around to the side of the house. "Are you sure you're all right?" she asked when Rage struggled with opening the side gate.

Rage ignored her.

"Where's everyone else?"

"Little Vinnie and Beast are about thirty minutes away. The big showdown is happening in the next hour." The gate came open. Rage headed for the car with Miranda on her heels.

"Showdown?"

"Yeah, it's a long story, but the gist of it is one of the ringleaders in the trafficking business is meeting with some important men at a warehouse in East Sacramento."

"And they left without you?"

"Damn straight they did, and I'm pissed."

"I can imagine."

Rage remembered why she liked having Miranda around. "Beast and Little Vinnie decided not to wake me before they left. I know their hearts are in the right place, but I'm not happy with them. All of you people seem to think you can just walk out anytime you see fit. It's not right."

"I understand." Miranda tried not to laugh when she saw the car. "That is the brightest color red I've ever seen."

"Got a problem with the color?"

"No. I love it."

"Well, good. Once I'm gone, the car is all yours."

"I can't take your car. That wouldn't be right."

"I'll tell you what's not right—dying too young from inoperable brain cancer. Do you want the car or not?"

"Wow," Miranda said. "You really know how to use the whole dying thing to your advantage, don't you?"

Rage smiled. "I take it that's a yes."

Miranda snorted.

Miranda and Beast are going to get along just fine, Rage thought as she slid into the driver's seat and turned the key. The engine coughed and churned, then rattled and died. Rage pumped the gas, waited, turned the key. Nothing. *Damn.* She didn't have time to adjust the valves.

"Can I do something?" Miranda asked through the window.

"I'm glad you asked. There is something you *can* do for me."

Miranda raised an eyebrow.

"When I'm gone, I need you to take care of Beast and Little Vinnie. Can you do that?"

"You're really sick, aren't you?"

"Did you think I was faking it?"

"I mean it's serious now, isn't it?"

"If you mean my time is almost up, as in days instead of weeks," Rage said, "the answer is yes."

They looked at each other for a few seconds before Miranda said, "If Beast and Little Vinnie will have me, I'll watch over them for you when you're gone."

Rage closed her eyes, thankful, grateful. "It won't be easy at first," Rage said. "Beast will fight you on every little thing. He'll disagree with you and piss you off more often than not. His stubbornness will make you crazy, but you have to know he's only testing you. He's not as tough as he looks or acts. He's a big teddy bear."

Before Miranda could respond, Rage turned the key and put her foot on the gas. The engine roared to life, and so did Rage as she felt her lifeblood course through her body. "If you want to come along," she told Miranda, "it's time to get in!"

TWENTY

On her way to East Sacramento, Faith had picked up Kirsten Reich from her office. For more than an hour the two of them had been sitting in her car parked on the side of the road. They were far enough from the warehouse where they wouldn't be noticed, but close enough to see cars coming and going.

They took turns using the binoculars, keeping an eye on the warehouse and the buildings surrounding it. Darkness settled across the sky. The trees rustled in the wind, but still no rain.

"Looks like we have someone positioned on the rooftop adjacent to the warehouse," Kirsten said as she peered through the binoculars.

Faith texted the group. Beast confirmed that two of his men were in place on the rooftops on both sides of the warehouse, giving them a clear shot at the front and back.

Kirsten handed Faith the binoculars and grabbed the bag by her feet. She had brought almonds, carrots, and a ham sandwich, and she offered to share her meal with Faith.

"No thanks," Faith said, her stomach twisting as her gaze settled on the clock.

"It's going to be all right," Kirsten told her, but to Faith they were hollow words that meant nothing.

Faith dialed a number. After no one answered, she disconnected the call. "I haven't seen Beth," Faith said. "She's still not answering her phone."

"I'm sure she'll be here soon," Kirsten said before she took a drink from her water bottle.

"Do you think I'm doing the right thing?" Faith asked.

"What do you mean?"

"Sometimes I wonder what I'm doing, you know—what's the purpose? Like now. What are the chances they'll bring Lara to this meeting?" A pause. "I never wanted this to be my battle. I didn't sign up for this. I never formed a group or had any intention of ever going after these people."

"I know how badly you want to find your daughter," Kirsten told her, "but you're also helping others. You're the spark that got people talking and doing. This is your chance to make a difference."

"I saw a couple fighting once," Faith told her. "It happened years ago. They were in the open, in the mall, where I was shopping with Mom. He hit her. Right there for all to see. Nobody did a thing, including me. We watched the woman cower and then drop to the floor. We watched her cry as he dragged her away. I did nothing to help. I can still see her face in my mind's eye."

"I think most of us have memories of a time where we wish we'd done something more or at least spoke up."

"My mom was attacked and my brother-in-law was stabbed," Faith went on. "It's one thing to put myself in danger, but something else altogether to ask them to do the same."

"They're adults. It's up to each of them to make their own decision." Kirsten looked Faith squarely in the eyes. "Listen. After your kids were taken, you could have sat back and done nothing and allowed the system to take over, but you didn't. You refused to let fear rule the day. You found the courage to go out there, despite the odds, and fight for your children. Every person in this world is capable of so much more. We are all worthy, but most people don't see it and therefore never realize it."

Faith nodded. Kirsten was right. People were stronger than they thought. Herself included. Nobody asked for bad things to happen, but such was life. Craig was dead. Nothing she could do would bring him back. Faith needed to suck it up for now and find her daughter. She could fall apart later.

"We have one life," Kirsten went on. "Standing up for a cause is never easy. It takes a brave person to stand up to their enemies. And now isn't the time to start doubting yourself."

"Thank you," Faith said, smiling.

Both of their phones vibrated. It was Eva, a member of Kirsten's group, letting them know she and others were ready and waiting.

Across the street, Faith could see Beast inside Colton's semitrailer. Dad and a few of his ex-military friends were in another truck, parked straight ahead next to the curb. The area was industrial, with good transportation access to road and rail. Trailer trucks and shipping containers were not unusual.

Colton had been in the building for forty-five minutes now. With nothing better to do, he'd shared a video with the group, showing the inside of the building. Upstairs was a nonworking bathroom and two empty offices. Downstairs was a vast warehouse space, devoid of any shelving.

The last time they'd heard from Colton was twenty minutes ago when he'd texted to let them know they wouldn't be hearing from him again unless there was a problem.

Faith wiped a tear from the side of her face. That it took the realities of child sex trafficking to open her eyes to the suffering happening all around her was beyond heart wrenching.

"Everything OK?" Kirsten asked.

"I'm sorry," Faith said as she stared out the window into the darkness shadowed by the moon and dotted by drizzly, misty rain. "Nothing is OK. The entire world seems as if it has been turned upside down. How did it come to this? My entire life has been spent waking up, going to work, making dinner, grading homework, worrying about a future that will never be now. For what? I don't understand the point of it all. It's all been for nothing. And I'm not exaggerating or looking for sympathy."

She looked at Kirsten. "I have witnessed the worst of humanity and more sadness in the past two months than I ever could have imagined. And yet, even wrapped in my own grief, I know there are others out there, hundreds, thousands, perhaps millions who were born into much worse. But the simple truth is that everything I've done is because I want my daughter back." She shook her head in wonder as she stared out into what suddenly looked like a dark abyss. "And to get my daughter back, I'm willing to risk your life and the lives of your friends, my neighbors, and my own family."

Kirsten remained silent.

"Everyone is busy. I know I've been busy," Faith said. "Too busy to open my eyes and take a good look at what was going on in my own backyard. How sad is that? Soccer practice and dance lessons. Teacher meetings and dentist appointments. Everyone talking about the weather and sports, their next vacation, and the best show on TV."

"This isn't anyone's fault," Kirsten told her. "Every day with your loved ones is precious. Ignorance is bliss, and smelling the roses is divine. Nobody wants to spend their days looking for something they really don't want to see anyhow."

A movement caught Faith's attention. She grabbed her binoculars and began counting vehicles as one car after another pulled into the unpaved parking lot next to the warehouse. Five sedans, all dark with tinted windows.

"One, two, three, four—eight men," Kirsten said as she texted the information to the group. "They're heading toward the loading dock."

"Hold on," Faith said. "Two more vehicles just came around the corner."

They waited. Faith kept her gaze fixed on the building. The other two vehicles drove past and disappeared around the corner, making it impossible for her to see where they went.

Their cell phones buzzed.

Kirsten read Eva's text aloud. "Fifteen men have now entered the building through the rollup steel door at the loading dock, bypassing the front entry altogether."

Faith's heart pounded against her ribs, her pulse racing. She worried about Colton, prayed he was well hidden. *Please let him be safe.*

A car passed by. Faith peered through the binoculars, watched one lone man climb out of the vehicle. "Aster Williams," she said as she watched him head for the building. She looked at the clock: 8:55.

Three people dressed in jeans and hoodies pulled low over their faces were walking on the sidewalk in front of Faith and Kirsten. As they passed by, one of them stopped, glanced their way, then walked toward their car.

Faith reached for her gun.

"It's Eva," Kirsten said. "It's OK."

Faith relaxed.

Kirsten rolled down her window. "What's going on?"

"Two men and three children exited a van around the corner," Eva told them. "They'll soon be escorted into the building." She signaled for the other women to go and she'd catch up. "We want to grab the children if the opportunity arises." Eva tapped a hand on the car. "Time to go. See you on the flip side."

Faith grabbed her bag from the backseat. She tucked her Taser in one pocket and her gun into the other.

"What are you doing?" Kirsten asked.

"Lara could be with those men. It's time for me to go."

"We need to be patient."

"Sorry, no can do." Faith stepped out of the car. She was done being patient. She couldn't sit still for another second.

Kirsten rubbed her temple, then exited the car on the other side and began gathering her gear from the backseat.

Faith didn't wait for Kirsten. She pulled a cap over her head and began walking in the same direction Eva had gone. Farther down the road, on the street corner, was a group of shadowy, indistinct figures huddled together. Across the street, she saw Beast, Little Vinnie, and one of their buddies exit the semi. All three men were dressed in fatigues, from tactical boots to helmets. Beast gave her a nod before the three of them headed for the warehouse.

Her phone vibrated. She stopped to read the text. Colton was letting them know the children were inside the building. He'd hoped to set off fire alarms, grab the children, and pull them to safety, but he couldn't reach the alarm without being seen.

Her nerves were raw. She looked around. Everyone had disappeared. The sky was dark and ominous, thick clouds ready to burst.

It was time to call Detective Yuhasz. She kept the conversation short. He was not pleased.

Faith slipped her phone into her pocket just as the dark clouds overhead broke open. She ran. As she rounded the corner, her dad called out to her. She turned back, saw him and three others near the chain-link fence surrounding the property. She ran to him and told him she'd called Detective Yuhasz.

One of the men pointed to a stream of thick gray smoke coming from the front of the warehouse.

"Looks like someone set off a smoke bomb," Dad said. He waved a hand, letting his group know it was time to move in.

Faith followed until Dad turned and stopped her. "I'd feel better if you went back to your car."

He knew better than to ask that of her, but before she could respond, he told her to stay safe, and then he took off with his friends.

The sharp retort of a gun being fired startled her and stopped her from moving forward. As her dad disappeared around the front of the building, the rapid, nonstop sound of gunfire sounded from every corner of the building.

What the hell was going on? Nobody was to fire a gun unless absolutely necessary. There were children inside the building. This was not how things were supposed to happen.

Another text from Colton: Lara was not among the children inside. People were scrambling to get out of the building.

Lara isn't here. No. No. No. How can that be?

For the first time in months, she didn't know what to do. Her heart thudded dully in her chest as she looked toward the sky. The rain, no longer a drizzle, came down in sheets. "Lara," she called out. "Where are you?"

She thought of Corrie Perelman and wondered how the woman continued on, day after day. For months Faith had hardly shed a tear, but now she couldn't stop them from coming, washed away by the rain.

Numb to the sounds around her, she saw a movement out of the corner of her eye. The shadow turned into a man. He was standing in the middle of the street, holding a gun, and lining up his shot. She tilted her chin downward until she saw a red dot on her chest. It wasn't terror that held her in place, but an intense feeling of loss.

She swallowed a painful knot in her throat, waiting for a bullet to strike her down.

Then tires squealed, rubber against pavement, as a car rounded the corner. The man with the gun looked toward the vehicle. He lifted his hand as if to shield his eyes from the bright light. Just as he was struck head-on, a shot fired. His body flew ten feet to the side of the road across from where Faith stood.

Numb with shock, frozen in place, Faith looked down at her chest. Her hands brushed over the front of her. She couldn't believe she was alive.

The bright-red Volkswagen Bug stopped in front of her. The engine released a long, squeaky hiss before it died. The passenger door flung open. Faith squinted, peering through the rain. She could hardly trust her eyes when she spotted Miranda in the passenger seat and Rage behind the wheel. What were they doing here? They had saved her life.

Before she could say a word, she caught sight of the man pushing himself to his hands and knees and crawling toward his gun.

Miranda jumped from her seat and charged across the street to stop him.

Faith followed a second later, intending to Tase him. Miranda, younger and faster, picked up his gun just as Faith got to him. He reached out and grabbed hold of Faith's ankle.

As she struggled to free herself from his grasp, he yanked hard, pulling her to the ground. She used her hands to break her fall, felt her wrist buckle on impact. She cried out in pain.

Miranda lunged for him, kicked him hard in the gut, forcing him to let go.

Faith found her Taser and gave him a jolt. He quivered, his eyes bulging. Writhing in pain, he gasped and clutched at his throat.

Faith checked his pockets for weapons and ID. There were none. She got to her feet and wrapped her arms around the girl, thankful to see she was all right. "Where have you been?"

"It's a long story, but I came back to help," Miranda said.

Faith pulled away, held her injured wrist close to her stomach. "You shouldn't be here. It's too dangerous."

"Go," Miranda said, obviously sensing her distress. "I'll keep an eye on this loser."

Faith looked over her shoulder at Rage and then back at Miranda. "I do need to check on my brother," she said. "Are you sure you can do this?"

Miranda kept the pistol aimed at the man's head. "I've got this," she said. "Go do what you have to do." Miranda gestured at Faith's hand. "Are you sure you're OK?"

"I'll be fine." She smiled. "We'll talk soon." Faith jogged across the pavement to the VW and leaned into the open passenger door. "You saved my life," Faith told Rage as water dripped down her face and over her chin and neck.

"Pretty much," Rage agreed.

Faith looked her over. Beneath the knit cap was a thin, pale face and eyes framed in dark shadows.

"You should have called me," Rage said. "I hate not being invited to a party."

"You're right. I should have called you. I'm sorry."

An explosion erupted. Windows shattered.

Faith ducked.

"Where's Beast?" Rage asked, her voice lined with panic.

"Last time I saw him he was headed for the front of the building." Her teeth chattered as the cold seeped into bone. "I've got to go. Three children were brought to the warehouse. I have no idea what's happened to them. And last I heard, Colton was trapped inside."

"Is one of the children Lara?"

Faith shook her head. She was about to shove off, but something stopped her. She looked back at Rage and said, "Thank you."

Rage tilted her chin in a subtle nod.

"For everything," Faith said. "I—"

"I get it," Rage snapped. "Now go!"

"Stay safe," Faith said, repeating her father's words before she ran off.

"You, too."

Searing pain shot through Faith's wrist as she ran toward the sound of gunfire. She stayed low, close to the side of the building.

A voice called out for help.

In the darkness, Faith saw a woman lying on the ground. She ran that way. It was Victoria Mitchell, bantamweight titleholder from Kirsten's group. Faith's stomach turned at the sight of so much blood. Her thoughts were scattered. Nothing made sense. Nobody was to be harmed.

Faith hooked her arms up and over Victoria's shoulders and dragged her toward the building. Victoria was wet and heavy. Every muscle strained as Faith pulled her to the side of the warehouse, crying out in pain until she was able to prop her up against the wall, where she'd be out of the worst of the downpour.

Blood gushed from Victoria's head, streaks of crimson trickling down the side of her face. Faith yanked off her coat, pulled her T-shirt over her head, then rolled the shirt into a ball and told Victoria to hold it against her wound.

Faith put her coat back on and zipped it tight. "Help is on its way," she told Victoria. She didn't want to leave the woman's side, but there wasn't anything more she could do for her. "I'll be back."

She passed more than one motionless body, making her way to the loading dock, where smoke plumed. Gunfire continued to erupt from inside the building, echoing off the walls and sounding like firecrackers on the Fourth of July. The rain wasn't letting up and neither was the small war going on around her. She kept wiping her eyes, trying to see. She used her right hand to hold her 9mm in front of her as she crept toward the loading dock.

A smoke grenade exploded close by. She dropped to the ground. After a few seconds, she continued on. Keeping her gun close to her chest, she used the thick wall of smoke as cover. If not for the heavy clip-clop sound of footfalls slapping against pavement, she might not have seen a man running through the smoky haze, heading for the parking lot.

It was Aster.

She couldn't let him get away.

Trying to keep her footfalls light, she kept a close tail. Aster didn't realize she was behind him until he got to his car. He turned slowly around, hands in the air.

Faith stood a few feet away. She didn't give him time to think about what his next move might be. She aimed low and fired, catching him in the hip.

He fell backward against his car, grimacing in pain as he reached into his pocket.

She fired again, hitting his right leg.

He fell flat against the ground. His gun dropped to his side. She stepped closer and kicked it away.

He was on his back, faceup, cursing as he rolled to his side in pain.

She clenched her jaw as she hovered over him, watching his face twist in agony. She'd never felt such hatred for anyone. She wanted to destroy him. He deserved to die. But not yet. "You son of a bitch," she said as she bent down and searched through his pockets. She found a pistol and tossed it out of sight, then patted him down, checking for more weapons.

His laughter caught her off guard. He really was crazy. They stared at each other through the downpour. She stood tall and aimed the barrel of her gun at his head.

"Go ahead," he croaked. "Put me out of my misery because I'll never tell you where your precious daughter is hiding out."

She blinked to keep her vision clear.

"You think you've made a dent in this billion-dollar business?"

This time when he laughed, Faith placed a foot on his injured leg and pressed down hard.

He grimaced. "Haven't you learned anything from all of this?" he asked. "You can't stop me. You'll discover soon enough you're fighting a losing battle."

"Tell me where she is, and I might let you live."

"You might as well shoot me now because I'll never tell you anything. You females don't know when to quit. You're all worthless, good-for-nothing whores who don't—"

Sirens sounded in the distance. "You don't know where she is, do you?"

She watched him closely. "You truly have no idea," Faith went on. "I've been questioning your idiotic men for weeks, and nobody ever mentioned Aster Williams," she lied, hoping to piss him off.

His eyes narrowed.

"You're not running this show, are you?" Judging by his expression, she'd struck a chord. "Who's the real man in charge?"

The sirens grew louder. Time was running out. Frustrated by his silence, she shot him in the foot.

He wriggled in pain, his face a maze of lines and deep grooves.

It took every bit of restraint she had within not to put a bullet between his eyes.

A police cruiser turned into the parking lot. Doors opened. "Put the gun down," an officer ordered.

She stared at Aster with regret. She should have taken him out while she had the chance. Slowly she bent down and placed the gun on the ground at her feet. Then she held her hands in the air.

Rage tried to fire up the engine again, but it was no use. She pulled her knit cap lower over her ears and climbed out of the car. Her legs nearly buckled from the weight. She'd never felt so weak. She thought she might collapse and never get up again. Every muscle felt fatigued as if she'd been lifting heavy weights.

Miranda hadn't moved. She stood in the rain, gun aimed at the guy's head as she interrogated him. "Where are you going?" Miranda asked Rage when she looked up and saw her exiting the car.

"I'll be right back," Rage said. "Does he know anything?"

"If he does, he's not sharing."

"Are you OK?"

"I'm good," Miranda said. "I'm not letting this asshole go anywhere."

Rage's heart was beating fast, so fast she thought it might explode. Her vision blurred as she walked in the same direction she'd seen Faith go. Again she worried she might pass out. She thought of Beast and Little Vinnie. She needed to find them. Not only to give them hell for leaving her but because she needed to make sure they were OK.

One step at a time, she told herself. One step at a time. She recalled the first time she'd gone running with Beast. She had been winded and wanted to quit. "You can do it," he'd told her more than once. She pretended he was there now, at her side, encouraging her onward. Over the past few days, as she lay sick in bed, she'd heard Beast talking to Little Vinnie about putting a small army together. Their conversation made sense because as she came around the corner, it looked and sounded like war: bodies everywhere, a constant stream of gunfire, people shouting orders, and piercing screams. Chaos.

Although her eyes had adjusted to the dark, the heavy rainfall and the smoke hovering around the loading dock made it difficult to see who was who and figure out what exactly was going on.

Sirens pierced the night as she crept closer. She found a place to hide behind a metal bin, trying to keep out of firing range as she maintained a lookout for Beast and Little Vinnie.

Faith was nowhere to be seen.

She heard shouting, recognized the voice of Russell Gray as he appeared from the smoke, barking orders before he ran to the glass doors at the front of the building. He sprayed the doors with bullets.

Rage covered her ears.

Glass shattered before he and another man made their way inside. The scene before her was surreal.

A massive figure burst from the smoke, firing a rifle as he made a hasty backward exit out of the loading dock area.

"Beast!" she shouted as he fell backward over a two-foot railing, landing with a hard thud onto his back.

He was alive. *Thank God.* Her heart skipped a beat as she called out his name again. Out of the corner of her eye she spotted a figure on the warehouse roof. A man was wriggling his way out of an escape hatch. He carried a gun.

Beast pushed himself to his feet and appeared to have no idea someone was looking down at him, making him a target.

"Beast!" Rage shouted for the third time as she ran his way. "Watch out!"

When he finally heard her, he turned toward her. "What are you doing here?"

"On the roof!" she shouted, tears mixing with the rain as she threw herself between the shooter and him, knowing what was coming next, welcoming the sting of the bullet as it tore through flesh and pushed her against Beast's massive chest. She would miss him. She'd had months to come to that realization. He was the only person who had ever loved her unconditionally. He loved her for who she was, with all her flaws and baggage.

Death was coming faster than she'd imagined. She could see it, feel it, taste it, and she welcomed it. She peered into Beast's warm eyes, glad to have it end this way instead of lingering too long in a hospital bed surrounded by pitiful, sorrowful looks.

The pain left her body, and in that moment she felt weightless and whole again. She thought of her little boy. Callan had given her life meaning. He was happy, and the thought cheered her immeasurably.

She'd made the right choice in saving Beast.

In his eyes, she saw only love—nothing but love. How beautiful, she thought, to realize what life was all about in that particular instant before death. No judgment, no silly games, no wondering about what came next . . . just love.

As he held her close, she felt the beat of his heart, rhythmic and strong against her ribs as she took her last breath.

———

Stunned and confused, Beast looked from Rage's round, wide-open eyes to the shooter standing on the roof.

He heard movement directly behind him. A shot rang out.

A bullet struck the rooftop shooter squarely in the chest, sending him toppling from the roof just as a string of police vehicles pulled in. The shooter landed with a thud on the windshield of the first cruiser in line.

The car door opened. Detective Yuhasz looked from the dead man on his windshield to Beast and then to Kirsten Reich, standing a few feet behind him, the one who had landed the fatal shot. Yuhasz ordered her to put her weapon down, which she did. Another officer cuffed her and put her in the back of his cruiser.

Detective Yuhasz shouted orders to his men before he disappeared inside the building.

With Rage's limp body cradled in his arms, Beast carried her over gravel and dirt, across the empty street, and to the back of the truck, where he could get her out of the rain.

His thoughts were everywhere and nowhere.

This couldn't be happening, Beast thought. He'd known this day would come, and yet it couldn't be here and it couldn't be now. Her face was gaunt and pale, her eyes shadowed by life and death.

This was not acceptable.

This was not real.

Anger enveloped him. He could feel it fold its wrathful tentacles around his organs, strangling his heart, crushing his spirit and will.

With one arm, Beast rolled the trailer door upward. He set her down, stepped inside, then scooped her up again with bloodied hands and carried her to the front of the trailer where he slid down, his back pressed against the siding, until he was seated, holding her all the while. The heavy rain sounded like battering rams above his head.

"Rage," he said, knowing there would be no answer.

She was gone.

He gently closed her eyes, kissed her forehead, then simply held her and told her everything he loved about her: the love she held for her son, her wit, her sarcasm, her ability to call him on all his bullshit. And as his thumb brushed lightly over her cheek, as he took note of the hollowness there, reality set in. She'd been so sick of late. Watching her, knowing she'd been hiding her pain from him, caused his anger to turn to something else.

She'd died on her own terms. She'd died saving his life.

And for the first time in a long while, maybe ever, he wept.

A woeful sound came from his throat. A sound he didn't recognize as he shed tears for all the pain she'd been forced to endure in her short life. He cried for all the happy times they'd shared, too, and for all she'd done to bring him back to life after he'd lost his wife and daughter. Rage had no idea the difference she made in so many lives. And he knew his world would never be the same.

TWENTY-ONE

"A confrontation between citizens and human traffickers became full-out warfare last night at a warehouse located in East Sacramento. Although it has yet to be confirmed, we've been told that a dozen businessmen allegedly involved in criminal activity were meeting there to discuss a recent string of arrests.

"Citizens have been taking it upon themselves to report suspicious activities, which have resulted in a high number of arrests this past week. Retired US Army Reserve Captain Bo DeLuc and retired Commander Charlie Ward, along with Russell Gray, the father of Faith McMann, and others, many ex-military, had reportedly planned to gather information on the group they consider to be part of the upper tier of the sex-trafficking hierarchy. But things got out of hand quickly after three children were brought to the site. No names have been released, but it's believed Lara McMann was not among the group. Aster Williams, the Sacramento businessman purported to be one of the ringleaders, was said to be in attendance when the first shot was fired. At this time many are speculating that Faith McMann—mother, schoolteacher, and, according to some, a vigilante—was behind this latest devastating event that has left five dead, two in critical condition, and six injured. All three children are safe. We'll keep you updated as more information comes in."

Dad shut off the television.

"Five dead," Lilly said as she helped Faith bandage her hand, keeping her pinkie and ring finger wrapped together in a makeshift splint. "And poor Rage," Lilly said, looking to Faith's dad for comfort.

"Are they going to put Mom in jail?" Hudson asked from the hallway.

They all turned his way.

"Nobody's going to jail," Faith said, hoping it was true, just before her cell rang. "It's Detective Yuhasz." She held up her good hand, asking for silence, before picking up the call.

After she ended the conversation, she asked Mom and Dad if they could watch Hudson for a couple of hours. The detective wanted to talk to her in person.

Fifteen minutes later, Faith was in her car headed for the police department in Auburn. So much had happened last night. It was difficult to concentrate. She couldn't stop thinking about Rage, who'd been so determined to live to see the day Lara was brought home.

"Stay safe" had been the last thing Faith had said to Rage. If only she'd known that would be their final moment together. She would have taken the time to let Rage know she never could have accomplished so much in such a short time without her help. Faith would have told her how special she was, a compassionate soul who would be sorely missed when she was gone.

So much chaos last night, Faith thought. *Smoke, rain, gunfire, and shouting.* If Rage hadn't shown up when she did, Faith wouldn't be here. It broke her heart to think of the moment she and Dad found Beast in the back of the semitrailer cradling Rage's lifeless body.

A squirrel skittered across the road in front of her. She hit the brakes. Her tires swerved. Once she had things under control again, she remained calm and kept her eyes on the road.

It was difficult to concentrate knowing Rage and two of Kirsten's friends had died. At times like this she wondered how much longer they could keep up the fight. Although arrests had been made and Aster Williams was in custody, it seemed the enemy was winning. How could they not be? It would take years of extreme focus and diligence to take these guys down.

Two of the five dead were on the list. Both recruiters and drug dealers, according to Richard Price. Two others were in critical condition: one of Aster's elite, and Victoria, the woman she'd dragged to the side of the building.

For the first time in a long while, Lara wasn't her only concern.

Faith had tried not to express worry in front of Hudson, but the truth was she had no idea if Detective Yuhasz would handcuff her and order her locked in a cell. It had happened before, and she imagined it could happen again. Two wrongs did not make a right. She knew that. Laws were put in place for a reason. She knew that, too. And yet she also knew that nothing the detective could say this morning would stop her from continuing her search for Lara.

The rain had stopped, but the roads were still slick from last night's downpour. It didn't help that people drove too fast on Auburn-Folsom, making it a danger to bikers, pedestrians, and other drivers. There were two cars ahead and one behind her. The forest-green Nissan directly in front of her kept braking. She held her good hand tight around the wheel and did her best to keep a safe distance away.

The car behind her, a silver Honda Civic, sped up, passing her and the two cars ahead at the same time a truck was coming from the opposite direction. Panicked, she pulled as far to the right as she could without going into the ditch. The Nissan in front of her did the same.

A horn blared as the truck passed by in a rumbling blur of watery spray. Faith waited a few seconds for the Nissan to continue on. When the car failed to move, she started to merge back onto the road. She wouldn't have given the Nissan another thought if it hadn't pulled out in front of her just as she was about to pass.

"Son of a bitch!"

She slammed on her brakes.

Her car fishtailed, but she managed to stay on the road.

Pulse racing, she looked at her rearview mirror and saw a line of cars approaching. Riled by what had just happened, she pulled to the side of the road again, deciding to let them all pass.

Up ahead she noticed the Nissan had pulled to the side again, too.

Something wasn't right. She stared ahead, tried to get a glimpse of the driver. This was getting weird. She grabbed her cell from inside her purse on the passenger seat. Before she could zoom in and take a picture of the license plate, the Nissan took off, tires squealing before getting traction.

The car disappeared. She counted to ten before merging back onto the road.

She jumped at the sound of her ringtone.

She was definitely losing it. Every nerve was shot. She hit the green "Call" button on her console and said hello.

There was breathing on the other end.

"Is anybody there?"

She was about to disconnect the call when she glanced in the rearview mirror and saw the same damn Nissan pull out from Horseshoe Bar Road and merge onto Auburn-Folsom Road.

He was back.

Focused on the road ahead, the caller all but forgotten, she sped up to fifty-five and then sixty, figuring she'd lead the asshole right to the Auburn Police Department.

The road became much narrower the farther she went. Sidewalks and ditches were now a steep embankment.

The Nissan sped up, too, staying uncomfortably close.

By the time she passed Newcastle Road, the speedometer had reached seventy. Her heart pounded, the adrenaline rush making it difficult to think. Up ahead a car pulled out of one of the developments, forcing her to slow.

Bam! The Nissan hit her from behind. She jerked forward, her chest hitting the steering column. She swerved into oncoming traffic, then yanked the wheel back the other way.

Her car did a 180. The engine stalled. Panicked, she turned the key. Nothing. She looked up and found herself facing the driver. His big eyes, dark and fearless, stared at her. Who was he?

She remembered the gun in the glove box. She leaned over to open the compartment.

Bam! Again she was jolted forward, her splintered hand caught between her chest and the steering wheel. She screamed out as intense pain swooshed through her body. About to reach for the glove box again, she noticed how close the Nissan's back wheels were to the embankment. Tires squealed as he put on the gas and came at her again. She used her good hand to grip the steering wheel and waited for impact.

Bam! This time when he reversed, she turned the key and stepped on the gas. Her car sped forward and slammed into the front of the Nissan, tires squealing as she kept her foot on the gas, pushing him backward, tires smoking, the undercarriage rattling.

His movements were frantic as he tried to find a way out of his predicament. It was no use. She had momentum on her side. She kept on the gas, pushing the car back an inch at a time until his back tires met with wet soil. He lost traction and disappeared over the edge.

She let off the gas. Her shoulders tight, she sat still for a few seconds. Her hands trembled. She didn't bother getting out of the car to see what happened. She made a U-turn and headed for the police station as planned.

Twenty-Two

The morning after losing Rage, Beast came out of his room, surprised to see Miranda sitting with his dad at the kitchen table.

"Scrambled eggs and sausage on the stove," Dad told him.

"I'm not hungry."

Little Vinnie frowned. "You didn't eat last night. What are you planning on doing, starving yourself to death?"

"Not a bad idea," Beast said. "The two of you can sit around and watch me slowly fade away and die because I'm sort of tired of always being the one left behind to pick up the pieces. It gets old real fast. Watching my buddies get their arms and legs blown off was nothing compared to what was waiting for me once I got home." He shook his head in wonder. "My wife and daughter and now Rage."

Nobody said a word.

"I hate that stupid name," Beast said. "Her name is Sally. Her name *was* Sally," he amended. "I hated it then, and I hate it now. For fuck's sake—*Rage*." Feeling as frustrated and mean as a caged animal, he let out a growl. "Sally didn't have an angry bone in her body," he ground out. "The only person she was mad at was herself."

Beast stomped across the floor, coming to a halt at the front door. He flung the door open, then stood there silently staring outside. He thought about taking off, but then thought better of it and stepped back inside. When he turned back to face Dad and Miranda, he gave the young girl a piercing stare. "What were you thinking bringing her to the warehouse last night? Didn't you know she was sick? Couldn't you see she could hardly take ten steps without having trouble breathing?"

"Leave Miranda out of this," Dad warned. "This is about you and your loss. You're not right in the head at the moment. What you're feeling has nothing to do with Miranda."

Beast didn't hear a word he said. His hand shook as he pointed a finger at Miranda. "If you had left well enough alone, Sally would still be alive."

Miranda jumped to her feet, nearly toppling the chair behind her. "You're so damn selfish. And you're a bully, too! Rage didn't want to sit in bed and wait for death to come. I was only here for, what, less than a week before I took off? And even in that short amount of time I saw that she was ready to die. If you'd ever stopped to pay attention to her, really pay attention, you would have seen that she'd been dying long before I ever met you crazy people. Why do you think she kept trying to talk to you? She knew her time was nearly up." Miranda took a shaky breath. "And for the record, not only were you in obvious denial; you were blind. Did you even see her dumping her food in her napkin and getting rid of it because she didn't want to be lectured by you all day about what she should eat and how much rest she should get?" Miranda paused before adding, "If you ever listened to what she truly wished to accomplish, you never would have left her here alone last night. That's not what she wanted, but you didn't give her a choice."

Beast was livid. His blood thickened; his face heated. "You never should have brought her there last night," he said, his tone deepening. "She was too sick to be out of bed."

Miranda tossed her napkin on the table. "She said you attended anger management classes for her. That's ridiculous because you're obviously the one with the problem."

His muscles quivered.

"If you stopped to think for a minute before accusing me of driving her to her death," Miranda went on, "you would see the truth. Rage had the keys to her car in her hand when I knocked on the door. She started that piece-of-shit engine right up and gave me two seconds to decide if I wanted to come along for the ride. I didn't know where you two were or what sort of crazy shit you were all up to. How would I know?" Miranda stopped talking and looked at Little Vinnie. "Thanks for breakfast and for letting me stay the night. I appreciate it." As she walked past Beast to grab her coat from the couch she said, "I'm sorry for your loss. She was a very special person, and I'm only glad I had the chance to know her."

After the door shut behind her, Little Vinnie began clearing the table.

"Go ahead and have your say," Beast told him. "You might as well."

But his dad merely dumped the eggs into the garbage and began cleaning the pan.

"That girl had no business sleeping in Sally's room. She's been dead less than a day, and you've already given her room away?"

Beast didn't wait for an answer. Instead he swept past him and entered the ridiculously small hallway leading to Sally's room. He flicked the switch. There was a sleeping bag and pillow on the ground. Apparently Miranda had a difficult time sleeping in Sally's bed.

He moved the blankets and pillow from the floor to the chair in the corner. He picked up Rage's favorite T-shirt, a soft gray fabric with a Ramones graphic, carried it to the closet, and slid it carefully on to a hanger.

He closed his eyes for a few seconds.

After a quiet moment passed, he rubbed the back of his neck and looked around. Peacefulness settled over him as he felt her presence. *Miranda is right,* he thought. Rage had known exactly what she was doing when she drove to the warehouse and straight into madness.

Rage had saved his life twice. The first time when he'd found her in the ditch, the same night he'd contemplated ending his own life. And again last night when she'd put herself in front of the shooter's bullet meant for him.

As he sat quietly, he found himself looking at the pile of papers she'd been working on these past few days. Rage had narrowed the ridiculous list of Patricks to three.

The fact that he still thought of her as Rage was not lost on him. Even if he'd never liked the nickname she'd chosen, she'd been relentless about making sure everyone called her that. His guess was that choosing another name had more to do with never feeling a connection to the name Sally, given to her by people who'd never treated her well, never loved her the way she deserved to be loved. Perhaps the name Sally had belonged to someone she wanted to forget.

With papers in hand, he plopped down on the edge of the bed and began looking through her notes: Patrick Monahan. Patrick Barnes. Patrick Fisher. There were no addresses, but she had scribbled down a few notes. For instance, Patrick Monahan had once lived in the Bay Area. In the margins she'd written down the name of a bank in Auburn with a question mark. She'd also printed and stapled a story about Patrick Barnes to her list. The guy had been arrested on drug charges and once worked as a pool maintenance man in Sacramento. And then there was Patrick Fisher. Again, in the margins, she'd written, "This could be the one. He recently sold a black BMW and he's a registered pedophile."

Beast leaned over and opened the top drawer of her side table. Inside was a stack of envelopes tied together with a satin ribbon. The envelope on top had his name written on it in beautiful cursive. He brought the stack of envelopes to his lap and untied the ribbon.

His chest ached.

She'd also written letters to Little Vinnie, Callan, Faith, and Miranda.

He swallowed the painful knot in his throat as he opened his envelope, his vision slightly blurred as he read:

Charlie (I don't think I've ever called you that), you already know how I feel about you and your dad, so I won't bore you with long, mushy prose. After you pulled me from the side of the road and brought me home to be a part of the family, I knew instantly that you and Little Vinnie were my people. Everybody needs someone, and I was so very lucky to get two of the best human beings on this earth. Treat your dad well. He loves you. Be kind to yourself because you deserve it. You've given so much, never taking a moment for yourself. It's time for you to let go of the anger inside and live a little.

All my love, Rage

P.S. Please make sure you find a reputable buyer for the coin you'll find in a plastic bag at the back of the drawer, and use the money to pay for Callan's college.

Deep inside the drawer he found the clear plastic bag holding the coin. He examined it closely, shaking his head, wondering when she might have gotten her hands on it as he read on:

P.P.S. Please read Sandi Cameron's letter and try to find a way to forgive her.

P.P.P.S. I forgive you for never being able to find the words to tell me how much I meant to you. It's OK because you were always there for me, and actions speak so much louder than words.

Faith entered Detective Yuhasz's office after he waved her in. He was on the phone, so she quietly took a seat in one of the two chairs in front of his desk. She'd decided not to tell him about her run-in with the man in the Nissan. Word would get out, and her father would be dead set against her leaving the house without protection. Bodyguards cost money, and she had better ideas of how to use the money hidden away in her parents' backyard. But that didn't mean she wouldn't do what she could to protect herself. For starters, she would trade her Camry in for a used car.

Not only did Aster Williams and his men seem intent on destroying her family; they seemed to put little value on life generally. It was all about money. The dollar was their god. Greed was their motivation.

Once Yuhasz finished his conversation, his attention fell to her bandaged hand. "Got hurt in the scuffle?"

She nodded. His sarcasm could not be missed. His annoyance with her was written all over his face, gouged in the deep grooves of his forehead.

He leaned back in his chair, hands folded. "I made a mistake in trusting you to keep your end of the bargain."

"How so?"

"You promised to let me know what you had planned," he said.

"I called you just as I said I would."

His frown deepened. "I trusted you."

"I couldn't risk having one of your men appear too soon. If that had happened, if a police cruiser was spotted, do you think Aster Williams and his men would have continued with their plans? Would they have brought those children into the warehouse?" She shook her head. "I think we both know the answer to that."

He wasn't merely annoyed with her; he was as angry as she'd ever seen him. But that didn't stop her from defending her position. "Why would you or the FBI have used the manpower to go to the warehouse in the first place based on the word of some loser in a bar who happened to talk to Beast?"

He said nothing.

"And, besides, no one involved was to make a move. Nobody was to get shot. No gun was to be fired."

"And why in the world would you believe that? Every person on the scene, mostly everyday citizens handpicked by you and your friends, was armed. And yet you thought you could somehow take control of some of the most ruthless men out there?"

"These traffickers are touching every walk of life. They have penetrated your department. They are everywhere." She sat up taller. "Even with all the tragedy, I would do it again."

His face reddened.

"This isn't about breaking the law. This is my daughter we're talking about," she said, her anger just as palpable. "I'll do whatever I have to in order to get my child back."

"You've gone from careless to reckless," he said flatly.

"Aren't you calling the kettle black, Detective? Didn't you bend the rules when it was your daughter's life at stake?"

"Enough is enough," he said.

"What do you mean?"

"The judge who agreed to your release after your last incident is reconsidering his decision. Within the next twenty-four hours, he'll be assessing the current situation and make the ruling as to whether or not to have you locked up again."

She leaned forward, her good hand gripping the edge of his desk. "Why would he do such a thing? My son is home. I need to be with him."

"You should have thought about that before you decided to go to that warehouse last night and wreak havoc."

"So you agree with him? You believe I should be locked up?"

"You shot a man."

"Aster Williams is not human."

"It's not my decision to make. The judge will do as he sees fit. You know that." Yuhasz waved a hand at her. "Look at yourself. You don't look well. You haven't taken care of yourself since the day your family was attacked." He shook his head.

She couldn't tell if her appearance sickened him, or saddened him.

"Surely you can talk to the judge, try to sway him somehow."

"You've gone too far," he said. "I tried to work with you, but in my opinion, you've become as dangerous as the men you're trying to stop. Five people died last night. *Five.* Two more are in critical condition. Does that mean anything to you? Anything at all?"

"It makes me sick to my stomach. We lost Rage and two other good people yesterday. Others are fighting for their lives. I haven't had a chance to mourn the death of my husband. A man I loved more than anything in this world. Once I find my daughter, I will allow myself to grieve for them all. But not before then." She stood, her chest tight, her emotions in check. "I have twenty-four hours?"

The detective looked baffled. "What?"

"You said I had twenty-four hours before the judge will be making a decision. Is that right?"

She watched Yuhasz rub his hands over his prickly head of hair, his frustration obvious. "And what will you be doing in the next twenty-four hours?"

"Looking for Lara—what do you think?"

"What information are you hiding from me now?"

"I have the same information as you, Detective." She paused before asking, "Any word about Aster Williams?"

"Despite being shot multiple times, he's alive, if that's what you're wondering."

"That's too bad," she said before clasping her hand around the door handle.

"Beth Tanner was attacked last night," he told her.

178

"No." Looking back at the detective, she touched her throat, unable to believe what he was telling her.

"A grisly crime scene, one of the bloodiest I've ever seen."

"Did you catch her attacker?"

"He's in the morgue, along with the neighbor, who had the incredibly bad timing to pick that moment to bring her donuts from his bakery."

"Mr. Hawkins is dead?"

He nodded. "Beth Tanner is at Sutter General in Roseville."

It took Faith a second for his words to sink in. "She's alive?"

"Last I heard she was still hanging on. She's a fighter. Killed her attacker with a three-pronged turning fork. I've never seen anything like it."

"She's a gun expert," Faith said quietly. "I would have thought she shot him."

"From the looks of it, he caught her off guard."

"Thank God she's alive."

"She was lucky," Yuhasz said. "Same goes for you and your family. One of the reasons I won't be upset if the judge sees fit to have you locked up again is because I have a feeling it might be the only way to keep you safe."

Faith stood quietly for a moment. So much had happened over the past few months, and yet they'd hardly scraped the surface. People were dying, and yet Lara still wasn't home. Her knees wobbled, but she refused to show any weakness at a time when she needed to be stronger than ever. Without another word spoken, she walked out of his office, taking the familiar path past O'Sullivan's desk, down a set of wide steps, and through double doors leading to the parking lot.

The moment she stepped outside, she bent forward, her right hand propped on her knee while she tried to suck air into her lungs. She wasn't afraid of these maniacs. They were scum. But keeping Hudson safe while doing everything she could to find Lara was wearing on her, making her question her strength and emotional toughness.

Upon hearing the door open and close behind her, she thought of Corrie Perelman's determination to find her own daughter. And what about Miranda? The girl had been forced into a life of sex slavery, struggling for much too long before escaping her own personal hell. And then there was Rage. Abandoned by those who were supposed to love her most, Rage had not only found the strength to give her son the best opportunity for a decent life; she'd fought valiantly every day to make a difference and to carry on.

Faith stood tall again, her head held high as she made her way to her car. She refused to break. "You will not win," she said aloud. "You will not win."

TWENTY-THREE

Beast was still sitting in Rage's room when his cell rang. He picked up and said hello.

"It's me," Faith said. "I had to talk to someone. Are you busy?"

"Shoot," he said.

"My neighbor Beth Tanner, the ER nurse—"

"I know who she is," he said. "What about her?"

"She and another neighbor of mine, Mr. Hawkins, were attacked at Beth's home last night. Mr. Hawkins was killed. And so was the attacker. Beth is in the hospital."

"I'm sorry."

"On my way to see Detective Yuhasz," she said, talking quickly, "a man driving a green Nissan tried to drive me off the road."

"Did you see his face?"

"I didn't recognize his face from our list of names, but I could probably pick him out of a lineup."

"What happened?"

"I drove him off the road instead."

Beast rubbed his jaw. "Did you get a license plate number?"

"No. I tried, but it all happened too fast."

"Did you tell Detective Yuhasz about this?"

"No."

"Why not?"

"I don't know," she said, frustration lining her voice. "These men are dangerous. They mean business, and I was afraid Yuhasz and my father might try to stop me from continuing on with my search for Lara."

"Nobody is trying to stop you. Your dad wants to find Lara as much as you do."

"I know. I'm tired, and I'm not thinking straight."

"Don't worry. I'll call it in. Tell me what happened and where."

After giving him the details, she said, "There's more you should know. The judge who let me off is considering reversing his decision and having me put back behind bars. He'll be making the determination in the next twenty-four hours. If that happens, I don't know what I'll do. Aster's men are obviously kicking things up a notch. I don't want my family hurt any more than they've already been. It's all starting to feel so—"

"Faith," Beast said. "Slow down. Take a breath."

"Innocent people were killed last night because of my carelessness. And now Beth and Mr. Hawkins. I never should have—"

"Knock it off," Beast cut her off again. "This poor-me attitude, look-what-I've-done, it's-all-my-fault whining doesn't suit you."

"But—"

"Kirsten Reich and her friends approached you. Not the other way around. You never asked anyone else to put their life on the line. What's done is done. We have work to do. If the judge decides to throw you back in the slammer, then that would mean your time is severely limited."

Faith grew quiet, which was a good thing because he needed to think. He scratched the side of his neck as his gaze fell on Rage's list of names. "I've got an idea. It's a long shot, but it's something. How quickly can you get over here?"

"Barring any more of Aster's men coming after me, I can be there in twenty minutes."

———

Eighteen minutes later, Faith pulled up at the curb. Beast waited for her at the door. As she walked toward him, she couldn't miss the sadness she saw. More than anything, she wanted to wrap her arms around him, try to comfort him, and tell him how sorry she was about Rage. But the seriousness of his expression and unfaltering stance caused her to reconsider.

"Where'd you get that car?" He looked at her bandages. "And what happened to your hand?"

"Probably just a sprain," she told him. "And I traded my Camry for the Corolla right after I left the police station. I was at a used car lot when I called you. After I got off the phone with you, the car salesman showed me the GPS tracker he'd found on the bumper of my Camry. Battery powered. Apparently he and his wife had purchased one just like it to keep track of their teenager. He said they could last anywhere from seven to thirty days." Seeing the GPS had only served to fuel her anger. Their enemies were getting smarter, bolder. Although she felt more secure driving a car nobody would recognize, she knew it wouldn't last.

Beast frowned. "Come on in."

She stepped inside, watched him take a look around the neighborhood before closing the door. She followed him across the living area, through the kitchen, and to Rage's room. The lights were on, and he opened the blinds, too.

"Is Little Vinnie around?" she asked.

"He's out looking for Miranda. Long story."

Judging by his tone, he didn't want to talk about it, so she let it go. He handed her a piece of paper.

She read it over. It was a list of three Patricks in the Sacramento area with scribbled notes in the margins. She looked up at Beast as he hovered close, waiting. "What is this?"

"Rage spent her last days looking up every Patrick she could find who lived within so many miles of Sacramento."

Faith nodded. "We talked about the mysterious man named Patrick on more than one occasion, but ultimately we both concluded it would be a waste of time, considering we didn't have much information and because there were so many people with that name."

He nodded in understanding. "I didn't try to stop her because it gave her something to do, kept her busy."

"I wonder how the process of elimination worked . . . you know . . . how did she narrow the list down to three?"

"I asked her about it the other day. Mostly she used instinct."

Faith had gotten her hopes up for nothing.

Beast went to the closet, scooped up a well-used backpack from the floor, then went to the bed and emptied its contents on the mattress: pens, sticks of gum, ChapStick, prescription medicine, tissues, and a crumpled piece of paper. He then proceeded to gather Rage's notes and papers from the bed, side table, and nightstand and shove it all into the backpack. Faith picked up a crumpled paper that had fallen to the ground and handed it to Beast to put with the rest of the papers.

Forty-five minutes later, after Beast called in a couple of favors to get addresses and backgrounds on all three Patricks left on the list, Faith waited at the door for Beast to join her.

Since Little Vinnie had taken the truck, they hopped into Faith's Toyota and drove off. Beast was a good sport, considering his head nearly touched the ceiling and his legs looked cramped.

The first house they visited belonged to Patrick Monahan in Auburn, located right off I-80. Beast jumped out of the car before she had a chance to shut off the engine. She exited the car and rushed to catch up with him.

On the way to Auburn, Beast had told her he would do the talking. That was it as far as plans went. Much too late now for strategizing. Faith stood at Beast's side while he knocked on the door loud enough to wake the dead.

An elderly woman with wiry hair answered the door. Her back was stooped, and she used a cane for support. Before she could say a word, someone called out "Mom" from inside the house.

"How many times have I told you not to answer the door? Jesus."

The voice belonged to a short, heavyset man. He grabbed hold of the woman's frail arm and pulled her none too gently out of the way. Before he could shut the door, though, Beast stuck a booted foot inside, stopping him from doing any such thing. Beast was in one of his moods.

"Is your name Patrick?" Beast asked.

"Yeah, so what's it to you?"

Beast stepped inside, pushing right past the man.

The elderly woman stood close by. She didn't appear all too surprised to see Beast barge into the house uninvited. With help from her cane, she walked back to the living area and sat down in a cushioned seat in front of an old television set.

Despite Patrick's threats to grab his gun if they didn't leave his house and get off his property, Faith followed Beast, peering around as he went down the hallway.

They moved from room to room, checking closets and any space large enough to fit a child. Upset, Patrick Monahan pulled out his mobile phone and threatened to call the police.

"Be my guest," Beast told him without slowing. He stepped into the laundry room filled with piles of dirty blankets and clothes. There wasn't much room, so Faith stayed in the hallway.

"As soon as the police arrive," Beast said, "I'll make sure they're aware of the criminal bench warrant that was recently issued for your failure to appear in court." Beast opened the washer and then the dryer before he set off for the next room.

Faith and Patrick followed. He looked over his shoulder at her with narrowed eyes.

"I'd probably be doing you a favor," Beast went on, "since it's always better to address these sorts of situations sooner rather than later. You know, so you don't risk being arrested when you least expect it."

Patrick Monahan's shoulders fell. "What is it exactly you're looking for?"

They were inside the master bedroom now. The bed was unmade, and the room was cluttered with unwashed dishes and old coffee cups.

"We're looking for my daughter," Faith said. "Lara McMann."

"Seriously?"

Before Faith knew what he was up to, Beast had a fistful of the man's shirt as he held Patrick against the wall. Beast's nostrils flared, and the veins in his neck bulged. Faith had only seen him turn into the Hulk a couple of times, but this time was definitely the most troubling to watch. Rage was gone, and he was going to find someone to take it out on.

Beast, she figured, had been set off by Patrick's seemingly complacent attitude. Faith was ready to step in if she had to. For now she waited.

"Do I look serious?" Beast asked through gritted teeth.

Patrick managed a nod. His voice squeaked when he said, "I sell drugs every once in a while, but I'm no pimp. I would never kidnap a child. I don't know who might have given you my name, but I have nothing to do with that little girl's disappearance."

Inwardly Faith began counting to ten. She got as far as five when Beast put the man down. "I'm going to finish having a look around. And then we'll leave. I suggest you shut up and stay out of my way."

TWENTY-FOUR

Patrick tapped his fingers on the table and stared at his phone, willing it to ring. Every television station had been playing bits and pieces of the battle fought last night at the warehouse in East Sacramento. Patrick had yet to hear from Aster. Had he made it out alive? If so, where was he? In the hospital? In a prison cell? At home?

"Shit. Shit. Shit," he muttered.

David Seamus was his last chance.

If the man didn't call him back in the next thirty minutes, Patrick would have no choice but to drag the girl off to the same abandoned construction site where he'd shot and buried Eddie and Gage. There was no possible way he could or would let the girl go and risk getting put away for life.

He stood, paced the room, then walked to the kitchen, opened the refrigerator, and looked around for something to eat. He shut the door when he realized he wasn't hungry. His stomach had been turning since he saw the first news story about Faith McMann and friends showing up at the warehouse with guns blazing. He was beginning to wonder if the woman was courageous or just plain crazy.

His phone rang. Music to his ears. "Hello?"

"We've got a deal. Meet me at the shipyard on Industrial Boulevard at six o'clock. Head for the North Terminal near the vacant lots. Make sure she has food and water. She'll be traveling in a crate along with the next shipment of rice."

"And where does she go from there?"

"Not your concern. Industrial Boulevard. Six o'clock. That's your drop-off point."

"What about the money?" Patrick asked. He wasn't putting the girl in any crate without the money. He'd drown her and toss her overboard before he'd let Seamus have her for nothing.

"Calm down. I'll have your money. Girl in exchange for cash. Quick and easy. Got it?"

"Sure. Yeah. Got it."

The line went dead.

Patrick cursed. He had a lot to do and not much time to do it. First things first. He grabbed his key, unlocked the door to the basement, and hurried down the stairs. The girl was asleep. He turned the light on. "Wake up. Time to get ready."

———

At the sound of his voice, Lara sat up, her mind hazy with remnants of last night's dreams swirling about. It took a moment for his words to register. What was Patrick talking about?

"Get ready for what?" she asked, her voice groggy with sleep.

Patrick seemed nervous about something. He was walking back and forth, muttering as he went, his eyes wild.

He was acting crazy, and she didn't like it. Hoping to get him away from the bed so he wouldn't see the words etched into the wall behind her, she slid from her cot and headed for the stairs.

He followed just as she knew he would. Although it had been days since he'd allowed her upstairs, she knew he didn't like her wandering around the house alone.

When she walked through the door into the hallway and toward the kitchen, he grabbed hold of her shoulder and pointed the other way. She followed his instructions, which were mostly hand gestures. She walked across the carpeted floor, past the TV, and into the hallway leading to the master bedroom. She'd never seen his bedroom before. His clothes were neatly folded and packed in open bags on the bed, everything orderly and in its place.

He pointed to the bathroom.

On the counter were a pair of scissors and a box of hair coloring—Clairol Nice 'n Easy. Natural black.

"Don't cut my hair," she pleaded. "I'll wear a hat. Nobody will recognize me, I promise."

"You can't promise shit like that." He grabbed her shoulder again and turned her about until she faced the mirrored wall behind the double sinks. She watched him pick up the scissors, tried not to cry as she watched strands and then clumps of long, blonde hair fall onto the counter and floor until she had nothing but jagged ends around her ears.

"Turn toward me," he said. He cut her bangs and any flyaway hair longer than an inch. After signaling for her to face the mirror again, he emptied the box, read the directions, and put on the plastic gloves. "Once I apply this, it's going to have to sit for a bit. So don't mess with it. Got it?"

She sniffled. "I don't want to go anywhere," she said. "I like it here." It was true. She didn't mind reading books all day in the basement. She didn't want to be sold to a crusty old man. She didn't want anyone touching her like she'd seen happen again and again to other girls at the farmhouse. Those men were disgusting old pigs with rotted breath and dark, soulless eyes. She would rather die than be stuck with some sick old man.

"You can take your books with you," he said. "You'll be fine. The people I'm sending you with are friends of mine. They're good people."

She knew when he was lying. He couldn't look her in the eye when he lied. He always cleared his throat, too, as if something was stuck. Dad had taught her a long time ago how to tell if someone was lying. It was the same day he'd caught her in a lie. Eager to go outside and play, she'd told him she was done with her school project. He'd known right away she was lying when she looked down at her feet instead of meeting his gaze.

"Why can't I go home instead?"

"Because you can't," he said. "Stop moving. If this gets in your eye, you'll go blind."

"Why are you doing this?" she asked. "For money?"

He squeezed the rest of the contents of the plastic bottle onto the top of her head, then massaged her scalp. His fingers pressed so hard it felt as if he might crush her skull.

"You're hurting me."

"Yeah. Good. No more questions."

She eyed the scissors, thought about grabbing them and plunging the tips into his stomach. But they weren't very sharp, and even if she did get a hold of them, there was no way she was strong enough to puncture him with them. She'd only make him angrier than he already was, and then what? No telling what he would do.

After making sure every blonde hair was covered in dark ooze, he peeled off the gloves and put everything inside the box, wrapped it all inside a plastic bag, and put the garbage with everything else on the bed.

She realized then that this was it. They were leaving for good, and he didn't want to leave any evidence behind.

Her hands trembled, and her stomach felt as if butterflies were flittering about.

What would her brother do in this situation? He'd always been a problem solver like their dad. He would find a way out of this; she knew he would. *Think, Lara, think!*

She needed to find a pen or pencil, something to leave a note in one of the books downstairs. That's what she would do.

TWENTY-FIVE

After checking in with Mom and Dad, making sure Hudson was OK, Faith told them she'd try to be back by dinner, but it was already three o'clock by the time Beast and Faith arrived back at Beast's house in Roseville.

Since they had two more Patricks they needed to talk to before dark, Beast and Faith decided to split up. One of the Patricks lived in Acampo about an hour and fifteen minutes away; that's where Beast would go. The third Patrick lived in North Sacramento; Faith would head that way.

They knew their chance of either one of them being the actual Patrick they were looking for was slim to none. But what other options did they have at this point? They needed to keep moving, keep looking. By this time tomorrow, Faith could find herself locked up in a cell.

Despite losing two friends last night, Kirsten Reich had texted her a few minutes ago. She was still out on the streets, talking to people, asking questions, finding out what she could. She insisted that her two friends would want Faith to continue with the search. They weren't finished yet, she told Faith. Her determination and willingness to keep on going were inspiring.

Since Beast's truck was now parked in front of the house, Faith decided to say hello to Miranda and Little Vinnie before heading off. Beast pulled the key to the house from his pocket and opened the door.

Miranda flew into Faith's arms the minute she stepped inside. Faith leaned back so she could take a good look at the girl. "You look good."

"I'm doing OK," Miranda said.

"Are you going to stick around for a while?" Faith asked.

Beast grunted as he proceeded to the kitchen, where Little Vinnie was doing what he always did, stirring something in a pot on the stove.

"I'm not staying," Miranda told Beast. "So don't get your panties all in a twist."

"You can stay with Mom and Dad," Faith said. "They would be happy to have you."

"Thanks," she said, "but I'll be fine."

"You're staying here with us," Beast told her. "No more running off without telling anyone. That's it. Discussion over."

"You're not the boss of me."

"Yeah, I am. You're what? Fifteen? Sixteen? I am definitely the boss of you." He used a spoon to taste his dad's concoction, then nodded his approval. He then pointed the spoon at Miranda. "Rage liked you. She'd be angry as hell if I didn't make you stay."

Miranda shifted her weight from one foot to the other. "I thought her name was Sally."

"She liked the name Rage," Beast told her, his tone gruff. "We'll call her Rage."

"End of discussion?" Miranda asked.

"Little Vinnie doesn't like smart-asses," Beast shot back.

"He doesn't like cursing, either," she told him.

Little Vinnie removed the towel from his shoulder, tossed it on the table, and disappeared into one of the bedrooms at the back of the house.

Faith said goodbye to Miranda and then followed Beast out the door. "You're a good man, Charlie," she told him.

He grunted.

She watched him climb behind the wheel of his truck and head south.

On the drive to North Sacramento, Faith thought about her other life, before the attack. She'd taken so much for granted. If she could relive those years with Craig, she would appreciate all the little things. Craig had a great sense of humor, and he knew how to listen. He was a wonderful and caring father. He had a generous spirit. No matter what, Faith thought, she would do her best to keep his memory alive.

It wasn't long before Faith pulled up to the curb in front of Patrick Fisher's small, one-story house. The bushes in front appeared to be well maintained. The grass was green and so were the vines covering the latticework. The cement walkway had been painted brick red and was swept clean of debris. The screen door covering the front door was locked, leaving her no choice but to ring the doorbell.

The curtain covering a large-paned window at the front of house moved. Somebody was watching her.

She slipped her right hand into her pocket and kept a tight grip on her gun. When the door opened, she did her best to appear relaxed. The man standing inside wore a flannel shirt, the sleeves pushed up to his elbows. Thick, dark hair covered his forearms. He was nearly as tall as Beast. His head had been shaved clean, and his eyebrows looked like giant caterpillars. "What do you want?"

Her plan had been to do what Beast had done at the last house they visited. She was going to take charge by simply stepping inside and giving whoever answered the door no choice but to let her in.

Having a locked screen door between her and the man changed everything.

She heard a noise. Someone was crying inside the house. It sounded like a child. Her insides twisted. "I—umm—I'm looking for a Patrick Fisher," she told him.

"Who are you?"

He obviously didn't recognize her, which meant he probably didn't watch a lot of news. "Susan Motts," she lied.

"Why do you want to see Patrick?"

She tried to get a good look at him through the screen. "Look, it's important that I talk to him right away." She held the gun tightly, the palm of her hand clammy.

Someone inside the house called his name. It sounded like a little girl, and she'd called him Patrick. Her eyes narrowed. She was talking to Patrick Fisher. Why would any child be calling him by his first name?

And why would he be afraid to tell her who he was?

He obviously wasn't the girl's father.

"I'm busy," he told her, about to shut the door.

"Please hear me out," Faith said. "There's money in it for both of us if you just listen to what I have to say." Another lie.

He whistled through his teeth as he unlocked the latch and let her inside. She tried not to let him see her surprise as she stepped inside. The moment he shut the door behind her, she pulled out her gun and aimed it at his chest. "Hands up! All the way!"

"Jesus Christ. I should have known better."

Faith took backward steps into the house. Two kids stood in the hallway. A boy she guessed to be around eight, half-dressed, and the same little girl she must have heard crying stood behind him. She looked younger than the boy. Her thumb was stuck in her mouth. They both looked wary. The girl's dirty-blonde hair was straggly and fell just past her shoulders. The boy's hair had been buzzed short. They both looked as if they could use a bath.

"Who do these kids belong to?" Faith asked Patrick.

"Niece and nephew. They belong to my sister, who got one DUI too many. I'm watching after them for a while."

"Does she know what you are?"

His jaw twitched. "What am I?"

"A sexual predator."

"Oh, I see. You've seen my name on some list recorded over twenty years ago."

"You're a registered pedophile."

"Yes, I am. And I've never touched a child or even looked at child porn."

She smirked.

"It's true," he said, whispering so the kids wouldn't overhear. "I made the mistake of admitting to a good friend that I was attracted to children. But I've never once touched a child sexually in my life."

Faith harrumphed. "People aren't registered as pedophiles for having thoughts."

"Innocent people are locked up all the time. My circumstances are no different. He accused me of touching his child. His word against mine."

She rolled her eyes. She didn't want to know his circumstances because she didn't care. When the small boy peeked his head into the room where they were talking, Patrick pointed the other way and told them both to go outside and play. They obeyed.

As soon as the kids were gone, Faith ordered him to give her a tour of the house. She made him open closets and lift bedcovers so she could see under the mattress. There was no one else here. No sign of Lara.

Patrick Fisher could not shut up. He talked the entire time, trying to get her to believe that not all pedophiles were monsters, that there were thousands of nonoffending pedophiles walking the streets, never so much as talking to a young child. He told her how his sexual preference was unknown to him until he hit puberty. He then went on to tell her about the time he was touched improperly as a child himself. It was an older man, he explained. Friend of their neighbors at the time—a man with sparse gray hair and spotted hands who had taken it upon himself to fondle Patrick's genitals.

Faith stopped to look at him for a moment. "So you don't believe the man who touched you is or was ever a monster?"

"No. I don't."

"And you don't think you were affected by what that stranger did to you?" Faith asked him as she resumed opening doors and cupboards.

"I absolutely wasn't affected by what happened."

"Well, I don't believe it for a minute."

"Why is that?"

Again she stopped moving so she could look at him. "You seem to have convinced yourself over the years that that one event was no big deal. Well, guess what? Until a child has grown into adulthood and can make his or her own choices in life, it is a big deal. What happened to you was and is a ridiculously momentous deal. You'll never really know if that one act stopped you from becoming who you truly are or who you were meant to be, or if that old man shaped you in a negative way."

"Or maybe what happened was all for the better," he said. "Maybe that one act made me fully aware of who I really am."

"Let's go to the garage," she told him, having a difficult time listening to him talk about his life. Either he was lonely, or he was trying to rid himself of guilt. Why he would tell his story to a woman threatening him with a gun, she'd never know. He talked about feeling inadequate as a child because of the taboo of his sexual desires. Overall what pissed her off the most, because of his own dealing with the old man, was that he didn't believe molesters should be scorned and hated. He didn't believe the act itself warranted analyzing or hatred of any kind.

And why would that be, unless he was a predator himself? She'd had enough.

She turned to face him and even went so far as to jab the gun his way in frustration. "These are kids you're talking about. Young, innocent children who all deserve to make their own choices in life when they're old enough to do so."

"And when is that?" he asked. "What age is appropriate for those sort of choices?"

Her eyes widened. "Did the fucker who touched you say, 'Hey, Patrick, mind if I touch your genitals?'"

"No."

"I didn't think so," Faith said. "You're in denial, Patrick. The old man with the spotted hands never gave you a choice."

She looked around the garage. There was one car inside, a red Mini Coupé. She stepped inside to have a closer look. No boxes or refrigerators lined the walls. No place to hide any bodies. She made him open the trunk, and then she checked out the rest of the car's interior. Nobody was inside. No tape or rope or streaks of blood.

Back inside the house, Faith waved her gun toward the sliding glass door leading outside. "Open the door, and then step outside."

He did as she said.

The kids stopped playing ball as she walked across the lawn and looked inside the shed on the corner of the property. "Has your uncle Patrick ever touched you inappropriately?" she asked the kids when she stepped out of the shed.

They both shook their heads.

"Are you absolutely sure?"

They both nodded.

"Do you feel comfortable living here with Uncle Patrick?"

More nods.

She looked over at Patrick. His arms were crossed over his chest, but he hadn't run off to call the police. In fact, he hadn't moved one inch from where she'd left him standing.

"I'll be back," she said as she passed by him and walked back into the house.

"I can't wait," he called out before she slammed the front door closed behind her.

———

It took Beast a little more than an hour to get to Patrick Barnes's place of residence in Acampo. A few minutes after taking exit 269 from CA-99 south, he turned right onto Acampo Road. He found a spot in front of the main entrance to the apartment building. The air was chilly but still no rain despite the dark, cloudy skies looming overhead.

Cans and bottles and fast-food wrappers littered the sidewalk around a too-full garbage can. There were no locks on the double doors, and nobody was inside the main lobby, so he took the stairs to apartment 21-B.

The hall carpets were stained and torn. The smell of cigarette smoke was strong, filling his lungs with ashy particles that made him cough.

He knocked twice.

Beast was glad to have something to do today—anything to keep his mind off Rage. He wasn't sure he'd ever be ready to deal with her absence.

She'd passed quickly. For that he was glad.

He wondered what kind of fool he was that he hadn't been able to tell her how he felt. Sure, he'd tried a couple of times, but it hadn't been enough. Maybe if he'd told her every thought he'd ever had, it still wouldn't have been enough.

The door opened. A woman peeked out through the crack.

He flashed a fake badge, one of Rage's toys. He didn't like to use pretend accessories, but he'd spotted it this morning in one of the kitchen drawers. He remembered the day Rage had opened the UPS package. She'd been excited to present him with his own authentic-looking undercover police badge.

This morning he'd thought, *The hell with it*, and he'd shoved it into his pocket. Why not? And now here he stood, facing a young woman who reminded him of his late wife, flashing a badge he had no business carrying. He looked heavenward.

"Can I help you?"

"I'm looking for Patrick Barnes."

"Oh." She angled hear head. "Were you a friend of his?"

"Not exactly. No."

"Is he in trouble?"

"I'm not sure," Beast said. "Maybe you can tell me." Beast raised an eyebrow. "Mind if I come in for a minute to talk?"

She looked suspicious, but she let him in just the same. He would never understand why people opened their doors to strangers, but more often than not, that's exactly what they did.

He took a look around the apartment.

Without asking for permission, he walked across the main living area, past a small kitchen, and into the bedroom at the back of the apartment. The bed was made, and there were hardly any knickknacks cluttering the room. After checking all the usual spots—bathroom, closets, and under the bed—he returned to the living area. The place was small but well kept. The floors were clean. No horrible smells like he'd experienced in the hallway outside her apartment.

The woman stood somewhere between the kitchen and the wide-open door, ready to run if need be. He didn't blame her. *Smart woman.*

"What's this all about?" she said, her shoulders stiffening as bravado set in. "You're not a cop, are you?"

Her eyes were blue, her lips nicely shaped and full. She stood no taller than five feet three inches. A simple black T-shirt and jeans revealed a semiathletic form. Maybe a runner.

"No," he said. "I'm not a cop. I'm a bounty hunter, but that little tidbit has nothing to do with why I'm here."

"I'm calling the police."

"I promise to leave as soon as you tell me where I can find Patrick Barnes."

"He's dead. I should know because he was my brother."

TWENTY-SIX

Lara stared at her reflection in the bathroom mirror. Her hair had turned black. Her scalp stung. The black dye looked like streaks of paint across her forehead and chin.

"Your name is now Sara," Patrick told her. "After you clean up, we're going to take a drive. Another man, a very nice man, will be meeting us upon our arrival. You'll be proper and polite. No talking and no sudden movements. I want you to smile and shake his hand."

"I'll never shake his hand. I'll run away."

Patrick got down on bended knee, looked her square in the eyes, and took hold of her shoulders. He squeezed hard, his thumbs digging into her skin.

"That hurts."

His face twisted in a way she'd never seen before. His eyes became squinty and mean. His mouth became a tight line across his face. His entire body trembled as he said, "You'll do exactly as I tell you. If you don't, I'll cut you into little pieces and feed you to the fucking fish. Do you hear me?"

She tried to nod, but she couldn't stop her shoulders from shaking and the tears from rolling down both sides of her face.

"Stop crying."

She whimpered. She couldn't help it.

He slapped her across the face so hard her neck snapped back from the force. "Knock it off," he said. "It's time for you to grow the fuck up!"

He walked into the bedroom, leaving her standing on the cold tiles. As he stood over the bed, going through his things, she opened one drawer after another, quietly but quickly, until she found a pencil. She slid it into her waistband.

Patrick returned with a long-sleeved dress. It was a flowery print with a crisp white collar. "Get in the shower. Leave the bathroom door open, or I'll kick it down. Make it fast."

She turned on the shower. When it was warm enough, she took off her pants and shirt and made sure to hide the pencil in the sleeve of the shirt folded on the floor. She used the soap to wash her arms and legs. Her muscles quivered as she began to cry. She was tired and more frightened than ever before. As the water drizzled over her head and turned black before rushing down the drain, she forced herself to stop crying, knowing she had to be strong if she wanted to find a way to escape.

Faith kept her eyes on the road as she drove.

She thought of Rage and how, just like Craig and the others who had perished last night, she deserved a moment of her time. The one thing Faith didn't have. On days like today, Faith had a difficult time sorting her thoughts.

People were dying.

Hudson was home.

And yet nothing had changed. Not really.

How could she ever help her son move on if she couldn't help herself?

She felt a sudden rapid fluttering inside her throat. Her chest felt tight. Worried about endangering herself and others, she pulled to the side of the road. She looked to the passenger seat for her phone and found it beneath the backpack Beast had left inside her car. Hoping Beast had found the Patrick they were looking for, she called him.

No answer.

As she settled down, as her heart rate slowed, she reached inside the backpack and looked through Rage's notes. The crumpled piece of paper fell to the side of the cracked leather seat. She picked it up, read the address, and noticed it wasn't Rage's handwriting. Someone, most likely Rage, had used the pencil-shading technique to reveal the address. Faith's eyes narrowed as she noticed something else: more indentations were beneath the address.

Faith grabbed the backpack and found a pencil on the bottom of the bag. She placed the crumpled paper on the dashboard and lightly ran the pencil over the indentation in the paper. She applied more pressure, using the lead to shade the indented letters, back and forth, until she could see what it said: *Patrick*. Her pulse raced. Then she noticed the *W* in a swirly font at the top of the stationary.

W for Williams. Aster Williams.

Rage must have retrieved the paper from Aster Williams's home when she and Little Vinnie were inside looking for information.

Rage would have mentioned the address if she'd had any idea it belonged to a man named Patrick. "Rage," she said aloud. "You did it."

Her pulse raced in earnest as she grabbed hold of her phone and called her parents' house.

Colton picked up.

"It's Faith," she said. "I think I might have found Patrick's address."

"What's his surname?" Colton asked.

"I have no idea, but he lives in Elverta." She gave him the address. "I'm going to call Detective Yuhasz and then head that way."

"How far away are you?"

"About twenty-five minutes."

"I can be there in ten."

"OK," she said and then hung up.

They were close, Faith thought. She could feel it. She called Detective Yuhasz next, and as she merged onto the highway she told him everything she knew, including the fact that it was a long shot, but she was letting him know what was going on just as she had promised.

Finished with her call to Yuhasz, she found herself worrying about Beast. Maybe her hunch was way off. Maybe he'd found the Patrick in question, and he was in trouble.

Keeping her eyes on the road in front of her, she couldn't miss the ominous gray clouds in the horizon, swollen and ready to burst.

Every once in a while she glanced in the rearview mirror.

Cars passed by in a blur. She had yet to spot a green Nissan. No one was following her.

———

Colton parked at the curb and jumped out of his truck. The house in Elverta, a light-yellow single-family home, was situated on a quiet street lined with trees. Colton knocked on the door. Waited. Rang the doorbell, then waited another twenty seconds. He put his ear against the door and listened, couldn't hear a thing.

He walked to his right, used his hands to cup around his eyes so he could look through the kitchen window. The blinds were cracked open, but it was dark inside.

Colton made his way to the side yard, where he was able to slide his hand over the fence and pull on a thin piece of rope to unlock it from the other side. He walked around the perimeter. All the doors and windows were locked tight. Determined to get inside, he headed back to the front, ready to kick the door down if he had to.

A concerned neighbor was crossing the street, waving a hand and asking him if he needed help.

"Yes," Colton said. "I could use some help. My sister is Faith McMann, and we have reason to believe her daughter has been kept hidden away in this house."

The man raised both hands, his expression one of shock, and then simply turned back around and disappeared inside his house.

Colton had no idea what the man was doing, nor did he care if the guy had gone inside to call the police. There was no time for playing games. He would tell the truth and be done with it. Besides, Faith had said she was going to call Detective Yuhasz. He could either try to knock the door down or wait for the detective to show up.

A few seconds later, Colton was surprised to see the neighbor return with a key. He held it above his head as he made his way back across the street. The guy wore a long, flowing robe over shorts and a T-shirt that hugged his round belly. "Here you go," he said. "My wife has had a key to this house since the last people who rented the place lived here. But the man who lives here now could have changed the locks. We have no idea."

Colton thanked him and followed him to the door. "It's worth a shot," Colton said.

The neighbor inserted the key. Click. The door opened.

Colton didn't wait for permission from the neighbor. He rushed inside, calling Lara's name as he ran down the hallway. In the bedroom he saw an assortment of suits hanging in the closet. Judging by the stringent smell of house cleaners, the bathroom had been cleaned recently. But the job had been done hastily because Colton noticed streaks of paint or dye on the tiles. At closer view he found strands of blonde hair on the floor, tucked in close to the baseboard.

The shower floor was still wet. He opened the glass door, stepped inside, and pulled a clump of black hair from the drain.

He felt a tightness in his chest.

Someone had taken the time to dye Lara's hair from blonde to black.

Lara had been here; he was sure of it.

He rushed down the hallway toward the front entrance, stopping at the door to his right.

The neighbor stood outside the main entrance. The expression on his face was a cross between curious and frightened. "Do you need any help?" he asked. "Did you find her?"

Colton shook his head.

No time for small talk. He opened the door in the hallway, hurried down a long flight of stairs. At the bottom he found a tin pail in the corner of the room along with a roll of toilet paper. In the other corner was a cot. He noticed a lump under the blanket.

He pulled back the cover and found a book, *The Book Thief* by Markus Zusak. He opened it. Right there on the first page was a note from Lara, written in her handwriting but messier, written in a hurry:

Port of West Sacramento. 6:00 p.m. Industrial Blvd. North Terminal. Rice Cargo.

About to run off to call Faith, he saw writing on the wall behind the thin mattress. He scooted the cot away. Scratched into the cement were random words, including the name Lara McMann in all caps.

Pulse racing, book in hand, he ran back upstairs, two steps at a time.

He could hear sirens in the distance.

"My wife wanted you to know that the man who lives here left about an hour ago."

"What kind of car was he driving—do you know?"

"A black BMW."

Colton thanked him, pulled out his cell, and called Faith as he ran to his truck.

Faith hit the "Talk" button the second the phone rang. "What's going on?" she asked, unable to calm herself. "Was it the right house? Did you find Lara?"

"It's the right house," Colton said, "but Lara's not here. It looks as if someone cut and dyed Lara's hair black. The shower is still wet, and the neighbor saw someone leave in a black BMW about an hour ago."

It was him, and they were close, Faith thought. Maybe closer than they'd ever been. Her mind reeled with speculation. Who had her daughter, and where were they taking her? Sick with worry and yet also filled with newfound hope, she asked, "What do we do now?"

"Detective Yuhasz has just arrived," Colton told her. "The neighbor had a key and let me inside. It looks as if Lara had been kept in the basement for a while now."

Faith had no words. Her stomach roiled.

"Yuhasz is coming this way. I need you to listen carefully, Faith, and then I need to go. Lara left a note inside a book on the cot where I'm guessing she's been sleeping."

Faith took the next exit, made a right, and pulled over, kept the engine running. A car honked.

"Her notes were scribbled, no details," Colton warned. "She was obviously in a hurry, but I recognize her writing. I believe she might have been taken to the shipyard in West Sacramento."

All the shipyards she knew of were huge, covering many acres. Where would they take her? Would she be put inside a shipping container? She recalled Hudson telling the FBI that's where he and other boys were kept for days if not weeks. *Breathe,* she told herself. *Stay calm. Stay strong.*

"I've got to go," Colton said.

"Do you have the address?"

"Rice cargo. Port of West Sacramento on Industrial Boulevard. North Terminal. Six o'clock. I'll be there as soon as I can."

The call was disconnected before she could ask any more questions. Faith wrote down the address. She used an Internet search on her phone to find the fastest route, and then she made a U-turn and got back onto the freeway headed west.

Could this truly be it? Could they find Lara in time? Her mind raced. Her mouth went dry. She looked at the clock. Twenty before six. What would happen at six o'clock?

She merged onto the highway, tires screeching as she laid her foot hard on the gas pedal. Her insides fluttered. *Lara, Lara, Lara. Hang on. I'm coming.*

Twenty-Seven

Lilly Gray was playing solitaire in the same room as her grandson when she heard the tiniest of whimpers. She had tried to talk to Hudson many times since his return, but for the most part he remained sullen and quiet.

Faith had told her to let him be . . . that he would open up about his ordeal when he was ready. Russell was upstairs in their bedroom, putting away the laundry, trying to keep busy.

Lilly walked to where Hudson sat on the couch, where he could usually be found playing video games. She stood behind him and watched. His hands, along with the controller, had dropped to his lap. His thumbs were no longer pushing buttons, his gaze no longer on the screen in front of him. She placed a gentle hand on his shoulder.

"I can't stop thinking about Lara," he said in a quiet voice.

She said nothing, simply waited to see if he had more to say. She wanted to tell him she felt the same—that every moment of every day was filled with thoughts of Lara.

"She's never been very fast," Hudson said of his sister. "She's the reason girls get a bad rap in the first place. She hardly has the strength to hold a bat in her hands without wobbling. She's weak. I always outrun her, and I'm younger. She's never been a good fighter, either. I can pin her to the ground in under a second." A short pause. "She didn't even like video games, Grandma. How is she ever going to survive out there with those people? Where is she? What are they doing to her? I wish they had found Lara instead of me. I could handle those guys."

Lilly came around to sit next to him. "She's stronger than you think. You used to be such a troublemaker, and your dad would be ready to punish you, but your sister would negotiate for you, for better terms."

Hudson wrinkled his nose. "What do you mean?"

"Your dad would threaten to not let you go to your friend's house after school and no outside activities for a week, but Lara would talk to him, using logic as she told him he was being too strict. She suggested he make you clean your room instead because it looked like a pigsty." Lilly smiled at the thought of it. "Lara always called it a win-win."

His eyes brightened a little bit. "That's why she was always helping me clean my room," Hudson said.

Lilly nodded.

Hudson eyes glistened. He'd been forced to grow up fast since the attack on his family. "Your sister can talk up a storm," Lilly told him. "I'm sure she's been talking those people to death."

He smiled then, a genuine smile that made it all the way to his eyes.

"And she can pinch," Hudson added. "I think I still have the marks from the last time she pinched the back of my arm."

It was Lilly's turn to smile. "And she beat us all at Monopoly during the holidays."

"Yeah," Hudson agreed, "but I don't know how that will help her."

"I don't, either, but who knows? I'm just glad you're talking about your sister because it's important that we all say what's on our mind."

"Why is Mom always gone?" he asked next. "Is she really looking for Lara?"

Lilly nodded. "Even if we locked your mother in her room and threw away the key, she'd find a way out so she could go in search of your sister. She would never stop looking for either of you. She's your mother."

"Do you think she'll find her?"

"I do."

It was quiet for a moment before Lilly patted him on the knee. "Want to go sit in the tree fort with me for a while? It's a nice day. Not too windy and hardly any clouds in sight."

"Are you sure you can climb that high, Grandma? Doesn't your leg still hurt?"

Lilly snorted. "I used to spend hours up there in the fort with your mom when she was small. We would play cards and talk all day about nothing."

"Mom played in the tree fort?"

"All the time."

"You always told me and Lara to stay away from there because it was dangerous."

She made a face and waved a dismissive hand through the air. "After your uncle Colton fell and broke his arm, I wanted to burn that tree house down."

"Ah, that's where Mom gets it," he said.

She stood and held out her hand.

Hudson pushed himself to his feet and put his hand in hers. He'd grown at least an inch over the past few months. And his mop of brown hair was getting long. Lilly made a mental note to make an appointment to have it cut. It was time for Hudson to get out into the real world again, time for him to start living.

Together they walked outside and made their way to the field of trees out back. Lilly knew she should probably tell Russell where they were going, but she didn't want to ruin the moment, so she looked back over her shoulder and smiled just in case he was looking from the bedroom window.

Russell heard a noise. A clank and a thud that sounded as if it were coming from the front of the house. Not wanting to concern Lilly or Hudson, he left a small mountain of laundry on the bed, walked downstairs, and slipped out the front door without being noticed.

He looked about, studying his surroundings. The water in the pond was still. All was quiet. He inhaled a breath of fresh air, crisp and clean after a good rain.

Colton had left the house thirty minutes ago after relaying all he knew about a man named Patrick and the three names Rage had left behind. Faith, Beast, and Colton were all out there somewhere, alone, looking for a man they'd never seen before. He didn't like it. Ever since the attack on Faith's family, they had put themselves out there, and that made them all targets.

The front of the property appeared the same as always. Nothing seemed out of the ordinary. And yet his senses were sharp, and something told him he hadn't been hearing things. Figuring it might have been the postman's truck he'd heard, he proceeded down the driveway toward the mailbox. Near the end of the drive he saw the same dark sedan that had been parked there earlier in the day. The news vans were usually lined up behind the sedan, but there had been a mass shooting in another country, killing dozens, so the media had other tragedies to focus on.

Farther down the road, he spotted one lone media van parked at the curb. He kept waiting for the van door to slide open and for some rookie reporter to pop out with a microphone, wide-eyed and eager for a story or an update on Hudson's health and well-being.

Russell kept a steady pace as he continued down the driveway, wishing he'd brought his cane. The only noise at the moment was the soft swoosh of his shoes against the pavement as he walked.

Although there didn't appear to be anything out of the ordinary, his skin prickled. His gaze moved from the mailbox to the white media van to the sedan's tinted windows. Most days the FBI agent stationed out front would roll down his window and give him a quick update or a thumbs-up, but not this time.

An intense pain shot up Russell's leg, made him wince. The aches and pains were always worse when he walked downhill. As he neared the sedan, he was able to make out the silhouette of the driver through the windshield. The agent looked to be asleep. By the time Russell drew closer, though, his instincts were on high alert, and he grew concerned.

A few feet away from the vehicle, he bent down to touch his toes under the pretense of stretching. Beneath the sedan he saw a wire on the other side of the car. The strand of metal fell from the bottom of the passenger door and then disappeared in the grass and fallen leaves at the side of the driveway. In case he was being watched, Russell tried to look nonchalant. He took his time returning to his full height, putting his hands on his back and then letting his head and neck fall backward for a full stretch.

He did his best to keep all emotion out of his face as he continued on to the mailbox. Once there, he collected his mail, sifted through it, and then turned toward the media van and gave a quick wave before heading back up the driveway.

Just another day. Nothing to see here.

As he passed by the FBI agent's car, he rested a hand on the hood under the pretense of keeping his balance. When he stooped over, he saw the agent clearly. The man wasn't sleeping at all. His eyes were open, unblinking. He was dead. A box and a tangle of wires were wrapped around his chest. The agent had been rigged with explosives.

His heart skipped a beat. A light sheen of sweat covered his brow. He could only assume the people inside the media van had experienced the same fate. Standing straight and tall again, he walked to the other side of the vehicle under the pretense of gazing out at the pond. Out of the corner of his eye, he followed the wire that led back up the hill. Well past the front entry, the wire crossed the driveway, partially hidden by leaves and pebbles.

With weak knees and trembling hands, Russell moved on up the hill. The wire weaved around a Japanese maple, then disappeared around the side and under the front of the house. Fearing the worst, that a bomb, maybe more than one, had been placed in or about the property, caused Russell to panic. He needed to get Hudson and Lilly out of the house. He was done pretending to be calm. He dropped the mail and ran for the front door.

———

Lilly was smiling at something Hudson had said, feeling better about his frame of mind, when she saw a hundred-dollar bill sticking out from beneath an old wool blanket in the corner of the eight-foot-square tree house.

"Is that real money, or does it belong to a board game?" she asked, pointing.

Hudson stooped slightly as he stepped that way. He picked up the bill and examined it closely. "It looks real to me." He lifted the blanket and saw two duffel bags.

"What's inside?" Lilly asked him.

He looked inside one and then the other. His mouth dropped open as he turned toward Lilly. "They're both filled with hundred-dollar bills."

Shouting in the distance took Lilly's attention away from her grandson.

Hudson must have heard the commotion, too, because he dropped the blanket and crossed the fort to have a look out the window.

She recognized her husband's voice. It was Russell, and he sounded panicked. Lilly's heart caught in her throat as she stuck her head out the door, getting ready to climb back down the tree. It would take her ten minutes, at least, to get to the bottom. Russell called out for the third time, loud and clear, the panic in his voice unmistakable. "There's a bomb! Get out now!"

She saw him inside the sliding glass door, frantically looking around as he continued to shout their names.

"We're outside," Hudson shouted back. "In the tree fort!"

Judging by the direction Russell went, he hadn't heard a word. He'd been having trouble hearing for a while now.

Her hands shook as she tried to get a foothold on a thick branch. "Russell!"

A deafening boom drowned out her voice.

She fell back into the tree fort, felt the ground shake beneath her as she reached for Hudson. She grabbed hold of his leg and pulled him close as debris hit the roof overhead. Pieces of wood and plaster poured from the sky, falling to the ground all around them.

TWENTY-EIGHT

Once Faith arrived at the shipping yard, driving no more than five miles per hour, she leaned into the steering wheel, looking from side to side, hoping to see any sign of life through the thick layer of fog.

Two trucks were parked outside a string of cream-colored buildings. She drove that way, parked, and climbed out of the car. Gun in hand, she ran toward the trucks. Keeping an eye out for any movement at all, hoping to find someone, anyone, who might be able to tell her where she could find the North Terminal.

The buildings were boxy and nondescript. The area was vast and deserted. The shipyard looked nothing like she'd imagined it would. There weren't many containers. As she came around the corner, she had to maneuver around equipment that looked as if it might be waiting to be shipped. There were wind turbines that looked like aircraft propeller blades, along with gearboxes and towers.

She walked at a good pace, more of a jog. It had been past six when she left the car. A strong breeze worked against her forward movement. She passed another vast, empty area and then came upon construction equipment secured by four walls of chain-link fence.

Frustrated that she couldn't find anyone, and feeling as if she was getting nowhere fast, she ran back the way she'd come to her car. She jumped inside, made a U-turn, and headed the other way. There were no signs telling her which way she was going, but she knew she was headed north. Again she drove along at no more than five miles an hour, hoping Colton would arrive soon.

Another half minute passed before she spotted a car parked at a weird angle, as if the driver had been in a hurry. She made a sharp left and headed that way.

The moment she saw it was a BMW, her pulse quickened.

She pulled up behind the car, jumped out, and ran to the BMW. She opened the passenger door. Inside was a bag, books scattered against the backseat. A lump formed in her throat. Lara had to be here somewhere. She needed to hurry.

She turned toward the shipping yard. Without the buildings to protect her, the wind hit her full force. Keeping her head down, her body bent forward, she moved toward the only two ships she could see from where she stood. She passed by endless stacks of empty wood crates, and then somehow managed to trap herself in a maze of orange, green, and gray shipping containers.

Cursing, knowing she was running out of time, she headed back the way she'd just come.

———

Yuhasz put on the flashing lights. Faith's brother, Colton, was in his truck behind him.

"Over there," Colton said to Yuhasz over the speakerphone. "Faith said she traded in her car for a Toyota Corolla. That has to be it."

They pulled up, one after the other, next to the Toyota and a black BMW. Colton jumped out of his truck and ran to have a look inside the vehicles.

Yuhasz climbed out of his cruiser and opened the trunk. As he put on his vest, Colton joined him. "Nobody is inside either car." Colton pointed to the left. "I'll go that way."

Yuhasz nodded. It would be a waste of time to try to stop him. The whole damn McMann clan had turned out to be an energetic bunch of stubborn human beings who regarded danger as a mere inconvenience. Not one of them knew how to follow orders. "Watch your back," Yuhasz said, but his words vanished within a gusty breeze before they ever reached Colton McMann's ears.

Yuhasz called for backup and then took off in the opposite direction Colton had gone. Although he had yet to regain full motion of his right arm, he wasn't worried. He could shoot just as well with his left. Yeah, he'd take hell from Lieutenant Harris and most likely Sergeant Bell, too, for heading out alone, but he didn't like the idea of sitting in his car staring out into what looked like a deserted ghost town covered in fog, knowing that two innocent civilians were out there, possibly three.

As he neared rows of containers, the only sound was the wind causing the metal to squeak and squeal. The place was eerie, devoid of people. The air smelled industrial and heavy. He kept his footfalls light, didn't want to alert anyone to his presence. As he neared the pier, he could smell wet wood, heard the sound of water lapping against the wood siding. The strong wind pushed against him as he made his way toward the ship docked up ahead.

He stopped and listened, his senses sharp.

He turned, slowly, staying in place where he stood, pivoting on the balls of his feet, making a complete 360-degree turn.

Something told him he was being watched. A hunch. A feeling. And then, out of the corner of his eye, he thought he saw a movement near the water.

He headed that way, every muscle stiff, every ounce of his mind and body focused. A strange sensation ran through him, as if someone or something was warning him to turn back the other way. He would do no such thing.

Ridiculous.

He trudged onward, doing his best to ignore the intense pain in his right shoulder, determined to reach the monstrous ship and get to the bottom of whatever madness had eluded him thus far.

———

Lara wasn't sure exactly what Patrick planned to do with her, but she knew they were waiting for someone. He'd made that clear. The ship they stood by was frightening, a huge metal monster ready to devour her. Water lapped between the hulk of metal and the dock. She didn't want to get on the ship or go anywhere at all. She wanted to be with her mom and dad. She thought about running, but instead stood rooted in place by fear, her body shivering, her teeth chattering.

"Knock it off," Patrick warned her, his fingers clamped around the back of her neck.

"I'm fre-eez-ing."

"Someone will be here soon. Remember everything I've told you."

"There's something in my eye. It hurts. I need you to get it out for me."

Patrick let out a frustrated groan as he bent down on one knee to take a look.

This was it, Lara decided. This could be her very best and last chance to escape.

She'd been practicing the move for days.

The top of his head was level with hers. She raised her arm high above her head. He looked up to see what she was doing, and that's when she brought her arm down hard, stabbing the nail she'd been holding into his face, hitting him in the eye.

He screamed, a horrible screeching, high-pitched noise. She'd never heard such a sound, like a wolf howling in the misty night. She saw blood, and she ran.

Just when Yuhasz was beginning to think the pain in his shoulder might stop him from going forward, he heard someone scream and saw something appear from the fog. It was a child, and he or she was heading his way.

With so little rest over the past few days, he thought he might be seeing things. But the feeling didn't last long. What he was seeing was real. The child was frantic, running fast, arms pumping at his or her sides.

Right as Yuhasz took a step toward the child, the sharp retort of gunfire pierced his eardrums and sent him two steps back. Unsure of whether he'd been struck but feeling no pain, he charged forward and scooped the child into his arms and ran toward the metal containers, hoping to find some protection there.

It was a girl, he realized as he ran.

She screamed at him as her small fists pummeled against his neck and face. Her fingernails dug into his ear and cheekbone, but he refused to loosen his hold. His good arm had most of her weight. He tried to use his other hand to cover her mouth and keep her quiet. It was no use. Her teeth connected with flesh. She bit down hard.

White-hot pain bolted through his skull. Still he held tight, running as fast as he could toward the thickest of fog in hopes the shooter wouldn't see where he was taking her.

Two more shots were fired in rapid succession. A bullet clipped the corner of the metal container in front of him, ricocheted and whizzed past his ear. Adrenaline pushed him onward. Every breath was a struggle, every step more difficult than the last as the little girl fought for her freedom.

Having finally reached cover, he almost lost his hold on the kid as he slid down, his back against metal, his hand wrapped tightly over her mouth despite the teeth digging deeper and breaking new skin. Up close, he recognized her at once. Those eyes. He couldn't help but feel as if he were looking at Faith. "I know your mom," he told her, his voice wavering.

She shook her head wildly. Focused on getting away, she didn't believe him.

"Your aunt Jana had a baby," he said, stringing words together as fast as he could think of them, knowing the shooter would be upon them soon. "They haven't picked a name yet, but it's a boy."

Her eyes narrowed; her cries went from sounding like a growl to a whimper.

"And your brother, Hudson, is home," he went on. "Grandpa Russell and your uncle Colton found him in the mountains with other boys who had been taken, just like you."

She stopped struggling. Finally.

Thank you, Jesus. But he knew better than to loosen his hold. His face was mere inches from hers. Her eyes were round and bright, still cautious and accusing. "I'm a detective with the police. I've been working with your mother since the beginning," he told her, his voice returning to normal.

Her head was pressed hard into his chest and shoulder.

He winced from the pain her movement caused. "Grandma Lilly misses you, and not a day goes by that she doesn't look through the photograph books she's made over the years, praying for your return."

Tears rolled down over his fingers still over her mouth. He felt her body sag and then fall limp.

"Everyone has told me you look like your dad, but you have the exact same eyes as your mother. I would have recognized you anywhere."

Her breathing grew shallow; her chest no longer rose and fell like a buoy in rough seas.

"If I take my hand from your mouth, you won't scream?"

She nodded ever so slightly.

He removed his hand from her mouth, then set her to the side, and told her not to move. He flattened his body against the container, readied his gun, and peeked around the corner.

The shooter had been waiting for a movement. A shot rang out. Yuhasz fired back. He then looked at Lara again, pointed in the direction Colton had gone earlier. "Can you run?"

She nodded. And he knew it was true. She'd been running like the wind when he'd grabbed her. "Your uncle Colton and your mom are close by. They're both looking for you." He pointed again. "I want you to run that way, but not until I get this guy's attention, OK?"

She nodded.

"Do not run toward the ship or the pier. Run straight toward those buildings over there."

"What about you?" she asked.

Just like her mom, he thought. *Always worrying about everyone else.* "I'll be fine. As soon as I take a shot, that's your signal to run."

Yuhasz stepped out from behind the containers, arms held straight out in front of him, gun aimed. The view before him was all gray and misty shadows. The wind had died down somewhat, but the fog was thickest by the water, making it difficult to see much.

Every step echoed off the wood planks as he walked toward the pier. His senses were on full alert. The air smelled of fish and metal.

"Don't move or I'll shoot," a male voice called out.

Yuhasz turned toward the voice. In the distance, he saw a dark form take shape. "Put your gun down," Yuhasz told him. "It's over."

"It's only just begun," the voice said. "I know who you are."

Keep talking, Yuhasz thought as he stepped closer.

"Your son-in-law was a talker, told me all about you," the voice continued. "He said you lacked courage and you always followed the rules." Laughter followed. "Where did that get you, Detective?"

As he grew closer, Yuhasz could finally see the man's face. His right eye was bloodied and swollen. "Put the gun down," Yuhasz said again, his tone firm.

"I'm not like you, Detective. I don't allow others to tell me what to do."

"Oh no? Aren't you one of Aster Williams's minions?"

"I'm afraid you have the wrong man."

"I don't think so," Yuhasz said as he took another few steps closer, keeping his eye on the gun.

"What kind of man sits behind a desk day after day, filling out paperwork, blindly following senseless laws created by the most corrupt of them all while letting a schoolteacher do his work for him?"

Yuhasz was thick-skinned when it came to criticism of himself and the department. It came with the job. He was used to it. "Put the gun down, and we'll talk about it on the way to the station," Yuhasz told him, intent on bringing him in.

"You have no idea who you're dealing with," the one-eyed man said, his weight shifting to the left as if a bit unstable on his feet. "I should let you take me to prison so I can give you a call after my lawyers get me out and I walk free." He chuckled. "All this trouble you've gone to, Detective, and for what?"

"Put the gun on the ground, and then put your hands behind your head."

The one-eyed man slowly dropped the arm holding the gun.

The relief Yuhasz felt was shortsighted, because the one-eyed man raised his arm again and fired.

The bullet grazed Yuhasz's leg, sending a wave of fiery heat through his body. The second shot hit his vest and pushed him backward, staggering and gasping for breath. The next shot hit his bad arm.

Mad as hell and cursing, Yuhasz raised the gun clasped in his left hand as he marched forward. His eyes shifted to the man's head. He pointed and fired.

Target down.

Yuhasz limped toward the man, knelt down and felt for a pulse.

There was none. The one-eyed man had taken a clean shot through the forehead. There was hardly any blood, just a grayish ring of discoloration around the entrance wound. He looked closely at the dead man's face. Dark hair, straight nose, square jaw.

He didn't know the man's name. And for the first time since he'd sworn to serve and protect, he didn't care who this man was or what his story was or if he even had one. Even so, taking a life felt no different than it always did—it felt like shit.

Yuhasz took a moment to look around, peering through fog, listening to the distant sound of water lapping against the dock.

Life and death were no joke.

In this day and age it wasn't always easy to maintain pride and idealism on the job. Human trafficking and the war on drugs on a good day seemed futile. On a bad day it was a collective problem society could not seem to fix.

Ignoring the piercing aches and pains sweeping through every part of his body, he pushed the button on his portable scanner and said, "Multiple shots fired. Suspect dead."

———

Faith had been running since she heard the first sound of gunfire. She felt as if she were on a treadmill, her legs churning, faster and faster, and yet she seemed to be getting nowhere. The fog grew thicker as she went along, causing her to lose her bearings. Disoriented, she stopped to look around, tried to calculate where she was and figure out if she was headed in the right direction. She swallowed. "Lara!" she called out as fear threatened to bring her to her knees.

Another shot rang out.

She turned toward the sound of the gunfire just as a child ran out from between two containers, headed right for her.

Faith froze. The child's hair was black and cut short around her ears. Colton had said he believed her hair had been dyed black. *Lara?* Could it be? Faith rushed toward the child.

"Mom," Lara cried.

Faith fell to her knees so she could take a better look. She lifted Lara's chin so she could see her face. The eyes were the same. Her turned-up nose and soft pink lips. *Her beautiful, heart-shaped face,* she thought as she smoothed back the hair away from her forehead. It was her. It was Lara. "I can't believe it's really you," Faith said.

Lara nodded, tears running down both sides of her face. Her lip trembled as she said, "I wasn't sure if I'd ever see you again."

Faith hugged her tight and then ran her hands over Lara's shoulders. Her daughter was thin and pale, her eyes fearful, her cheeks hollow, but it was her. She'd found Lara.

For months she'd dreamed about this moment. It was hard to believe it was real. She kissed her daughter's forehead, her cheek, her nose. "You're here," she said. "My little girl is coming home."

Lara nodded between sobs.

"I've missed you so much it hurts."

"I've missed you, too," Lara said. "I never want to leave home again."

"Everything is going to be all right." They held each other close, neither wanting to let go of the other, not even for a second. The ache, the horrible, heartbreaking ache she'd felt for too long, lifted within, leaving her weak and frail. Faith breathed in her daughter's scent. Touching her, seeing her, holding her. It was a miracle.

It took another shot being fired to remind Faith that they needed to keep moving, find a place to hide until Colton arrived. "We have to go," she told Lara, pushing herself to her feet and lifting her daughter into her arms, despite the searing pain in her hand. Lara's thin legs wrapped around her waist as Faith headed off in the opposite direction from where Lara had come.

Sirens sounded in the distance. *Thank God.*

Faith kept running, except she wasn't running at all, she realized. She was limping, walking as fast as she could but definitely not running. Every part of her was shutting down, but they had come too far to stop now.

No sooner had she made her way past the same equipment she'd seen earlier than she saw a man heading in their direction. Unable to see him clearly, she turned around, ready to run.

"Faith!"

She stopped, looked over her shoulder at the sound of a familiar voice.

It was Colton.

He stepped forward, hands out, palms up. "It's me," he said.

Faith's knees wobbled.

Colton lunged forward and caught her, stopped her from falling to the ground.

"I'm OK," she said once she regained her balance.

As he stood there looking at her, he shook his head as if in wonder. His gaze shifted to the child in her arms, his brow lifting in question.

They had all been disappointed too many times to assume it was Lara. Faith nodded.

Colton stepped behind Faith so he could get a better look at his niece. He ruffled Lara's hair and broke out laughing, causing Faith to do the same, brother and sister sharing in a moment of delirious glee.

"You two get back to the car, and get the hell out of here," Colton said, unable to hide his happiness. "Drive straight home, and don't look back," he said.

"Where are you going?" Her insides did somersaults. "Don't leave us."

"Detective Yuhasz is out there somewhere battling it out with a lunatic. I can't leave him here to fight on his own. He's practically a part of the family now."

"Did I hear you correctly?"

They both turned toward the sound of the detective's voice.

Yuhasz was hobbling toward them, his arm dangling limp at his side. He was a mess. Colton went to him, hooked the detective's good arm around his shoulder.

"Did he get away?" Colton asked.

Yuhasz shook his head. "I got him, but not before he shot me a couple of times. Can't anyone hit the damn vest? I'm going to call the manufacturer first chance I get."

Faith set her daughter on the ground and clasped her hand in hers. Her eyes glistened as they walked ahead of the two men. She looked over at Lara. Her daughter. Surreal. Against all odds they had found Lara.

She had both of her children back.

She glanced heavenward, thinking of Craig, wishing he were here.

The sirens grew louder.

Lara peeked back over her shoulder. "That man," Lara said, "helped me get away."

"Detective Yuhasz?"

Lara nodded, her eyes brighter than before.

"He's a good man," Faith said. "A very good man."

Twenty-Nine

"Grandma! Grandma! Are you OK?"

Lilly opened her eyes. Hudson was hovering over her, concern in his eyes, tears dripping off his face.

She tried to sit up, but she couldn't manage. Hudson helped her.

It took only a few seconds for everything that had happened to come flashing back. The panic in Russell's voice as he shouted her name. Seeing him near the family room door. And then an explosion that sounded like a sonic boom as the ground rumbled beneath them.

"Russell," she said as she crawled to the small window. She looked out through the trees with their twisted limbs, trying to make sense of what she was seeing. Half of their house was gone. A noise caused her to turn and see that Hudson had vanished. She crawled on all fours to the exit, saw her grandson scrambling down the trunk of the tree.

"Get back here, Hudson. It's too dangerous."

"Grandpa's in there. I've got to find him."

"Listen to me," she said as his feet hit the ground. "Come back here. Wait for me." Afraid another bomb might go off, she backed out of the door and started the long climb down.

By the time she made it to solid ground, Hudson had disappeared somewhere within the piles of debris. Lilly walked stiff-legged over pieces of siding from the house. Her arms and legs trembled as she negotiated a path through the rubble. She noticed fragments of aluminum and plastic from her refrigerator, picture frames, and bricks. How could anyone live through such destruction?

The thought of losing her husband was incomprehensible.

She had to find him. He was alive, she repeated over and over again. He was alive. He had to be. He meant everything to her. He was her rock, her world.

She stopped in her tracks. The center of the house had caved inward, leaving gaping holes. Smoke seeped out of nooks and crevices. One of Faith's bedroom walls on the second floor was gone, plaster and sheetrock blown to bits.

"Hudson!" she called, praying for an answer.

Nothing.

Her insides twisted. "Don't you dare leave me, Russell. Where are you?"

She walked over debris, nearly fell as she tried to get to the spot where she'd last seen her husband. Leaning over to peer into a dark hole, she strained every muscle to lift a section of wall, careful not to cut herself on broken glass. It was no use. The wood and stucco were too heavy. She listened for any sound, wondering how he could possibly have lived through such destruction. Wiping tears from her eyes, she walked to the other side of the house. Her legs stiffened, knees locking. "Hudson," she called again, her voice quivering with desperation.

"I'm coming," Hudson called back. "He's here."

Hudson! Thank goodness! A fluttery feeling rumbled in her belly and worked its way to her brain. She'd misheard her grandson; she was certain of it. A split second later her breathing was suspended as Hudson rounded the corner. "I found him, Grandma. He's OK!"

"He's alive?"

"His leg looks bad, but I think he's going to be OK."

She followed Hudson, moving as fast as she could. They rounded the side of the house, then skidded, side by side, down a slippery slope of dead leaves and dirt. Her husband was lying on his side, grimacing in pain. Even from a few feet away she could see that he was in bad shape, his leg twisted at an odd angle.

"I'll get help," Hudson told her, and he ran off.

She hurried to Russell, fell to her knees, and began checking the rest of his body for cuts and bruises. She unbuttoned his shirt. Other than his leg, he appeared to be in good shape. She smoothed his hair away from his face and then leaned forward and kissed him soundly on the mouth.

She pulled away, her eyes bright. She couldn't believe how lucky he'd been. "Where does it hurt?"

He winced. "Everywhere."

"What were you thinking running around inside if you knew there was a bomb?"

"I couldn't find you, couldn't bear the thought of losing you." He reached out a hand.

"Don't you ever scare me like that again," she told him.

"Never again," Russell told her. "I promise."

"Help is on the way," a neighbor called from their driveway. She could see Hudson was there, too.

She waved a hand, then turned back to Russell. "We're going to be all right. Everything is going to be OK."

———————

Beast hung up the phone. He'd just talked to Faith. Lara was safe.

He plopped down on the edge of his bed, unable to wrap his mind around everything that had happened. If not for Rage's list. If not for her courage, determination, and perseverance, they would never have found Faith's daughter.

Rage had found Lara.

She'd accomplished what she'd set out to do the moment they met Faith McMann.

A bit of time passed as he sat in silence before he noticed the letter from Rage on his nightstand, reminding him of her plea that he read the letter from Sandi Cameron. He came to his feet and retrieved the letter from the top drawer. Turning the envelope over, he peeled it open.

Dear Mr. Ward,

I've made many mistakes in my life, but none so awful as the one I made the day I took the lives of your wife and daughter. I never should have turned down your request to speak to kids about texting and driving, but at the time, the thought of standing in front of a roomful of my peers and telling them what I had done seemed worse than being burned at the stake. I was a socially awkward child and teenager. The boy I was texting that day had asked me to meet him. I was beyond thrilled to receive his text since I had a feeling he might ask me out. Turned out the joke was on me. Had I made it to the yogurt shop instead of slamming into the car coming the other way, I would have merely had my heart broken when I arrived and realized he and his friends were having fun with a prank.

It wasn't my heart that was broken that day, but yours. I don't know why I felt the need to tell you the whole story. I'm not asking for sympathy. Maybe I just needed to get it all off my chest, let you know what happened, why I was stupid enough to text when I knew better. The truth is, within days of turning down your offer, I knew I couldn't live with myself if I didn't follow through with your request. For the past few years, I have been traveling from city to city, school to school, talking to classrooms and auditoriums filled with people, sometimes only ten, sometimes hundreds. And I tell them what happened that day. I talk about the little sister who used to look up to me. I talk about my parents and the relationships they lost and how my mistake affected so many. I talk about your wife and your little girl, and I talk about you, Charlie Ward. Nothing I could ever say or do can bring them back. I'm not writing you to ask for forgiveness, because the truth of the matter is I'm not sure if I could forgive someone for taking my sister or my mom or dad because of their lapse in judgment. But I can tell you how very sorry I am.

    Sandi Cameron

His chin fell forward, and once again he let the tears come.

These tears were for his wife and daughter, the two people he'd loved most in the world. Two people he'd lost and yet never mourned because anger had shut off his emotions. Anger, he realized, had in a sense crippled him. No matter what he did, he hadn't been able to find a way past or through the fury and resentment that were always there. It was a teeth-clenching, aching, heated, skin-prickling sensation that had turned into an impenetrable brick wall and refused to budge. Until this very moment he'd never felt responsible for his anger. He'd put the blame solely on society's shoulders. War and death had framed his life, made him who he was. Anger had lived heavily in his heart for too long.

He was done.

It was time to forgive . . . not past or current circumstances, not Sandi Cameron or any other person who had crossed his path. It was time to forgive himself. He inhaled a cleansing breath and then slowly exhaled, letting it all go.

Could it be that simple?

He folded the letter, slipped it into the envelope, and then put it back into the top drawer of his dresser.

There was a soft knock on the door before his dad stepped inside. "Are you going to stay in your room all night?"

Beast looked at his dad, glad his old man was still around. His emotions clogged his throat, preventing him from saying anything.

"Are you all right?" Dad asked.

"No," Beast said. "How about you?"

"The same," Little Vinnie said matter-of-factly. "How are we going to go on without her?"

"We'll figure out a way," Beast said, pulling himself together. "We always do."

He went to his dad's side, put an arm around his shoulder, and ushered him from the room. "I love you, Dad."

Little Vinnie stopped outside the bedroom door, long enough to give him a hard look.

Beast lifted an eyebrow. "What is it?"

"Should I be worried?"

Beast walked into the kitchen ahead of his dad and said, "I'm going to help you make dinner tonight. So yeah, you should probably be worried . . . very worried." He looked to the living room next, where he saw Miranda glance his way. "Are you just going to sit there doing nothing?" Beast asked her. "Or are you going to make yourself useful and give us a hand with dinner?"

"Since you put it that way," she said, pushing herself to her feet, "I guess I'll help. I make a mean liver pâté," she said with a devious smile. "Maybe we could make that tomorrow night."

Little Vinnie and Miranda laughed.

Beast ignored them both as he opened drawers and cupboards in search of a pan. He knew Rage would be his first thought in the morning and his last thought at night, as she had been for so long now. But her memory would bring him happiness instead of sorrow, and he would never forget what she'd done for him. She'd given him life. He would not squander it.

THIRTY

Faith's entire family gathered at Jana and Steve's home in Rocklin, awaiting the limousines that would soon take them to the cemetery.

While Jana dressed in the other room, Faith held the newest addition to their family, Landon Adam Murray, in her arms, enjoying the feel of his warm body cradled against her chest as she sat in the rocker in the corner of the family room.

Unlike her brother, Lara pretended everything was OK. But Faith knew otherwise. Faith had been staying by her daughter's side at night until she drifted off. She heard the cries for help, and she saw the way her daughter jumped at every noise. Lara had insisted they dye her hair back to blonde immediately, which had left her with an orange tone. It might take a few weeks, but her own color would return, and her hair would grow long again, if that's what Lara decided she wanted. Like Hudson, her daughter had lost a lot of weight. Unlike Hudson, Lara was talkative, in a nervous sort of rambling way that seemed forced at times. Her tattoo would be removed in a few days, and her first session with Kirsten Reich was set for the end of the week. It would be a long road to recovery.

Mom and Dad were living here with Jana and Steve and the new baby. Dad's leg had been shattered in dozens of places. He would be in a wheelchair for a while. But he was alive, and after seeing the devastation at their parents' home, every one of them knew they were lucky Dad was still around.

Lara wasn't ready to go back to the house on Rolling Greens Lane, so the three of them—Hudson, Lara, and Faith—had agreed to live at a hotel while they decided whether or not to sell the house. Colton had said they could come live with him, but Bri and the kids would be coming home soon, and Faith didn't want to intrude. They needed time alone.

Since Lara's return, Faith had found herself thinking only of Craig. It wasn't forced. It just was. She cried at night, every part of her feeling the loss of him. But during the day, Faith left her tears behind and did her best to be strong for her children, encouraging them to say whatever was on their minds, letting them know they were safe and that she would be with them every step of the way while they all found their bearings in this new, strange world they lived in.

"There," Jana said as she came to stand before Faith, reaching out for Landon. "Look at that. You got him right to sleep."

"I still have the magic touch," Faith told her.

Their eyes met. "If I can ever be one-hundredth of the mom you are, I will consider myself lucky," Jana whispered in her ear.

Faith said nothing as she held back tears.

"Let it go," Jana said. "Today is for Craig, and Rage, too. If you want to cry, you should cry."

Faith nodded.

"I want you to know that Steve and I talk about Craig all the time. He will not be forgotten. He was truly a brother to both of us. It will never be the same without him. Everyone who knew him feels the same. He deserves this day."

Tears fell freely from both of them. Jana took Landon in her arms and carried him to his bedroom down the hall.

Faith wiped her eyes, then came to her feet. It was time to get ready. On her way to the bedroom where she'd left her clothes, she heard Lara and Hudson talking in another room. The door was ajar.

"Did you really stab a nail into the bad guy's eye?" Hudson asked.

"I had to," Lara told him. "I would have done anything to get away."

"I don't even know if I could have done that. Did he hurt you?"

"No. He just scared me."

"After they took you away, I couldn't stop thinking about one of them hurting you."

"We're lucky we had family to come find us," Lara told him.

"Yeah," Hudson agreed. "A lot of the kids I met had no one. Joey's family sold him and his brothers to those people. I never once believed them when they told me Mom and Dad didn't want me any longer."

"I didn't believe them, either."

Faith swallowed the lump stuck in her throat, glad they had each other to confide in, and then she proceeded to Jana's bedroom and dressed quickly. It took her only a moment to slip into her black sheath dress and heels. She brushed her hair back into a French twist and then applied lipstick. Mom joined her just as Faith was about to leave the bedroom.

"With everything going on, I've been meaning to ask you about the money I found in the tree fort."

The statement surprised Faith. "That's trafficking money," Faith told her. "That money is the reason we're getting ready to attend Craig's funeral. It's what destroyed our entire family. I'm going to use it to open a shelter for victims of trafficking. There are so many women who need a place to live, a place where they can get the help they need while they figure out their next step." Faith looked at Mom. "You didn't move the money, did you?"

"Of course I did. You can't just leave two million dollars in a tree fort. But don't worry—Colton has it in a safe place."

"I'm sorry about your house," Faith said, not for the first time.

"It's just a house, Faith, and none of this was your fault. I've been badgering your father for years to remodel the kitchen. Now I get to live with Jana and be close to my newest grandson while the house is redone. It's a win-win," she said. Mom placed her palm on Faith's cheek. "I'm so sorry, honey. I wish it didn't have to be this way. I know you miss him."

"I do."

"You're stronger than I ever was," Mom told her. "You didn't think twice about journeying into a world of darkness, a world nobody wanted to believe existed. You fought them all and took back what was yours."

Faith gazed fondly at her mom, knowing how lucky she was to have her love and support. "I know you as well as anyone," Faith said, "and I know you would have done the same."

Mom smiled. "Come on. It's time to go."

Together they exited the room and joined everyone outside where they would pile into the line of vehicles waiting to drive them to the cemetery.

An hour later, Lara stood to Faith's right while Hudson stood to her left behind a podium facing a large crowd of people—friends, family, and many she'd never seen before and might never see again after today.

The wind had settled down, and the sky was a deep shade of blue. No rain. No thunder or lightning, a peaceful day.

Faith looked out at all of Craig's friends, old and new, people who had gathered today to pay their respect. Most of Faith's immediate family, she noticed, had dry eyes. They had been mourning Craig for months, and they were all cried out. Her family was strong and resilient, and that's one of the things Craig always used to tell her he loved most about them. The tears would come later on their own terms. Today they would celebrate Craig's life. Talk about all the wonderful things he did, and recall the happy memories.

Dad sat in his wheelchair in the front row next to Mom.

Beth Tanner would not be in attendance today, but Faith had visited her in the hospital more than once. She was expected to fully recover.

Kirsten Reich, Eva, and other members of her group were there. Colton sat beside his wife, Bri, and his two daughters. Bri and kids had returned last night from Florida. Colton and his family had some work to do, but Faith felt certain they would pull through.

She nodded at Detective Yuhasz sitting in the back row with his two daughters and grandchildren. Detective O'Sullivan had come. Same with Judge Lowell, who had decided not to reverse his original decision as long as Faith agreed to return to anger management classes.

Marion Carver, advocate for antitrafficking, and her daughter, Emily, were seated in the third row next to Miranda.

Faith cleared her throat. "Thank you for being here today. Many of you never got to know my husband, Craig, but trust me when I tell you he was a wonderful husband and father. His children meant the world to him, and there wasn't anything he wouldn't have done for them." Faith stopped to unfold a piece of paper. "Hudson and Lara wrote a few things about their father that they asked me to read. 'Our dad was a hard worker,'" Faith began. "'He was honest and he cared about people. He was proud of us, too. He always asked about our friends, and he made us laugh every single day. He was our best friend.'"

Faith wiped a tear from her eyes, grateful when people who knew Craig from work and golf and all the other things he enjoyed in life came up to the podium to have a word.

Twenty minutes later, since Beast had declined to speak about Rage, Little Vinnie stepped up to the podium. His hands shook as he held his crumpled notes in front of him. Then he cleared his throat. "Rage was a scrawny little thing when she came to live with my son and me," he told the crowd. "She'd been dealt a tough hand when it came to life. She was beaten and abandoned, betrayed by the people she loved. And yet, despite all of her hardships, it didn't take me long to see that she was as beautiful inside as she was outside." He put a hand to his heart. "Rage might not have been born into a life of love and laughter, but that's exactly what she gave to all of us who knew her best." After a short pause he added, "Rage loved life. Although she would never have admitted it, she loved people, too. She wanted a happy ending, not for herself but for everyone around her. Rage loved life even when she was complaining about it."

He waited for a bit of laughter to subside.

"Rage had a son at a young age. One of her deepest regrets was giving him up for adoption. But then she met Sue and Danny, and she loved them almost as much as she loved her son. She died in peace knowing he was in good hands."

Little Vinnie paused again, swallowed, then said, "Rage enjoyed the little things in life like sunflowers, ladybugs, and pickles." He smiled as he remembered her joy in most things. "Rage was unselfish. She always wanted to help people in any way she could. As an example, one day at the grocery store she talked to a teenager standing in front of the store with a cardboard box filled with kittens. He was going to take the animals to the pound if he didn't find them homes." Little Vinnie wagged a finger at the crowd. "I can tell you this, I didn't get any shopping done, but you can bet every kitten had a home by the end of the day."

He shook his head. "I don't mean to take up too much of your time. Rage wouldn't like that. But I have this sudden need for all of you to know how special she was and how important it was to her that she help Faith find her children." He wiped his eyes. "Lara and Hudson, Faith McMann's children. That's all she talked about. Every news report reminded us of the odds of a happy outcome, but Rage didn't care about odds. She never once doubted that Lara and Hudson McMann would find their way home." He nodded. "A true miracle. Just like Rage." Little Vinnie nodded at Faith, letting her know he was finished before turning the podium back to her.

Apparently Faith's family wasn't done crying after all. Everyone was a mess, and tissues were being passed down every aisle. "Some of you didn't know Craig and some of you didn't know Rage," Faith told the crowd, "but after hearing these stories, you can see how their lives crisscrossed. I knew Craig for thirty years. He was handsome and smart. He made me laugh. Craig was the father of my children. He was my best friend. He was my person."

She looked down, took a long moment to compose herself. She felt Lara's hand touch her arm, giving her strength. "He was so very special. He'll never be forgotten. And I can tell you this with one hundred percent certainty . . . if he'd known Rage, if he had an inkling about all she did to help me find Lara and Hudson, he'd be happy to share this day with her."

Faith stopped for a moment to collect herself and let the emotions rush over her and through her as she did her best to regain her composure. "Rage and Craig never met, of course, but they meet today, spiritually and in our hearts. They were both well loved. They will be missed."

Epilogue

Faith was one of the last to arrive at anger management class.

After ZZ Top, tonight's instructor, told her to sign in, he motioned for her to take one of the empty seats at the front of the class.

He spent the first ten minutes talking about setting boundaries, waiting until you're calm before you talk to a loved one, and removing yourself from any situation where the angry person will not settle down.

She'd heard it all before, but Faith remained still and listened closely.

When the door opened, everyone turned that way. Latecomers were frowned upon. Faith was surprised to see Beast and Miranda. They came to the front and took seats next to her.

Faith smiled up at him.

Beast merely grunted.

"Everyone must have a nickname," the instructor told Miranda. "Please stand up and tell everyone the name you have chosen."

Miranda pulled a face, making it clear she didn't want to be here and certainly wasn't interested in standing in front of the class.

"Faith," the instructor said, "do you mind telling our newest member your nickname and how it came to be? Maybe that will help our new friend choose a name she thinks might suit her."

He obviously had no idea she and Miranda were already well acquainted, but Faith didn't mind at all. She stood, turned toward the other people in attendance, and said, "On a Friday, a warm November day, my family was attacked by three men. My husband, a wonderful and decent human being, was killed that day. My two children were taken. The nightmare they endured while being held captive is something you and I will never understand. But I do know my family will never be the same." She paused. "The bastard who started it all, Aster Williams, is alive and well in prison. If he's ever released, he'll do what he does best. He'll find new ways to destroy lives. If his wife and children allow him back into their lives, he'll have family to greet him." She swallowed. "I will never see my husband again, never hold his hand, never see him smile like he used to every day when he walked through the door after work. My family, every single one of us, is working hard to get our lives back and find some sense of normalcy." Her heart pounded, and a tiny light flickered within, bouncing around, refusing to be extinguished. "We're forever changed," she said. "I no longer live in a bubble. My eyes have been pried open, and they see everything." Her hands had become fists at her sides. "My name is Furious."

AUTHOR'S NOTE

The world is filled with evil, and you don't have to look very far to find it. Darkness lurks in many corners. We all like to think the worst crimes happen far away from where we live. But, sadly, that's far from the truth. Right now, at this very moment, innocent people, including young children, are being lured into some form of human trafficking. It's happening in my own backyard, and it's probably happening in yours. Trafficking is the subject of my current work, the Faith McMann trilogy. I was looking forward to getting a break from writing about serial killers. Little did I know that I was about to jump into something much worse, a place where not one single monster was hiding among us, but many. Despite the enormity of this growing problem, awareness is the first step in preventing these crimes. And because I believe good can triumph over evil, I like to think that if the community works together, we can take these monsters down, one at a time.

I am about to begin writing my tenth thriller, the first book in my new Jessie Cole series. Writing a gritty thriller where good conquers evil, where victims don't just learn to survive but thrive, where readers can find a sliver of light in the darkness, makes me happy. I hope you'll come along for the ride.

ACKNOWLEDGMENTS

I have been writing for a long time, and, up until a few years ago, it was always a solitary journey. Not any longer. The people at Thomas & Mercer have offered their support every step of the way. I am extremely grateful for Liz Pearsons, the amazing Charlotte Herscher, Robin O'Dell, Sarah Shaw, and so many others. Thank you.

And, Colton Alan Johnson, I can't end this trilogy without a mention of the little boy who left us too soon. Thank you for being the inspiration for Faith's brother, Colton, the best big brother in the world.

ABOUT THE AUTHOR

Photo © 2014 Morgan Ragan

New York Times, *USA Today*, and *Wall Street Journal* bestselling author Theresa Ragan has sold more than 1.8 million books. Under the name T.R. Ragan, she writes thrillers, including *Furious*, *Outrage*, and *Wrath* in the Faith McMann trilogy and *Abducted*, *Dead Weight*, *A Dark Mind*, *Obsessed*, *Almost Dead*, and *Evil Never Dies* in the Lizzy Gardner series. Theresa also writes medieval time-travel stories, contemporary romance, and romantic suspense. She and her husband have four children and live in Sacramento, California. To learn more about Theresa, visit her website at www.theresaragan.com.